SILENT NIGHT, DEADLY NIGHT

Jemima Ames—she was usually a flamboyant personality, but that night she was the death of the party.

Tim Ames—the stay-at-home husband, whose wife was very hard to live with. Question was, how hard?

Hannah Cadwall—the dead woman's best friend, she was also Jemima's second in command. How tired was she of playing second fiddle?

Bob Dysart—he was the open-handed host . . . with a hidden source of cash.

Heidi Hayhoe—with a name like that and her sweet, sexy girl-next-door personality, nobody would suspect her of anything. Ho ho ho. . . .

"AN ELEGANT AND WITTY MYSTERY . . .
by an author one hopes has many more
stories up her talented sleeve."
Publishers Weekly

Rest You Merry

CHARLOTTE MACLEOD

AVON
PUBLISHERS OF BARD, CAMELOT, DISCUS AND FLARE BOOKS

AVON BOOKS
A division of
The Hearst Corporation
1790 Broadway
New York, New York 10019

Copyright © 1978 by Charlotte MacLeod
Published by arrangement with Doubleday & Company, Inc.
Library of Congress Catalog Card Number: 77-27713
ISBN: 0-380-47530-8

First Avon Printing, November, 1979

AVON TRADEMARK REG. U.S. PAT. OFF. AND IN
OTHER COUNTRIES, MARCA REGISTRADA,
HECHO EN CANADA

Printed in Canada

UNV 10 9 8 7

For Helen and Glenn

Chapter 1

"Peter Shandy, you're impossible," sputtered his best friend's wife. "How do you expect me to run the Illumination if everyone doesn't co-operate?"

"I'm sure you'll do a masterful job as always, Jemima. Isn't that Hannah Cadwall across the way ringing your doorbell?"

With a finesse born of much practice, Professor Shandy backed Mrs. Ames off his front step and shut the door. This was the seventy-third time in eighteen years she'd nagged him about decorating his house. He'd kept count. Shandy had a passion for counting. He would have counted the spots on an attacking leopard, and he was beginning to think a leopard might be a welcome change.

Every yuletide season since he'd come to teach at Balaclava Agricultural College, he'd been besieged by Jemima and her cohorts. Their plaint was ever the same:

"We have a tradition to maintain."

The tradition dated back, as Professor Shandy had taken the trouble to find out, no farther than 1931, when the wife of the then president had found a box of Japanese lanterns left over from some alumni ball of more pros-

7

perous days. Combining artistic yearnings with Yankee
thrift, she decided to stage a Grand Illumination of the
Balaclava Crescent on Christmas Eve. The professor had
come to feel a deep sense of personal injury because it
hadn't rained that night.

The Grand Illumination, blotting out for one night the
drabness of the Great Depression, had been such a smash-
ing success that the college had repeated the event every
year since, with accumulating embellishments. Now during
the entire holiday season the Crescent became a welter
of twinkling lights, red sleighs, and students in quaint costume chanting totally superfluous injunctions to Deck the
Halls. Those faculty members whose houses faced the
Crescent threw themselves into the jollification. No energy
shortage dimmed the multicolored blaze because the college generated its own power from methane gas.

From near and far came tourists to bask in the spectacle
and be milked by the lads and lasses of Balaclava. Students
sold doughnuts and mulled cider from whimsical plywood
gingerbread houses, hawked song sheets, ran parking lots,
or put on the guise of Santa's elves and hauled people
around on old-fashioned sleds at a dollar a haul. Pictures
appeared in national magazines.

However, the photographers always had to shoot around
one dark spot on the gala scene. This was the home of
Peter Shandy. He alone, like a balding King Canute, stood
steadfast against the tide.

In the daytime his stubborn refusal to assist at the Annual Fleecing didn't matter so much. The small house of
rosy old brick, framed by snow-covered evergreens, looked
Christmasy just as it was. Still, it was this very pictur-
esqueness that galled the committee most.

"You could do so much *with* it," they moaned.

One after another, they showered on him wreaths made
of gilded pine cones, of stapled computer cards, of stuffed
patchwork, of plastic fruit, of lollipops wired to bent coat
hangers with little scissors attached so he could snip off
goodies as desired. He always thanked the donors with
what courtesy he could manage, and passed on their offer-
ings to his cleaning woman. By now, Mrs. Lomax had the
most bedizened place in town, but the small brick house
on the Crescent remained stubbornly unadorned.

Left to himself, Peter Shandy would willingly have made some concession to the event: a balsam wreath or a spray of holly on the front door, and a fat white candle guttering in the parlor window after dark. He rather liked Christmas. Every year, he sent off a few decently restrained cards to old friends, attended those neighborhood parties he couldn't in decency avoid, and went off to visit relatives.

Cousin Henry and his wife, Elizabeth, were quiet people, older than Peter, who lived a three hours' journey by Greyhound from Balaclava Junction. They would thank him for the box of cigars and the basket of assorted jellies, then sit him down to an early dinner of roast beef and Yorkshire pudding. Afterward, over brandy and the Christmas cigars, Henry would show his stamp collection. The professor had little interest in stamps as such, but found them pleasant enough things to count. Late in the afternoon, Elizabeth would serve tea and her special lemon cheese tarts and remark that Peter had a long ride ahead of him.

Agreeably stuffed and warm with familial attachment, the professor would slip back into the brick house somewhere around nine o'clock in the evening and settle down with a glass of good sherry and *Bracebridge Hall*. At bedtime he would step out the back door for a last whiff of fresh air. If it was a fine night, he might feel the urge to stay outside and count stars for a while, but for the past couple of years the Illumination Committee had scheduled fireworks, which wrought havoc with his tallies.

Altogether, too many of Shandy's Christmases had been blighted by the overwhelming holiday spirit around the Crescent. On this morning of December 21, as he stood automatically counting the petals on the bunch of giant poinsettias snipped out of plastic detergent jugs which Jemima had just forced upon him, something snapped. He thrust the loathsome artifact at Mrs. Lomax, grabbed his coat, and caught the bus for Boston.

On the morning of December 22 two men drove up to the brick house in a large truck. The professor met them at the door.

"Did you bring everything, gentlemen?"

"The whole works. Boy, you folks up here sure take Christmas to heart!"

"We have a tradition to maintain," said Shandy. "You may as well start on the spruce trees."

All morning the workmen toiled. Expressions of amazed delight appeared on the faces of neighbors and students. As the day wore on and the men kept at it, the amazement remained but the delight faded.

It was dark before the men got through. Peter Shandy walked them out to the truck. He was wearing his overcoat, hat, and galoshes, and carrying a valise.

"Everything in good order, gentlemen? Lights timed to flash on and off at six-second intervals? Amplifiers turned up to full volume? Steel-cased switch boxes provided with sturdy locks? Very well, then, let's flip on the power and be off. I'm going to impose on you for a lift to Boston, if I may. I have an urgent appointment there."

"Sure, glad to have you," they chorused, feeling the agreeable crinkle of crisp bills in their hands. From a technical point of view, it had been an interesting day.

Precisely forty-eight hours later, on Christmas Eve, Professor Shandy stepped outside for a breath of air. Around him rolled the vast Atlantic. Above shone only the freighter's riding lights and a skyful of stars. The captain's dinner had been most enjoyable. Presently he would go below for a chat with the chief engineer, a knowledgeable man who could tell to the last pulse how many revolutions per minute his engines made at any given speed.

Back on Balaclava Crescent, floodlights would be illuminating the eight life-size reindeer mounted on the roof of the brick house. In its windows, sixteen Santa Claus faces would be leering above sixteen sets of artificial candles, each containing three red and two purple bulbs, each window outlined by a border of thirty-six more bulbs alternating in green, orange, and blue.

He glanced at his watch and did rapid calculations in his head. At that precise point, the 742 outsize red bulbs on the spruce trees would have flashed on for the 28,800th time—a total of 21,369,600 flashes. The amplifiers must by now have blared out 2,536 renditions each of "I'm Dreaming of a White Christmas," "I Saw Mommy Kissing Santa Claus," and "All I Want for Christmas Is My Two Front Teeth." They must be just now on the seventeeth bar of the 2,537th playing of "I Don't Care Who You Are, Fatty, Get Those Reindeer off My Roof."

Professor Shandy smiled into the darkness. "Bah, humbug," he murmured, and began to count the stars.

Chapter 2

The enormity of what he had done did not hit Peter Shandy until he was halfway through breakfast on Christmas morning. Then his right hand froze in the very act of conveying a forkful of excellent pork sausage to his expectant mouth.

"What's wrong, Mr. Shandy?" asked the sympathetic purser. "Not getting seasick on us, are you?"

"It's the engines. They've stopped."

Though this was not the real cause of Shandy's perturbation, it happened to be true. For no apparent reason, the ship's great pulse had suddenly ceased to beat. The engineer threw down his napkin, made a blasphemous utterance, and leaped for the companionway. The captain rushed to the bridge, followed in order of rank by his first, second, and third mates. The steward cleared his throat deferentially.

"Well, Purser, it looks as if you and Mr. Shandy will have to finish the sausages."

"Please present my share to the ship's cat with the compliments of the season," replied the professor. "I believe I'll go try on my life jacket."

He was not particularly alarmed. Compared to what might be in store for him back at Balaclava Junction, the prospect of sudden death by drowning was not without some attraction. Also, there seemed no immediate danger, especially since they had been traveling southward along the coast. A sea anchor was thrown out to keep them riding comfortably until seagoing tugs could arrive to tow them to port. A helicopter flew overhead taking pictures for television. Shandy stayed out of camera range and meditated on his infamy.

An honorable man withal, he could see only one course of action, and he took it. When they put in at Newport News to dry-dock, he repacked his bag, bade farewell to his new-found comrades, and caught the next Greyhound to Balaclava Junction.

It was, as the bus driver remarked at rather too frequent intervals, one hell of a way to spend Christmas. Eating a greasy cheeseburger at a rest stop, Shandy thought of Elizabeth's roast beef and Yorkshire pudding. Jolting along slick roads in freezing sleet, he brooded on her lemon cheese tarts. Dozing fitfully, stiff and chilled, he would wake to regret those sausages he had donated to the ship's cat, and drop off again to dream there was somebody waiting back in the brick house on the Crescent to cook him a hot supper.

There wouldn't be, of course. Mrs. Lomax was away visiting her married daughter over the holidays and she wouldn't have worked today in any case. As he alighted in the chill dawn of December 26, not a leftover reveler, not even the tar-and-feathering committee he half expected, was to be seen. The professor turned his coat collar as high as it would go and began the precipitous climb to the Crescent, wondering at what point he would be confronted with the blinking and bellowing evidence of his ill-judged prank.

He wasn't. The brick house stood dark and silent. He might have known the doughty men of Balaclava would cope with trivia like locked doors and break-proof power boxes. Some student in the Engineering School doing a minor in felonious entry must have thrown the switches.

Relieved, yet nettled at finding his aesthetic bombshell so completely defused, Shandy jabbed his key into the lock, swung open the front door which his accomplices had wrapped like a giant Christmas present with a tumorous growth of pixie mushrooms in the middle, and stumped inside.

He took off his coat, hat, and muffler and hung them in the hall closet. He took off his galoshes and also his shoes, for his feet had swelled from cold and too long sitting. He wiggled his toes. In spite of everything, it was good to be home.

Now for some food. In sock feet, the professor padded down the narrow hallway. The faculty dining room wouldn't be open for hours yet. In any event, he had no wish to venture out from sanctuary so hardly attained. There must be something edible in the kitchen. Hot soup would be just the ticket. Shandy was quite good at opening tins.

Intent on sustenance, he failed to watch where he was going. A sharp pain pierced the sole of his right foot, the floor moved, and he landed flat on his back.

Peter Shandy was not hurt, for the floor runner was thick, but he was extremely put out. Remembering what the engineer had said on finding the engines had stopped, he addressed the same remark to the men from Boston, and turned on the overhead light to hunt for whatever they had so carelessly dropped where he would be sure to step on it.

He borrowed another expletive. The cause of his downfall was a marble, one of his own, that had been given him long ago by a niece of Elizabeth's. This elfin sprite, Alice by name, had loved to visit at the brick house. Alice was married now and living far away, sending him snapshots of her babies instead of the paste-and-crayon creations over which she had so lovingly labored in years gone by.

Most of Alice's gifts had distintegrated, but Peter Shandy still kept her thirty-eight fried marbles in the little glass bowl they had come in. He counted them over sometimes, remembering a little girl's breathless account of how the fascinating inner crackling was achieved.

It was a blue marble he had stepped on. There were seven blue marbles, four light and three dark. This was a dark one, hard to see against the figured runner. That explained his downfall, but not why the marble was on the floor instead of the parlor whatnot.

Temporarily diverted from his quest for soup, Shandy

stepped into the living room. More marbles rolled under his unprotected feet. All thirty-eight must have been spilled, but how? The Boston workmen had been deft and efficient. Furthermore, they'd had no occasion to go near the whatnot, which stood well away from any door or window, in the same corner where he'd found it when he first took over the house from a departing professor eighteen years before.

He recalled having made a final tour of the rooms just before he'd left, to make sure all parts of his plan were duly consummated. He couldn't remember noticing the marbles on the whatnot, but he'd surely have felt them underfoot. Could some tiny animal, a mouse or squirrel, have pushed them off the shelf? It would have to be a muscular rodent. Anyway, he'd better pick them up before he took another toss.

The bowl lay on the carpet, luckily unbroken. Shandy went crawling around the floor, counting aloud as he dropped the errant spheres into their receptacle.

"Thirty-four, thirty-five, thirty-six, and the one I stepped on in the hall. Must be another somewhere. Yellow with brown streaks."

But where? The rooms were small and uncluttered. Even crouching down and squinting along the pile, Shandy could detect no crackly gleam. He searched the hallway, moved chairs, at last thought to look behind the sofa. He didn't find his marble. He found Jemima Ames.

The assistant librarian was dead, no question about that. She was lying on her back, looking up at him with the same cold, fishy stare he'd seen when she handed him the bouquet cut from detergent bottles. Her mouth was slightly open, as though she might be about to deliver one last exhortation about the duty of a Crescent resident, but she never would. There was a settled look about the body, as though it had been there for some while.

The manner of her death seemed plain enough. A small stepladder brought from the kitchen lay beside her, her head propped against the edge of its flat metal top. As to why she'd climbed the stool, a plastic Santa Claus face lying across her chest gave silent answer. Feeling like a murderer, Shandy padded over to the telephone and rang campus security.

"Grimble, you'd better get over here. This is Peter Shandy."

"Yeah? Where you been?"

"I was—er—called out of town unexpectedly."

"Didn't happen to take Miz Ames with you, by any chance?" Grimble evidently thought he was being funny.

"No, but I—er—have her with me now. That's why I'm calling."

"Hang on. I'll be right over."

Shandy put down the receiver. Grimble had been on the lookout for Jemima, therefore she must have been reported missing on Christmas Day, or even the day before. That could mean she'd been lying here almost the whole time he'd been gone. It would take her husband at least twenty-four hours to realize Jemima wasn't where she ought to be.

In the midst of his perturbation, the professor was ashamed to realize he was less upset over having inadvertently killed his best friend's wife than he was over not having got to heat his soup. Blaming himself for his lack of proper feeling, he nevertheless made a tentative move toward the kitchen. Then he stopped.

He might be in an even worse spot than he thought he was. Had Jemima still been alive when he skipped out of town and took ship for foreign parts without telling anybody he was going? His opinion of the assistant librarian, her ridiculous title, and her eternal badgering were well known. Everybody else thought she was a pest, too, but nobody else had gone to such lengths to spite her, and nobody else had her corpse behind his sofa.

He had little time to brood. The security chief was already hunting among the mushrooms for his knocker.

"Come in, Grimble. Come in. Good of you to get here so quickly."

"Sure, Professor, any time. Where is she, and what's she been up to?"

"Well—er—I think the circumstances speak for themselves."

"Why can't Mrs. Ames speak for herself? She generally does." The security chief wouldn't have dared say such a thing if he hadn't been seriously annoyed. "Where is she?" he repeated.

"In here. Behind the sofa. I didn't move anything."

"You mean you—oh, my God!"

Grimble stood goggling down at the corpse for at least a minute. Then he shoved his cap forward and scratched hard at the base of his skull.

"What do you know about that? Looks as if she butted in once too often."

"Yes." Professor Shandy found that his lips were so dry he had trouble articulating. "Apparently she took exception to my—er—decorations."

"Well, now, I don't want to hurt your feelings, Professor, but some of the folks around here do think you've kind of overdone it. They think you're trying to outshine 'em, see?"

That was the one possible interpretation of his outrage that Shandy would never have thought possible.

"Of course," Grimble went on kindly, "most of us figure you're just making up for all the times you wouldn't be bothered. I think it's kind of cheerful myself, with the music and all. Even Professor Ames noticed that part. First time I ever seen him take any interest in the Illumination. Too damn bad he couldn't take a little more interest in his wife."

"How long has she been missing?" asked the professor with his heart in his mouth.

"Best I've been able to find out is that she went to a party at the Dysarts' last Thursday night. You know that big wingding they always throw at Christmastime."

"Yes. Come to think of it, I was intending to go myself. I quite forgot to let them know I wouldn't be there. I shall have to make my apologies."

Realizing he had an iron-clad alibi, Shandy became voluble. The invitation had been for eight o'clock, and at that hour he was in Boston, picking up his ticket to board the *Singapore Susie*.

Grimble wasn't interested. "Well, anyway," he cut in, "she stayed at the party till half past nine."

"Was her husband with her?"

"Hell, he don't remember where he was. Home with his nose in a book, or up at the soil lab making mudpies, most likely."

"I expect so," Shandy agreed.

Timothy Ames never left his study if he could help it, except to teach a class or immure himself in his soil-testing laboratory. He was deaf as a haddock and hopeless at small talk, so there was nothing unusual in Jemima's attending a social event without her spouse.

"Where did she go when she left the party?"

"Looks to me as if she come straight here. She was wearin' that purple cloak thing she's got on now, they said. Professor Dysart says he helped her on with it an' saw her out the door. Prob'ly tripped on the end of it an' that's how she upset the ladder. She was all steamed up about these decorations of yours, they said. Must o' got a few drinks under her belt an' decided to come an' take 'em down. See, she's got one o' them Santa Claus faces on top of her. It's the sort o' thing she'd do."

"Yes," said the professor sadly, "it is. I ought to have known better. I feel personally responsible for this terrible—"

He intended to add "accident," but the word wouldn't come out. Professor Shandy was a truthful man, and there was that missing marble still to be accounted for. Should he explain that odd circumstance to Grimble, or should he not?

On the whole, he thought not. The college security force was trained to cope primarily with unauthorized prowlers and overexuberance within the student body. Chief Grimble was a man of good heart but limited intelligence. The police would have to be called in anyway, so he might as well tell his story where it would do some good. The sooner the better. He was feeling more exhausted every second. But Grimble was making no move.

"Would you like to use my phone?" he prodded.

"Don't you think we ought to go over and tell Professor Ames ourselves?" said the security chief. "He'd never hear the telephone in a million years."

"Yes, but aren't we supposed to notify the police first? We do have an unexplained death on our hands."

"What's so unexplained? She fell an' bashed in her skull."

"Still, don't you have to observe certain—er—formalities?"

"Search me. All I know is the president's goin' to raise holy hell if this gets into the newspapers."

Grimble wasn't so stupid, after all. The Grand Illumination was slated to last through New Year's. At least half the student body had given up the chance of spending

Christmas with their families in order to run the parking lots, the sleigh rides, the refreshment stands; to sculpt the giant snowmen, sing the carols, build the bonfires, sweep the skating ponds, or put on costumes and stand around in picturesque attitudes for the benefit of those golden calves, the tourists.

Proceeds were handled on a fifty-fifty basis: half to the student, half to the college. Many of these young people depended on Illumination earnings to help pay their tuition. The college used its half for scholarships and loans. It was excellent business both ways and the president would have good reason to be upset if unfavorable publicity kept visitors away. A braver man than Grimble, or than almost anybody, might well think twice, and perhaps a few more times to be on the safe side, before inviting the wrath of Thorkjeld Svenson.

Nevertheless, Shandy replied, "Then we'd better let him know at once."

"He's off skiing, thank God," said Grimble. "I guess I better get hold of Fred Ottermole down at the police station. He's not a bad egg."

"Yes, do that. Er—while we're waiting for him, why don't I make us a cup of coffee?"

"Great idea. Three sugars in mine, if you can spare it."

The security chief stuck a thick finger in the telephone dial, and Professor Shandy at last managed to reach his kitchen.

Chapter 3

With a hot drink and a couple of stale doughnuts under his belt, Shandy felt queasier but less defeated. He managed to greet Chief Ottermole with a decent mixture of distress and dignity.

"This how you found her?"

Ottermole was a large, youngish man wearing a sheepskin-collared leather jacket over his uniform. He refused to take it off, perhaps because he realized the added bulk enhanced his already impressive appearance. He had his gun, his flashlight, and his notebook at the ready, but his ball-point pen wouldn't write. Professor Shandy lent him a pencil and answered his question.

"Yes. I haven't touched her. She was obviously beyond help."

"How did she get here?"

"I wish I knew. I've been away since Thursday evening myself. I hadn't been in the house more than a few minutes before I called Grimble."

"How come him instead of me?"

"We always call security when anything goes wrong. It's just habit."

"Um. Where were you?"

Shandy drew a long breath and chose his words carefully. "As you can see, I'm a middle-aged man of quiet habits. Living here on the Crescent, I get the—er—full impact of the Grand Illumination. I expect you don't have to be told what that entails."

"I sure don't," said the policeman gloomily. "Okay, so you cleared out."

"Exactly. I—er—had contributed my share of the decorating—"

"Oh, boy, you can say that again! How the hell did a guy like you ever get those eight reindeer up on your roof?"

"Actually, I didn't. Being without experience in such matters, I simply hired some decorators and told them to—er—decorate."

"Oh, yeah. People have been kind of wondering how come you picked out all those funny colors. S'posed to be artistic or something, huh?"

"Er—they seemed to know what they were doing. It took a great deal longer than I'd thought it would. I had made arrangements to go off on a short cruise over the holidays, and was supposed to be in Boston by seven o'clock in the evening. Since I couldn't very well go off and leave the workmen unattended, I had to stay in the house till they'd finished. By that time I'd missed the six o'clock bus, so I asked them to give me a ride, which they were quite willing to do. What with one thing and another, it got to be a scramble and I forgot to tell anybody I was leaving. That didn't seem to matter much, because the men assured me the mechanisms were perfectly safe and I knew the neighbors would keep an eye on the place. They always do."

"So you figure this woman came in to check things out? What would she be doing up on a ladder?"

"Presumably she was altering the decorations in some way. Mrs. Ames was chairman of the Grand Illumination Committee, and she took her responsibilities with great seriousness. I suppose that Santa Claus object she seems to have taken down was—er—bothering her."

"How could she get in? Don't tell me you went away and left your door unlocked, with tourists milling around here thick as flies on dog-do in August."

"Oh no, I'm always careful about locking up. I don't

know how she got in, unless Grimble opened the door for her."

"I never," said the security chief. "What the hell, Professor, you people are always leaving keys around at each other's houses and forgetting to take 'em back. She prob'ly had one herself."

He and Ottermole exchanged grins over Shandy's head. The security chief shrugged.

"Doesn't look as if there's any mystery about what happened here. Everybody in town knew Mrs. Ames. She wouldn't let a little thing like breaking and entering stop her if she thought there was something that needed to be fixed. Only thing surprises me is that she bashed her own head in, when there were so many people around who'd have been glad to do it for her."

Ottermole grinned again. "If you repeat that, I'll shove you in the clink. Well, I guess we might as well get the wagon up here."

"The sooner the better," said Grimble nervously. "I just hope to Christ we can get her out of the Crescent without anybody spotting us. Boy, Professor, I'm sure glad you got home when you did. Say, how come you're here at all? That must have been some short cruise."

"It was shorter than we expected," the professor explained. "The ship developed engine trouble and had to put in at Newport News. You may have seen the—er—thrilling rescue on television. Since there was no telling how long she'd be disabled, I decided I might as well give up the idea and come back. She's the *Singapore Susie,* if you care to make sure I was actually aboard. I can write down the names of the captain and officers for you. I'm afraid I never did learn who the men were with whom I rode to Boston. However, I do have the firm's invoice in my desk, and could easily find out."

"That's okay, Professor. I guess we can take your word for it. Mind if I use your phone?"

"Not at all."

Ottermole went into the study and dialed. "Hello, Doctor. Sorry to get you up, but we've got a little problem up here at Professor Shandy's house on the Crescent. No, he's okay, but he just came home from being shipwrecked and found Mrs. Ames dead on his parlor floor. Yeah, some days you just can't win. Looks to me as if she fell off a

stool and cracked her skull. She was in here fixing the
Christmas decorations. Okay, I'll tell him you said so.
Look, do you think you could get over here right away?
Eddie Grimble's having a bird. He wants to take her
out before the gawkers start coming. President Svenson
wouldn't like the publicity, he says. Good. See you."

He hung up. "Relax, Eddie. Dr. Melchett's on his way.
Soon as he gives us the go-ahead, I'll have Charlie Forster
bring that old pickup of his around."

Ottermole went back to the telephone and chatted with
one of his cohorts until the doctor arrived. Melchett's ex-
amination took about thirty seconds.

"She died instantly of skull fracture at least three days
ago. The wound in the cranium is consistent with the shape
of the object she fell on. Anything else you need to know?"

"Nope. That wraps it up. Thanks, Doctor."

"I'll drop off a certificate at the station on my way to
the hospital."

Melchett left, and within a few minutes, a plain blue
pickup truck arrived. Two men wearing noncommittal nylon jackets carried out a large brown paper parcel. The
townsfolk, too, were sensitive to the good will of Thorkjeld Svenson.

Peter Shandy attended the swathing of Mrs. Ames with
anxious care. He was still fretting about that marble. He
had thought it must be under the body, but it wasn't. At
last he had to tell Chief Ottermole what he was looking
for.

"That was how I happened to find her, you see. I
stepped on one of the spilled marbles and took a rather
painful toss in the hallway. Then I thought I'd better pick
them all up before I fell again. But after a thorough search,
I've found only thirty-seven out of the thirty-eight."

"Wait a second. Are you saying you know for a positive
fact how many marbles were in that dish?"

"Of course," said Professor Shandy, astonished to be
asked such a question. "The missing marble is yellow with
brown streaks. I wish you'd have the undertaker look for
it among her—er—personal effects."

"Sure. I'll tell Harry you haven't got all your marbles."

Shandy refused to be baited. "Thank you. They were
given me by a little girl of whom I'm very fond. I

shouldn't wish to hurt her feelings by appearing to be careless of her gift."

The child in question was now twenty-six years old, but he hoped such an explanation might persuade Ottermole that he was less cracked than his marbles. Apparently, it did.

"Oh, I get it," said the chief. "Well, I guess we'd better put this show on the road. Say, you know Professor Ames a lot better than I do."

"Yes, Tim and I are old friends. I'll tell him, if you want."

"Thanks a lot. That's one job I'll gladly pass up any day. See you later, Ed. So long, Professor. Don't find any more bodies."

"I earnestly hope never to find another. But you will tell them about that marble, won't you? I know it sounds trivial at a time like this, but if the child should come and find one gone—"

"Look, I know all about it. I've got kids of my own."

The policeman climbed into the back of the truck. Ed Grimble stayed where he was, looking at Professor Shandy and scratching the back of his head.

"Say, Professor, I don't suppose it's any of my business, but that story of yours about the marbles, I don't get it. You used to have that little girl of your cousin's here sometimes, but, hell, that was a long time ago. She must have kids of her own by now."

"Three," said Shandy. "You're quite right. I expect Alice has forgotten all about her fried marbles. I was only—er—trying to add verisimilitude to an otherwise implausible request. Do you ever have hunches, Grimble?"

"Once in a while. Like I had a hunch right now you were givin' Fred Ottermole the business."

"It's important that he hunt for that missing marble. If it turns up in Mrs. Ames's clothing, we can safely assume she knocked over the dish herself. If it doesn't, we'll have to re-examine our data."

"What are you driving at, Professor?"

"Grimble, I do not understand how those marbles got spilled. I was the last one out of here Thursday afternoon, and I'll swear they were on that whatnot over in the corner then, not because I noticed them particularly, but because I didn't. Small round objects on the floor have a way of making their presence felt." He rubbed his left buttock thoughtfully.

The security guard shook his head. "I don't see what you're so fired up about. Mrs. Ames was a big woman, and she had that damn fool cape flappin' around her like a washing in a windstorm. She must o' been hell on bric-a-brac."

"I grant you that, but why should she have gone anywhere near the whatnot? As you see, it's out of the path from the door to the window, and she knew her way around this house well enough."

The Restaurant Management students ran a superb catering service and Shandy was never stingy about doing his fair share of entertaining. Jemima had always come with Tim to his parties, and dropped in altogether too often between times to bullyrag him about one thing or another.

"You see." He pointed to the ostensible cause of her death. "She even knew where to find that step stool, which belongs in the kitchen, though she could perfectly well have stood on a chair."

"Cripes, I don't know, Professor. Maybe fumbling around in the dark—"

"But it would not have been dark. With all those candles and whatnots in the windows, the place must have been lit up like—er—a Christmas tree. That is, assuming the lights were on. I gather somebody has been manipulating my switches."

"Well, what happened was, everybody started getting on my neck about the music. It was drowning out the carolers and the bell ringers and driving the neighbors nuts, if you'll pardon me for saying so. We tried to get hold of you to tone things down a little, but you were nowhere to be found, so I told Jamie Froude from maintenance to jimmy open that switch box your guys had attached to the side of the house here, next to the light meter. That way, we managed to turn off the music. Some people wanted us to douse the lights, too, but the little kids were getting such a kick out of the blinking Santa Clauses and all that I said to Jamie, 'What the hell, they came to see lights, didn't they?' So all we did was adjust the timers so the damn things wouldn't blink so fast, and gave the night watchman instructions to shut 'em off when he made his one o'clock rounds. Since then, we've been turning everything but the sound on manually every afternoon at dusk and having the watchman throw the switch after everybody leaves. Your place is the hit of the show."

"My God," murmured the professor. "So the long and the short of it is, if Jemima came any time before one o'clock in the morning, the lights would be on, and if she came afterward the place would be in darkness."

"That's right. Now that you mention it, I shouldn't think a woman would want to go prowling around somebody else's house in the middle of the night by herself."

"Neither should I, in this instance. Mrs. Ames was more a charger than a sneaker. I daresay she'd intended to tackle me at the Dysarts', and when she found I wasn't at the party, she came straight here. We'll have to make inquiries."

"You can if you want to," said the security chief. "I'm not sticking my neck out for no yellow marble."

Professor Shandy sighed heavily. "I suppose I can't blame you. No doubt it's all a mare's nest. I've been traveling all night and perhaps I'm not thinking straight. You might as well go along about your business. I'm going to fix myself a bite of breakfast, then go over and try to make poor Tim Ames understand what's happened."

Chapter 4

There were a couple of eggs in the fridge. Shandy fried them and made himself another cup of instant coffee. Then he took a hot bath and a shave. After that, he felt a trifle less like the way Jemima Ames had looked. He put on a light gray shirt, a dark gray suit, and a reticent tie, not because they were appropriate for the errand he had to perform but because he owned no other sort of clothing, aside from the corduroys and flannel shirts he kept for field work.

Standing in front of the mirror, he brushed his graying hair. He wore it trimmed rather short, making no effort to cover his bald spot. Peter Shandy liked to be neat and he wore garments of excellent quality which lasted for years and saved fuss in the long run, but nobody could have called him a vain man.

He'd never felt that he had anything to be vain about. He was neither short nor tall, neither fat nor lean. His face was not regular enough to be handsome or ugly enough to be interesting. He thought of it mainly as a place to park his glasses. He put them on, went downstairs for his gray felt hat and gray tweed ulster, and set out to find Timothy Ames.

How was old Tim going to take the news? It was foolish

to speculate, since Shandy would find out soon enough, but natural to be concerned. Ames was his oldest and closest friend at Balaclava. The soil specialist had been the first to understand and sympathize with Shandy's ideas for improving strains of plants. Over the years, his help had been invaluable. Together, the pair of them had worked, studied, rejoiced, grieved, and fought quietly but tenaciously for research grants, for added laboratory space, for better equipment, for all the perquisites true scholars need but grandstanders are apt to get.

They had won more often than not because Thorkjeld Svenson was no fool and because they got results. Shandy, Ames, and the college had all made a killing on the Balaclava Buster, a giant rutabaga so prolific and so nutritious as cow feed that it alone generated most of the manure to produce the methane that ran the college power plant, not to mention a stream of royalties from seed companies far and wide.

The Buster was their greatest but far from their only triumph, and in all the eighteen years of collaboration, their relationship had been marred by only one minor rift. This concerned an extra-fast-sprouting viola which Shandy had wanted to call Agile Alice, while Ames held out for Jumping Jemima. Dr. Svenson had finally appointed himself arbiter and they settled perforce on Sprightly Sieglinde, in honor of Mrs. Svenson.

Shandy wished now that he hadn't been so pigheaded. Jumping Jemima was by far the best name of the three. Except that it was too apt. He thought of that dented-in skull and wished he hadn't eaten those eggs.

The moment of truth was at hand. He went up to the Ameses' front door and began his accustomed fusillade. No ordinary knocking could attract Tim's attention.

Today, however, Professor Ames must have been on the *qui vive*. Shandy had been hammering a mere three minutes or thereabout when his old comrade appeared.

"Pete! Glad to see you."

This was no idle platitude. Ames was grinning like a jack-o'-lantern, slapping him on the back, and going into a fit of chortling that threatened to land the man writhing on the door mat. Shandy got them both inside fast and shut the door. A public display of mirth was hardly the thing in a fresh-made widower. It was after seven o'clock by this time. At least one neighbor must be up and watching from a window. Seldom did any event around the Crescent go unobserved or unremarked, even in Illumination time. That was what made it so hard to believe that not one of them knew Jemima had been inside the brick house for three days.

Reminded of his painful errand, Shandy tried to speak. Tim was in no mood for doleful news.

"That," he gasped, "was the funniest—God, Pete, I've prayed for twenty-seven years that somebody would have guts enough—" he found an unused chuckle or two, got them out of his system, and wiped his eyes. "How in hell did you ever have the nerve?"

"I don't know," Shandy replied in perfect honesty. "I just did."

"You're a great man, Pete. Care for a drink?"

"Bit early, isn't it?"

Professor Ames considered the question. "Maybe you're right. How about coffee, then? I don't think I've had breakfast yet. Come to think of it, I'm not sure I ate any supper. Want some eggs or something?"

"No, I've just finished. I'll cook for you, though."

Shandy was no brilliant performer in the kitchen, but he was less incompetent than his friend, as the state of the never very neat room testified.

"Been keeping bachelor quarters," Ames explained as he pottered about, searching in vain for a clean frying pan. "Jemima's off somewhere. This time of year she's generally some damn place or other, but lately she hasn't even come home to sleep, far as I can tell. I asked Grimble if he'd seen her around and he got all excited. Asked me when she was here last. How the hell am I supposed to know?"

"When did you first miss her?"

"Yesterday afternoon at exactly three o'clock. I remember that because Jemmy phoned from California to wish us Merry Christmas. That reminded me we hadn't done anything about Christmas dinner and the presents were still sitting on the table. We hadn't intended to make any big thing of the holiday with both the kids gone and her so wrapped up in that goddamned Illumination, but I did think she might stick her nose in long enough to open her packages. I wish to Christ she'd turn up. We're out of everything. Now I can't find any coffee."

"Look, Tim, why don't you come over to my place?" said his friend in desperation. "I've got coffee. We can—er—talk about Jemima there."

He involuntarily turned his head away as he finished the sentence, so that Ames had no chance to lip-read more than the invitation, which he seemed ready enough to accept. He put on a threadbare tweed jacket which was the only outer garment he ever wore, winter or summer, and shambled alongside Shandy, across the Crescent.

Regrettably, the sight of those eight plastic reindeer set him laughing again. Shandy could only hope that whoever was watching would decide after the news of Mrs. Ames's death got around that her husband had been hysterical with grief.

After the gloom and clutter of Tim's place, the brick house seemed a cheerful haven in spite of the brown paper parcel that had so recently been taken out of it. Professor Shandy had never thought a great deal about his home before. He'd liked the previous tenant's old-fashioned furnishings well enough and made few changes, except to weed out the clutter and bring in some of his own, mostly books and potted plants he got to do research on and kept around for company. There was also a handsome water-color portrait of the Balaclava Buster, the work of a lady botany professor who had hoped to reach her colleague's heart through his rutabaga. Cross-pollination had not been successful. The lady married somebody else and Shandy continued his comfortable bachelor's life with Mrs. Lomax keeping him tidy and the faculty dining room keeping him fed.

Insofar as he thought of the future at all, he'd pictured himself going on more or less as he'd been doing. Now for the first time he wondered whether that would be possible.

He had always managed not to get personally involved in any of the blood feuds that had raged around the Crescent during his occupation, but he knew only too well how high passions could run over acts far less outrageous than the one he had committed. He had not meant to kill Jemima, of course, but he had deliberately and with malice aforethought made savage mockery of the Crescent's most cherished tradition and the college's chief extracurricular money-maker. If Tim had the wit to see his

act for exactly what it was, so would the rest of the faculty
and so, even more to his peril, would those Stymphalian
birds, the faculty spouses. And it was inconceivable that
President Svenson would mistake his motive.

Shandy wasn't worried about losing his job per se. He
had tenure, to begin with, and it would take something
like an act of Congress to remove him. Moreover, President Svenson would not hasten to kill, so to speak, the
gander who laid the golden eggs. There was always the
chance Shandy might hatch another Balaclava Buster.

In any event, his own share of royalties from that and
other successful experiments, coupled with his salary as a
full professor and his relatively modest life style, had made
Peter Shandy a rather wealthy man. He could retire tomorrow, if it came to that.

But he didn't want it to come to that. Fifty-six was
ridiculously young to step down. He would miss his work,
his colleagues, his students. He would miss the sociabili-
ties of campus life, tiresome as he sometimes found them,
and he would miss his house.

Yet he knew perfectly well that if the full force of his
peers' disapproval was turned on him, it would be impossible to stay here. His life would be made miserable in
countless little ways. His lawn would die, his spruces get
budworm, his power would fail and his pipes would freeze
and nobody would know why. Secretaries would forget
to notify him of faculty meetings, hostesses would absent-
mindedly leave him off their guest lists, his students would
transfer. At the faculty dining room his food would be
served cold and late and no colleague would dare to share
his table. By the end of the next semester, he would either
have quit of his own accord or turned into a curmudgeonly
recluse. And he'd have nobody to blame but himself.

Well, at least he'd given old Tim a good laugh. How
much was his friend going to enjoy the joke, when he
learned it had cost him a wife?

Shandy fussed around his own immaculate kitchen,
heating water and laying out what he could find in the
way of eatables. Then he motioned Ames into what Mrs.
Lomax insisted on calling the breakfast nook.

"Sit down, Tim, sit down. I'll get the marmalade. Oh,
and what about some fruitcake? Elizabeth always sends
me a fruitcake."

"I know Elizabeth always send you a fruitcake. What the hell's wrong with you, Pete? You're flopping around like a hen with its head cut off."

Shandy sat down opposite him and propped both elbows on the table for support.

"The fact is, Tim, I have some bad news for you."

His guest set down the mug he'd got halfway to his lips.

"Pete, it's not—not the Portulaca Purple Passion? Oh, my God, don't tell me those seedlings have damped off?"

"Oh no! It's—" Shandy started to say, "It's not that bad," but caught himself in time. "It's Jemima, Tim. I found her."

For a long time, Ames showed no reaction. Shandy began to wonder if he'd heard. Then he said, "You mean she's dead, don't you?"

Shandy nodded. His friend bent his head and sat staring down into his coffee mug. At last he picked it up, drank off the cooling liquid, and wiped his mouth with a fairly steady hand.

"How did it happen?"

"I don't know."

Now that the barrier was broken, Shandy found it easy enough to keep going. "I came home this morning—I'd been gone since Thursday evening—and found her stretched out behind the sofa with her skull fractured. Dr. Melchett said she'd died instantly, if it's any comfort to you. She'd been there pretty much the whole time I was gone. She had on that long purple cape and an evening skirt. It looked as though she must have come in to take down those cursed decorations, and had a fall. She'd apparently brought in a little stepladder from the kitchen here—"

"What for?"

"To stand on, they assumed."

"Who assumed?"

"Grimble and the police chief, a chap named Ottermole. Know him?"

"Snotty young bastard about four sizes too big for his britches? I damn well ought to."

Ames breathed fire through his luxuriantly haired nostrils for a while, and Shandy recalled that it was Ottermole who had taken away Tim's driving license.

"Look here, Pete, I wish to hell you'd quit pussyfooting. All that 'apparently' and 'they assumed' . . . why don't you just say the sons of bitches misread the evidence, which is exactly what I'd expect a pair of nincompoops to do. Show me where you found her."

"Finish your breakfast first."

The widower shoved a whole slab of fruitcake into his mouth, and got up from the table. Chewing hard, he followed Shandy into the living room.

"The sofa wasn't pulled out as it is now," Shandy explained. "We had to move it to get at the—at Jemima."

"Show me."

Shandy pushed the heavy piece of furniture back into its usual place, parallel with the window, a few feet out from the wall.

"And the stool was how?"

"Like this." He laid the small ladder back where he'd found it. "And Jemima was lying on her back with her head resting against the top edge, and this Santa Claus thing on top of her. Shall I demonstrate?"

"Yes."

Shandy joggled himself into position as best he could.

"Is that how she was lying," Tim asked, "in a straight line with the stool?"

"Just about. She wouldn't have been able to fit any other way. There's only about three feet of width back here."

"Mh. How did you happen to find her?"

"Now, that's something that puzzles me, Tim. I stepped on a marble."

Shandy went over to the whatnot and picked up the little dish Alice had given him so many years before. "I don't know whether you've ever noticed these, but Elizabeth's niece gave them to me a long time ago. You remember she used to visit me sometimes?"

"Of course I remember. Nice little kid. Damn sight better behaved than my own."

"Er—at any rate, I've always kept this bowl of marbles here on the whatnot. There were thirty-eight."

Ames nodded perfunctorily. He took it for granted Shandy would know.

"When I got home this morning, the marbles were scattered over the living room floor and out into the hall. I might not have noticed, since I was cold and hungry and in a state of—er—general perturbation, but one of them tripped me up. So I went hunting for the rest. At first I didn't think to look behind the sofa because it seemed impossible any could have got there. The base is solid right down to the floor, as you can see, and besides, the floor slants a bit in the opposite direction. It's an old house, you know. But I knew I was one short and I'd looked everywhere else, so—"

"Did you find the marble?"

"No. I've asked them to search her clothing. It might be in her pocket or somewhere. But, drat it, Tim, I don't see how she could have spilled those marbles. There was no need for her to go anywhere near the whatnot."

"What gets me is that step stool," said Ames. "What the hell would she bother to drag that in here for? These ceilings aren't very high, and Jemima was a big woman. She could have reached that mask easily enough from the floor. You try it. You're taller than I am."

"And she was at least a couple of inches taller than I."

Shandy went to another window and reached up. He had no difficulty in touching the plastic ornament.

"There, see," said the husband. "Anyway, it wouldn't have been like Jemima to bother about that stool. Damned awkward place to put it, for one thing. She'd have been more apt to shove the sofa over against the window and jump up on that, if she needed to, which she didn't. Jemima spent half her life leaping around on the furniture. That was why I wanted to call that viola the Jumping Jemima. Remember the one we had the fight about that time? I was trying to get back at her about some damn thing or other, I forget what. Water over the dam now. Well, that's one less thing on my conscience, thanks to your pigheadedness."

"Thanks to me, she's dead," said Shandy bitterly. "If I hadn't lost my temper with her and pulled this damn fool stunt, she wouldn't have come here in the first place."

"You sure she came by herself, Pete?"

The two old friends looked into each other's eyes. Shandy shook his head slowly.

"The only thing I'm sure of is that I found her dead in my house. Melchett says—"

"That horse's ass would say whatever he thought Dr. Svenson wanted to hear. You know that."

"Yes, I know. And Grimble says she probably came straight here from the Dysarts' party, about half past nine on the evening of the twenty-second." Shandy's lips twisted. "At least that gives me an alibi. I was running away to sea by then."

He gave Ames a brief rundown of his short-lived adventure aboard the *Singapore Susie*. His friend nodded.

"Stroke of luck for you, Pete. At least you're in the clear. Leaves me in the soup, of course."

"You?" Shandy stared at him in astonishment. "Tim, if you were going to murder your wife, you'd have done it a long time ago."

"That's opinion, not evidence."

Nevertheless, Professor Ames's grin returned for an instant. "She was an awfully exasperating woman to be married to, Pete. She was the world's rottenest housekeeper, she minded everybody's business but her own, and she never once shut her mouth that I can remember. Nevertheless, being her husband had its good points. For one thing, it stopped me from thinking of my deafness as an affliction."

He emitted an odd little wheeze that would under other circumstances have become a chuckle. "It's good to have one friend I can say rotten things to without feeling like a skunk."

"That's not so rotten," Shandy replied. "Hell, Tim, you do have to live with your deafness. Living with anybody but Jemima, you'd have felt constantly frustrated at the thought that you might be missing something by not hearing what she said. With a less assertive woman, your conscience would have driven you to make social efforts that are hard for you to handle. As it was, you could do as you pleased and still have somebody to send out your shirts. I'm putting it badly but you know what I mean. I suspect there are a few people around here who might have envied your situation."

"I know damn well there are. I may be deaf, but I'm not dumb. Don't suppose one of 'em killed her out of spite?"

"That's a supposition I shouldn't care to make without something to back it up," said Shandy. "Er—are you quite sure somebody did in fact kill her?"

"Christ, Pete, you've been sure of that fact yourself,

from the moment you found her, and don't try to tell me you haven't. I can read you like a book. What was your first impression?"

"That somebody had been clever," Shandy admitted. "Smart-aleck clever. The spilled marbles were a piece of utterly tasteless embroidery. I suppose they were supposed to create the impression that she'd been blundering around in the dark, possibly because she'd had one too many at the Dysarts'. Jemima did like a drink, you know."

"I ought to. I've been accused often enough of driving her to it. But she never got drunk, Pete, not that way. Her face would get red and she'd start telling somebody off or hurling the furniture around. That's why I'm so sure this scene was staged. She wasn't clumsy, she was belligerent. She'd have been much more apt to just reach up and rip those lights down regardless of any damage to the woodwork, or else to stomp all over your upholstery in her muddy boots. Where do you keep that stool, anyway?"

"In the back hall closet. Once in a while, when Mrs. Lomax feels especially put-upon, she gets it out and starts performing some herculean feat that involves a great deal of grunting and groaning and climbing up and down and sloshing soapsuds around. Except for those few times, I don't believe it gets used very much. I'd wondered about that myself. It did seem out of character."

"Damn right it does. More of your tasteless embroidery. I agree with you, Pete. We're dealing with somebody who's clever but not very intelligent, which in my opinion includes just about everybody on the goddamn faculty. What do you think, Pete? You know 'em better than I do."

"That's open to challenge. I socialize more than you, because I'd be a lonely man if I didn't, but I'm not on particularly intimate terms with any but the Enderbles. Why do you think it has to be a faculty person?"

"Well, hell, Pete, it has to be somebody who knew Jemima well enough to want to kill her."

"Yes, but was she killed as herself, so to speak, or for some reason—er—exclusive of personality factors?"

"How should I know? All right, I'll grant you she didn't make the usual distinctions between town and gown when it came to butting in and making a nuisance of herself, but I'm going on the evidence. We have to assume, at least in my opinion, that she was murdered by somebody who knew how steamed up she was over this joke of yours, who knew how to get into your house, and who knew where you keep your step stool."

"I'll grant that. And also by somebody who knew I'd gone away. Since I left in a hurry without notifying Grimble, that does seem to narrow the field."

"To some extent, at any rate. I think we can take it as given that every single resident of the Crescent was peeking around the curtains by the time you climbed into that truck. I know I was."

Despite his preoccupation with the hypothesis of his wife's murder, Ames chortled again. "Damn, that was the most amusing afternoon I've spent since President Svenson lost his footing while he was showing the Secretary of Agriculture how we make methane gas. It was an awful disappointment when I saw you were carrying a suitcase. I'd hoped we could get together during the evening and enjoy the reactions."

"I wish we had!" cried Shandy. "Tim, I can't tell you how sick I am about this ghastly business."

"Hell, Pete, you don't have to. I expect I'll feel pretty rotten myself, once I get used to the idea that she's really gone. After all, damn it, Jemima was my wife. I didn't like her very much, but I sort of loved her, in a way. Personal feelings aside, I think what we ought to bear in mind is that if you hadn't provided a convenient parking place for her body, another would have been found."

"Then you think the murder was premeditated."

"It must have been. Look at this room. Do you honestly believe anybody could have brought Jemima in here alive, bumped her off with the blinds up and all those lights in the windows and God knows how many people milling around outside, gone through that folderol with the step stool, thrown marbles all over the floor, and got away without one person's looking in and noticing what he was up to? In the first place, Jemima wouldn't have been all that easy to kill, unless you made damn good and sure to sneak up on her and land one clean blow that did the job. And it had to be done in the right spot, with the right kind of weapon. Even that jackass Melchett would have noticed any real discrepancy between the shape of the wound and the shape of the stool, wouldn't he?"

"Yes, and so should I, and there wasn't. The only alternative suggestion is that there actually was a quarrel and somebody shoved her from in front, so that she fell and struck some hard object similar to the stool."

"Who, for instance? Name me one person in Balaclava Junction, except for President Svenson and that behemoth he's married to, whom Jemima couldn't have licked with one hand tied behind her back. Anybody who tried to knock her down would have to be mopped up with a blotter."

"Er—in any event, the incident would have caused a stir, since it must almost inevitably have taken place in front of witnesses. I see your point. The tidiness of the room and the—er—staging of the scene indicate that Jemima may have been killed elsewhere and brought here sometime after the lights were turned out."

"Can you think of any other logical explanation?"

"I can't think at all any more." Shandy slumped down on the sofa and buried his face in his hands. "Dear God, I'm tired."

"Sure you are, Pete."

Ames whacked his friend on the shoulder. "Why don't you take a nap? I've got to call the kids, then I suppose I'd better get downtown and find out what they've done with her. I'll get back to you later."

"Thank you, Tim. I'll be here."

Shandy let his old friend out, locked the door, and went upstairs to his bedroom. He ought to call the Dysarts. He ought to go with Tim. He ought to have his head examined for ever having started this terrible chain of events. What he did was to fall asleep.

Chapter 5

Professor Shandy slept a good deal longer than he'd meant to. By the time he woke, stiff and chilly, the early dusk was already gathering. So, evidently, was the crowd. He could hear a babble of voices down in the Crescent, and a preliminary ripple of bongs from the chapel carillon. As he lay collecting his wits and easing his cramped muscles, the bedroom was suddenly bathed in multicolored light and those accursed Santa Claus faces began flashing on and off. Grimble must have thrown the switch. Cursing, he sat up and reached for his shoes.

His intention was to take down those hideous masks and jump on them, but as he reached for the first one to hand, a shrill young voice from below piped, "Aw, mister!" He settled for drawing the blind, realized the cloth would be apt to catch fire from being pressed against the hot bulbs, and had to put it up again. From his folly, there was no escape.

At least he could flee temporarily to the faculty dining room. Both he and Tim would feel better with a hot meal under their belts. He'd go round up his old friend.

It was curious, now he thought of it, that the police had not fetched the husband over here this morning, instead of trundling Jemima's body straight downtown without even letting Tim know where it was. True, he mustn't have had to look far. Balaclava Junction had only one undertaker, who belonged to the same lodge as Grimble and Ottermole and would surely get the business. Still, they might have asked Professor Ames's consent before turning his wife over to Harry the Ghoul. The fact was, people did not take Tim seriously as a human being.

Shandy could understand why easily enough. Ames was not totally deaf. He did own a hearing aid, but peculiar bone formations in his ears sometimes caused the device to act as a built-in scrambler. One never knew whether he was hearing the right words, the wrong words, or a jumble of unrelated sounds. He could lip-read very well, but was so near-sighted that he had to get close to the speaker, and so shy that he didn't always care to do that.

Perhaps as a result of his affliction, Ames concentrated so fiercely on his own subject that he was usually oblivious to everything else, thus a natural butt for all the absent-minded professor jokes. Even his appearance was almost risible: diminutive, gnarled, bald on top and hairy everywhere else.

Jemima, probably not on purpose but out of her own need to be important, had fostered the myth of her husband's general uselessness outside his particular field. His children liked him well enough as a sort of family pet but never seemed to accord him the respect due a father. Yet Professor Ames was an exceedingly bright, capable, and above all logical man. Whoever had done this dreadful thing to Jemima didn't know that.

Shandy couldn't honestly see that this narrowed the list of suspects much. Not many people did know, aside from himself and President Svenson and perhaps a few of the more observant students. It was always hard to tell what students took in and what they didn't.

This was no time for such musings. Shandy put on his good gray overcoat and good felt hat and added a dark red cashmere muffler Alice had sent him, for there was a chill in the air that penetrated the walls of the brick house, probably because he'd set back the thermostat earlier and forgotten to turn it up again.

He remedied his omission before starting out. Tim might want to come back and sit awhile, and it would be good to have the place comfortable for him. It was too bad they'd have to put up with that lurid glare, but he realized at this stage that his only hope of averting general obloquy was to brazen it out and pretend he thought his decorations handsome. Instead of being obliged·to declare open warfare, his neighbors could work off their resentment by despising his rotten taste behind his back.

That meant he would have no defense next year, assuming he managed to stay, against whichever Illumination stalwart caught up Jemima's fallen torch and offered to decorate his house for him. It was, he supposed, only a fair price to pay. Perhaps the *Singapore Susie* would be repaired by then, or he could fly out and spend the holidays with Alice, as she'd been begging him to do ever since she got married. Maybe Henry and Elizabeth would enjoy an expense-paid trip as a Christmas present, instead of the accustomed cigars and jellies.

He doubted it. They were a pair of contented old fogies, such as he himself had so short a time ago looked forward to becoming. Sighing, Professor Shandy opened his front door and eased himself out into the maelstrom of merriment.

"Watch it, Professor!"

He leaped just in time. One of the sleds, carrying a gaggle of shrieking tourists and propelled by a blond Amazon in a bulky red sweater, no pants to speak of, and heavy rib-knit green tights, hurtled down the sidewalk.

The sled pullers knew perfectly well they were supposed to keep the sleds off the walkways and never let go of the towropes, but the rule was constantly being violated, especially by those of the girls who were pretty enough to think they could get away with anything. Professor Shandy was by no means indifferent to feminine pulchritude, but beefy blondes left him as cold as he would have thought those minuscule pants left them. He would have a word with that young woman if he could ever get her to stand still long enough and if he managed to find out who she was. They all looked much alike in those ridiculous costumes, which were meant to represent Santa's elves. He wouldn't even have known this one was female if she'd been obeying another of the rules and wearing the knitted face helmet that was supposed to go with the costume.

Muttering, he elbowed his way through the strollers and gapers, and managed to reach Ames's house more or less unscathed. Before he'd even started knocking, Tim opened the door.

"Hi, Pete. I thought you'd be over. Been watching out the window."

"Good thing you were. I'd never have been able to make myself heard above this God-awful racket. It gets worse every year."

"You contributed your share. God, that was funny."

Ames made the statement automatically, showing no inclination to throw another laughing fit. Shandy could understand why.

"How did you make out with Ottermole?"

"All right, I guess. He asked me a lot of damn fool questions about when did I see her last and so forth. Seemed to think I was mentally defective because I couldn't tell him. But, damn it, that was the way Jemima operated. She'd breeze in and change her clothes or grab a basketful of junk for one of the booths, go charging out again, and stay till the last gun was fired and the smoke cleared away. We've had separate rooms since the kids moved out, so how the hell would I know whether or not she came in to sleep? Asked me if the bed was made, for God's sake. Nobody's made a bed in this house for thirty-seven years. Well, maybe that's a slight exaggeration. I guess she used to change the sheets now and then, but you can bet your sweet Alice it wasn't while the Illumination was going on. You want a drink?"

"I daresay I could use one. I was going to suggest that we go over to the dining room."

Ames snorted. "You sound like Jemima. 'If you want any dinner, you'd better go up to the college. I have more important things to do than stand around a kitchen.' Of course she'd spend all day baking those damn fool coconut cowpats for the cookie sale. I never knew why it was she could handle everybody's job but her own. Now, where the hell did she put the whiskey?"

He maundered off, searching for a bottle that would likely as not be empty if he ever found it. Shandy didn't offer to help. He only hoped Tim would tire of hunting soon and they could get out of here. The dismal confusion of the Ames house had always depressed him, but it seemed even deadlier now without Jemima's boisterous presence actual or impending.

Could he possibly be missing the woman? He supposed it was possible. Tim had said, "I didn't like her, but I sort of loved her, in a way." That was more or less how he himself had felt about her; not love, certainly, nor friendship, but the grudging fondness one had for one's tiresome but well-intentioned relatives.

For a wonder, Tim managed to locate not only the whiskey but a couple of clean tumblers. Shandy pretended he was glad to get the drink, because old Tim was so pleased with himself for succeeding at this essay in housewifery. How in God's name was he ever going to manage here alone?

"Have you called the children?" he asked.

"Called the Oceanographic Institute to see if there was any way I could get hold of Roy. They say he's still at sea, headed for Ross Bay. They're going to send a wireless to the ship. Best they can do right now. Later they'll try to set up some kind of radio relay so I can talk to him at the base."

"That's good. What about Jemmy?"

"She doesn't think the doctor will let her come. Baby's due in a few days. Jemima was going to fly out. Had her ticket all bought. All Jemmy could say was, 'Now Mummy can't be with me.' I didn't think she'd take it so hard. Suppose it is sort of a jolt, 'way the hell and gone the other side of the country with none of her own folks around her."

"Why don't you go on Jemima's ticket?"

"Huh? Me? What the hell could I do?"

"You could be with her."

"For what that's worth."

"It might be worth more than you think, Tim. Why don't you call her back and suggest it?"

"I wouldn't even know what to say."

"Say you'll go as soon as the funeral's over, if she wants you to."

"What if she doesn't?"

"Then you stay here."

"You make it sound easy."

"Why shouldn't it be? She's your own daughter, isn't she?"

"Oh yes, no doubt about that." A smile flickered across the gnomish face. "Jemima had her faults, but that wasn't one of them. All right, Pete, if you say so."

"Want any help getting the number?"

"No, I can manage."

Ames set down his tumbler and went to wherever the phone might be lurking. Shandy stayed where he was. He didn't want to hear the hurt in his old friend's voice if Jemmy turned her father down.

Apparently she didn't. Ames came back looking sheepish but happy.

"She's tickled pink. Told me when the plane leaves and says I damn well better be on it because Dave's taking time off from work to pick me up. Laying down the law just like her mother."

"I'm glad, Tim," said Shandy with all sincerity. "It will be a great thing for both of you. I can keep an eye on the house while you're away."

"Hell, she's got that fixed, too. Some old-maid aunt of Dave's was there, bringing over her plants. She just got fired from her job or some damn thing and was leaving town anyway, so Jemmy had the bright idea of sending her here to housekeep for me."

"Why not? You probably won't have her underfoot for long. There's nothing to keep a woman in Balaclava Junction unless she decides to marry you or take over Jemima's job on the Buggins Collection."

That last was a particularly nasty thing to say and Shandy was at once sorry he'd said it, but Tim well knew what a sore point the Buggins Collection had always been with him.

Back in the 1920s, some distant connection of the founder took exception to the fact that Balaclava Buggins had preferred his first name to his last. In order that the family name might be preserved in college, he bequeathed his personal library to the institution with the proviso that it be housed as a separate unit and known as the Buggins Collection.

As he left only a small sum to maintain the collection, and as the books had nothing to do with agriculture, they were dumped into a room at the back of the library building and locked up until such time as somebody got around to straightening them out.

The college grew. The librarian got busier. The Buggins Collection got dustier. Once in a while, somebody would unlock the door, sneeze a few times, shake his head, and lock it again. The books couldn't be circulated, or even consulted, because they had not been catalogued. Nobody cared because nobody wanted to read them anyway, until Peter Shandy joined the faculty.

Professor Shandy had a pleasant, old-gentlemanly taste for verse as distinct from poetry. He had grown up on Macaulay, Joel Barlow, and John G. Saxe. He could never read "Jim Bludsoe of the Prairie Belle" without choking up on those immortal lines, "I'll hold her nozzle agin the bank/Till the last galoot's ashore." He could recite "The Dinkey Bird goes singing/In the amfalula tree," although he had not done so since Alice grew up.

He thought of the treasures in rhyme that must be lurking among those cobwebbed piles, and wished to Christ somebody would get busy and straighten them out. He would gladly have taken on the job himself in his spare time, but Porble the librarian never let anybody have the key to the Buggins Room because the books couldn't be circulated since they hadn't been catalogued and it was against library rules for nonstaff people to go in there and mess around.

So Shandy, once tenure had made him bold, started chanting at faculty meetings, "We ought to do something about the Buggins Collection." First it was a joke, then a bore. Nothing happened until he did what he should have done in the first place and voiced his concern to Mrs. Svenson at a cocktail party. Jemima Ames, who had a knack for popping up in the wrong place at the worst time, overheard and at once volunteered herself as assistant librarian for the Buggins Collection.

Sieglinde Svenson knew Mrs. Ames as a tireless worker in college causes. She spoke to Thorkjeld. President Svenson knew there was money in the Buggins fund that couldn't be touched for any more useful purpose. He did not know Mrs. Ames's total inability to stick to anything she was really supposed to do, so he hired her.

At the time of her demise, Jemima had held the appointment for almost a year. She had requisitioned card files and made great play with Library of Congress lists. She had spent much time and energy promoting a contest to design a special bookplate for the Buggins Collection which nobody bothered to do because there were no prizes and which would in any case have been redundant as the late Mr. Buggins had already put in his own bookplates. She had flaunted her title and talked of the great work to be accomplished, but not one book had got dusted, much less shelved.

If Shandy had in fact been the one to slaughter Tim's wife, it would have been the Buggins Collection that drove him to it. Since nobody else gave two hoots about the old books, however, some other frustration must have triggered the deed.

But how could he know frustration was the motive? Jemima had been putting people's backs up for years, and nobody had murdered her before.

"More whiskey, Pete?"

"Er—no, thanks." He set down the glass he'd emptied without realizing it. "I think we ought to get along to the dining room, or they'll have nothing left but turkey hash. To tell you the truth, I've been wondering why anybody wanted to kill Jemima. I mean, wanted to so badly that he or she actually did it. Oh, damn, you know what I'm trying to say."

"I know, Pete. She could be the most exasperating woman on earth, but she wasn't basically ill-natured. I've been wondering about that myself."

"Did you tell Ottermole we'd decided it was murder rather than accident?"

"No, I thought I hadn't better. He thinks I'm about one step ahead of the funny farm anyway, and I figured he wouldn't listen to me. He's convinced he did a brilliant piece of detecting."

"I expect he wants to think so, anyway. The townees don't want to run afoul of Svenson any more than we do. Did you manage to find the marble?"

"No sign of it. I made Harry the Ghoul search her clothes while I stood there and watched. That was another thing that made Ottermole sure I was rounding the bend."

"I'm sorry."

"What for? Damn it, I'm sorry, too, but not about what that jackass thinks of me. Come on, Pete, we might as well tie on the feed bag."

Chapter 6

They picked their way among the cider-swiggers and gingerbread-nibblers, the sliders and the strollers, up the slippery, trodden Crescent toward the college. Shandy marveled that so many humans were willing to drive long distances over secondary and often tertiary roads for the privilege of being fleeced by Balaclava's car-park bandits and joggled by fellow gapers as they milled around ankle-deep in slush. To his horror, he could see that Shandy's Folly was indeed the hit of the show.

"Boy, whoever lives in that place believes in giving us our money's worth," he heard one tourist exclaim. "I'd hate to have their light bill."

The professor winced. He hadn't thought of that. Power from the Cookie Works, as it was irreverently called, was not precisely cheap. No wonder Svenson encouraged the Illumination in all its excesses. The college must do a tidy business in electrical fees on top of everything else. Shandy observed as much to his companion.

Tim didn't hear. He was rambling on about his own problems, mouthing words without realizing no sound was coming out. This often happened. Shandy nudged him in the ribs.

"Speak up, Tim."

"Eh? Oh, I was just sounding off about Harry the Ghoul." Undertaker Goulson was well liked in town, but the nickname was irresistible. "He was pestering me about what I wanted Jemima laid out in. Showed me a bunch of fancy dresses with no backs to 'em. Most indecent things I ever saw. Told him I wouldn't stand for anything so disgusting, and so I won't. Pete, I can't handle this thing. I wish to God Jemmy could have come."

He kicked at frozen slush and took another tack. "I don't know if it's occurred to you, Pete, but we're going to be about as popular around here as a couple of skunks at a lawn party. All the people who couldn't stand Jemima when she was alive are going to feel guilty and blame us for her getting killed. You'd better come to California with me."

"No, I'll stand the gaff. You had nothing to do with it."

"I let her lie there for three days. They'll call me a callous brute. Suppose I was."

"No, you weren't," said his friend loyally, even though he knew the neighbors must be saying that and a great deal more. Confirmation appeared in the shape of Jemima's staunch ally, Hannah Cadwall, bearing down on them with blood in her eye. Knowing his only defense was in attack, Shandy beat her to the draw.

"Hannah, we came out looking for you."

His outright lie stopped her in her tracks. Shandy pressed his advantage.

"Tim was just saying we need a woman's help in this terrible time. I expect you've heard about our—er—tragedy?"

Mrs. Cadwall nodded, not quite sure how to reply. Professor Ames nodded, too, and had presence of mind enough to leave the talking to Shandy.

"Perhaps you wouldn't mind walking along with us to the dining room. I'm trying to get him to eat something," Shandy added in a conspiratorial murmur.

"Why, of course. Anything I can do—such a dreadful— still can't believe she's—" Mrs. Cadwall's earnest incoherencies were a welcome switch from the reproaches she no doubt had ready framed. She did show a distressing tendency to lead the shattered widower by the arm, but that would have to be borne. If he could get her to see Ames as victim instead of villain and himself as a well-intentioned blunderer, public opinion might still be swayed in their favor, because Hannah was a talker and so was her husband. Shandy eased the tremolo stop out another notch.

"Unfortunately, he won't be able to have either of the children with him. Roy's at the South Pole and Jemmy's about due to have her baby, as you doubtless know. She's so dreadfully cut up about her mother that Tim's promised to go out there right after the funeral. Rather heartbreaking, don't you think?"

Mrs. Cadwall obliged with a sniffle. "Poor soul, whatever will become of him? Jemima was so—so—"

"Indeed she was. It's a sad loss for us all. I'll confess to you, Hannah, as an old friend, that I'm having strong guilt feelings about this awful thing. After that—er—little talking-to you two gave me, I—er—tried to make amends, as you must have realized. You can't say I didn't try."

"No, you certainly tried," Mrs. Cadwall had to concede.

"Chief Ottermole feels that Jemima must have been in the process of—er—modifying my efforts when she slipped and fell. I'll never forgive myself." That last bit, at any rate, was not humbug.

"Now, Peter, there's no sense in your brooding over what can't be helped. In a way, I suppose it's as much my fault as yours. I nagged at you enough about decorating. Next year, I'd be glad to—"

"It's right this minute we need you most, Hannah. Do you think you might possibly be willing, as Jemima's—er—closest friend and confidante, to do her a last favor?"

"Oh yes, anything!"

"Tim was just saying—Tim," he bawled into the widower's ear, "why don't we ask Hannah about the dress?"

Ames, who had been lip-reading as best he could, picked up his cue.

"Goulson wants to know what to lay her out in. Tried to talk me into some piece of nonsense he's got down there. Didn't look like her style. Can't you pick out something of hers that she liked, that she'd feel comfortable in?"

The last words came out jumbled, probably because his teeth were slipping. Hannah took it for emotion and was won.

"Leave it to me, Tim. I'll straighten out Harry the Ghoul. Shall I order the flowers, too? The florist's his brother-in-law and they'll skin you alive between them if you don't put your foot down."

"Hannah, you're a good friend. You go ahead and do it the way you think Jemima would have wanted, and send the bills to me."

Mrs. Cadwall blew her nose. "Peter," she choked, "see that he eats a good dinner."

There was a fair amount of shoulder-patting and hand-squeezing before Mrs. Cadwall sped off on her errand of light. This took place directly in front of the dining hall and was witnessed by a satisfying number of faculty members. Ames almost queered the performance by remarking, "God, Pete, you played her like a violin," but fortunately he forgot to turn up the volume. Shandy got him inside fast and asked the waitress in properly subdued tones for a table in a quiet corner.

They got through the meal rather quickly. The student waitress was brisk and efficient. Those fellow diners who came over to offer condolences didn't linger at the table. It was never easy to make small talk with Professor Ames, and the subject was not a pleasant one.

"The funeral?" Tim answered the question for the sixth time. "It's tomorrow morning at ten o'clock in the college chapel. Don't want to drag it out and put a damper on the Illumination. Jemima wouldn't have liked that."

He sighed and picked up his dessert fork. The inquirer took the hint and left.

Tim was looking awfully tired, Shandy thought. This must be a terrible strain on the deaf man, so used to living in his own silent world. Probably the best thing would be to get him straight home. For Shandy himself there could be no rest. Among other things, he must call on the Dysarts, not only because he owed them an apology but because he wanted to know more about Jemima's last actions of record.

He signed the check, left a lavish tip feeling that he'd better get as many people as possible on his side, and shepherded his old friend back down the hill. Neither of them said much until they were inside the house that its late mistress had bedecked so exuberantly without and allowed to remain such a dismal mess within.

"Do you mind staying here alone, Tim?"

"Why the hell should I? Anyway, I expect Hannah will

be along pretty soon to get that dress. I forgot to give her my key."

"Speaking of keys, I've been wondering whether you or Jemima had a key to my house."

"Damned if I know." Ames glanced around the cluttered room helplessly. "If we did, it's buried somewhere. It wasn't on her, anyway. She wasn't even carrying a key to this house. She knew I'd be here."

"Then I wonder how she got in. She or whoever took her. I could find no sign of forced entry."

"Maybe they picked the lock."

"They're supposed to be the nonpickable kind. You have to use a key both coming and going. Tim, that's another mistake! I had to use my own key to get in. If there was no key on her, how in hell did the doors get locked? I think we'll have to go back and try to pound some sense into Ottermole's head."

"Can't be done, Pete, believe me. He'll claim the door was unlocked and you didn't notice or the key was there and you hid it or some damn bunch of horsefeathers. He doesn't want a murder during the Grand Illumination and he's not going to have one and that's that. Oh, Christ, Pete, I can't handle this."

"All right, Tim. You concentrate on getting through the funeral and out to be with Jemmy. I won't do anything you don't want me to."

"At this stage, I don't know what I want except a few hours' sleep. I'm not going to ask you to sit on this. You're a scholar. If one of your plants died, you'd think it was part of your job to find out why. If somebody gets killed in your house, the same principle has to apply, I suppose. You know I've always worked with you as best I could, and I'm not backing off now, especially when it's my own wife that's dead. I'm just asking how much you think you're going to accomplish by raising a ruckus when you're already in the doghouse for trying to sabotage the Illumination. You know damn well that's what you had in mind and so does everybody else around here who isn't an utter jackass, regardless of your fancy footwork back there with Hannah Cadwall. Aren't they going to think this is just another scheme to stir up trouble because your first one laid an egg?"

Shandy hunched his shoulders. "You've never given me

bad advice yet, Tim. I'll wait until I have something more tangible to show. Er—you're not by any chance planning on cremation, are you?"

"No, we have a family plot up near Groton. I'm having her buried there as soon as the ground can be dug. In the meantime, they'll keep her in some damnable cold storage vault they've got somewhere. So we can get at the body without having to order an exhumation for the next couple of months, I daresay. That what you had in mind?"

"Er—yes. Though the cause of death seemed obvious enough. Tim, I can't leave this awful business lying on my doorstep. Surely it won't hurt to keep nosing around in a quiet way?"

"It might hurt a great deal, if the wrong person got wind of what you're up to. You know yourself that students in Poultry Management are always squeamish about killing their first chicken, but after that they take it in stride."

"For a man who doesn't talk much, you have quite a gift for words, old friend. I'll try not to wind up in the soup." Shandy rewrapped his muffler. "Florence Nightingale is about to ring your doorbell. I'll leave you to her."

"Thanks, pal. Care to walk me down to the funeral? I'm supposed to get there early so people can cry over me."

"I'll pick you up at a quarter past nine."

Shandy opened the door for Hannah Cadwall, pressed her hand and was rewarded with a watery smile, and went out to breast the tide of jollity once more. He had no scruples about leaving his friend with Hannah, as Tim could always turn off his hearing aid.

That remark of Tim's about chickens was uncomfortably perspicacious. He hadn't thought of the possibility for himself. There seemed to be a great many things he hadn't thought of. At least he ought to be safe enough making his apologies to the Dysarts.

"Watch it, Professor!"

There was that accursed girl again, trundling some squealing wretch over the iced-in ruts on her confounded sled.

"Watch it yourself, young woman," he snapped. "You're supposed to keep those sleds out of the walkways."

She sped past before he got the words out, with a provocative waggle of her backside. Some other bogus elf, anonymous in a knitted mask, yelled from one of the gingerbread houses, "Don't be a party-pooper, Professor. How about a hot cider to melt that cold, cold heart?"

"I've just finished dinner, thank you," he replied with what fragment of dignity was left to him. "However, I'll take a packet of those—er—coconut cowpats."

The Dysarts went in rather heavily for whimsy.

"You'll never regret it," the student assured him, accepting a five-dollar bill and returning a shockingly small amount of change.

"I regret it already," the professor replied, gazing in dismay at the pittance in his glove. "In any event, I don't intend to eat them myself so the worst will be spared to me. Er—speaking of survival, can you tell me the name of that—er—blond bombshell who keeps trying to run me down with her sled? I've been wondering if she does it out of personal animosity or near-sightedness."

The elf stared through its yarn-fringed eyeholes. "You mean you don't know Heidi Hayhoe?"

"Obviously not. Is there any reason why I should?"

While the elf was still groping for words, its stand was suddenly inundated by a horde eager to exchange cold cash for hot cider. Shandy grabbed his bag of cowpats and fought his way loose.

The Dysarts lived in the last and largest house on the Crescent. Actually, it faced Shropshire Avenue, the road that meandered down from behind the college to cross Balaclava Junction's Main Street. However, the Crescent counted the handsome fieldstone and clapboard residence as its own because it did the neighborhood credit. So, most people felt, did the Dysarts.

They were the only faculty couple who did mad, sophisticated things like hopping down to New Orleans for the Mardi Gras or over to Milwaukee for the Oktoberfest. They were the only people in town who owned a Porsche and among the few who knew how to pronounce it. They also owned a beat-up old Volkswagen.

Nobody needed two cars in a village where everything was within walking distance, but that was part of the Dysart mystique. Adele made a point of driving the VW to the supermarket about once a month. The elderly vehicle was apt as not to break down in the parking lot and give her an opportunity to demonstrate that she was just a harried housewife like the rest of them. Adele was the one with the money.

She also had a great many teeth. Professor Shandy was always aware of Adele Dysart's teeth, but never more so than now, as he handed over his sack of bucolic ribaldry and stammered out his apologies for having cut their Christmas party without notice.

"I was—er—called out of town unexpectedly."

"So we heard, only that wasn't the way we heard it. Hiya, Pete."

Bob Dysart surged forward. Bob always surged. He reminded Shandy of the *Singapore Susie,* now that the professor was in a position to make the comparison.

"Have a drink and tell us all about it."

"There's—er—not a great deal to tell. Thanks, I will. A small scotch and water, if you don't mind. About half of what you'd consider a reasonable allowance for an elderly lady in poor health."

Bob dispensed liquor as he did everything else, in a big way. Shandy did not wish to complete his roster of social gaffes by having to battle his way back up the Crescent half sloshed. He picked his way among the Dysarts' assortment of furniture, avoided the camel bench and the chair made entirely of buffalo horns, and settled on a wicker throne with a back like a peacock's tail. The seat wasn't too bad, and he wouldn't have to look at what was behind him.

"How's that?"

His host thrust a tumbler with a large orange D on it into his hand. Shandy tasted the mixture with apprehension and decided to let the ice melt a little.

"Fine, Bob. I suppose you've heard the—er—terrible news?"

"We've heard Jemima Ames fell and cracked her nut, if that's what you mean." Bob made a thing of calling a spade by a more vulgar name. "As to whether it's terrible, I haven't made up my mind."

"Pay no attention to him, Peter," said Adele. "He's in one of his Oscar Wilde moods. I think it's perfectly awful myself. Poor Jemima was such a vibrant personality."

"That depends on how you define vibrant," her husband quibbled. "Constantly in motion and not getting anywhere but making a lot of noise about it, like a tuning fork? If that's what you mean, I agree absolutely."

"That's not bad, sweetie. Perhaps you'd better go write it down. Bring me a bourbon on your way back."

"You've already had a bourbon."

"I've had two, but who's counting? Tell me, Peter, was she all bloodied up and horrible?"

"No, nothing like that. Just—er—lying there."

"Oh."

Adele struggled not to look disappointed. "Hannah told me she tripped on a ladder or something while she was trying to take down those fantastic Santa Clauses of yours. She said she was going to, you know."

"Did she? No, I didn't know."

"You would have, you bad kid, if you hadn't skipped out on my lovely party. Who's the woman?"

"What woman?"

"The one you went to spend Christmas with. Why else would you walk out on me?"

Shandy felt himself gripped by another of those hellish impulses.

"Er—her name is Susie. In strictest confidence, of course."

"I won't breathe a word," said Adele with an earnestness that fooled nobody. "What's she like?"

"Well—er—she's very fond of the water. You say Jemima was trying to take down my Santa Clauses? I think they're rather colorful myself."

"They're that, and then some," roared Bob. "Come on, Pete, you can't kid us. Everybody knows what you were up to."

"That's distressing. I'd hoped I might be able to—er—persuade you otherwise."

"Forget it, pal. Feeling was running pretty high at the party. No higher than the guests, I have to admit."

"You know what happens when Bob makes the punch," said Adele. "I'm not sure whether it was the cherry brandy or the tequila this time."

"Too bad I missed it," said Shandy, unable to repress a shudder. "Then Jemima was a trifle above herself, so to speak?"

"No worse than anyone else," Adele started to say, but her husband cut in.

"No use trying to paint the lily, Dell, or whatever it is you do to the damn things. Pete would know, I expect. Jemima was drunk as a skunk, to coin a simile. Don't you remember how we all stood at the window watching her weave herself down the path with that purple cape flapping out behind her? Christ, we laughed ourselves sick."

"Well, don't do it again," said his wife. "Peter, you wouldn't believe the mess I had to cope with next morning. Next time you drop one of your time bombs into the punch bowl, sweetiekins, you clean the bathrooms."

"Isn't she cute, Pete? How's your drink? Ready for the dividend?"

"No, thanks. I'm still working on the—er—principal. I wonder if you have any idea who let her in?"

"Who can remember?" Adele replied. "Either Bob or myself, I suppose, or else she just barged in without ringing the bell. She'd do that."

"I meant into my house," Shandy explained. "She couldn't have barged in there because I'd locked up carefully before I left."

Dysart shrugged. "She must have found a key somewhere. I know Adele and I are always leaving them with the neighbors when we go away and so does everybody else. You probably gave her one yourself at one time or another."

"I'm quite sure I didn't. Jemima wasn't particularly reliable. Anyway, Mrs. Lomax generally takes care of the place while I'm gone."

"She didn't this time."

"No, but—"

"Damn it, Pete, there's no use making a mystery over a little thing like this. You've passed one out to somebody or other so long ago you've forgotten about it, that's all. What about the Feldsters? They're the most logical, being your next-door neighbors."

Shandy didn't think so. Mirelle Feldster had been trying for fifteen years to take poor, lonely Peter Shandy under her motherly wing. He couldn't believe he'd ever have been fool enough to give her a key to his house and not get it back. Still, there was always the possibility she'd managed to get hold of one somehow.

"Were they at the party?"

"Sure. Everybody was but you and the Cadwalls, naturally. I'll bet a nickel it was either Mirelle or Jim who gave Jemima the key. You can imagine how they're feeling about this cute trick of yours, with eight plastic reindeer leering straight into their bedroom window. Must be putting old Jim right off his stroke."

"If you ask me, he quit stroking a long time ago," Adele put in, but Shandy paid no attention.

"But you don't actually remember anyone's mentioning a key?"

"Hell, I don't remember anything at all with any great degree of clarity from about half past eight on," said Dysart.

"I'll drink to that," said his wife.

"That and whatever else comes handy. You were feeling no pain yourself, tootsie."

Shandy was not about to let them get sidetracked. "But you do recall Jemima's leaving, Bob? Who let her out?"

"You mean held the door and waved 'by-'by? I didn't. I believe I went upstairs with her to get her blanket and war bonnet mainly because I had to go to the bathroom and the one downstairs was in use. I presume she got down on her own while I was making my tinkle."

"And I know I didn't," said Adele. "Contrary to what my loving husband is trying to make you believe, I was cold sober. I wouldn't dare be anything else in front of that crowd. I couldn't go to the door with Jemima because I had something in the oven. She'd come to me a few minutes before and said she must be going and I said she couldn't go yet because she hadn't had any of my squid puffs."

"Your what?"

"Squid puffs. It's a Greek recipe. They have to be timed to the minute. I rushed out to put a batch under the broiler and the next thing I knew, Bob was yowling, 'Hey, everybody, get a load of the mountain going to Mohammed.' So I glanced out the window and there was Jemima lumbering down the path to the short cut. I must say I was a bit miffed, when I'd gone to that much bother especially for her."

"Do you happen to remember the exact time?"

"Yes, I do, because I was timing the puffs. I had to take them out at precisely nine twenty-nine. Funny how things like that stick in your mind."

"That's right," said Bob. "The carillon started ringing while we were still gathered around the window, laughing our fool heads off. God, that was funny!"

"Don't kid yourself, darling," cooed his wife. "The others just went along with your lousy joke because you were buying the booze, which needless to say you weren't. I hope you don't honestly believe you're fooling anybody about who pays the bills around here."

The conversation had worked around to where the Dysarts' badinage usually did wind up sooner or later. Shandy set down his still nearly full tumbler and got up.

"I'm afraid I'll have to be going. I promised Tim I'd make some phone calls for him. The funeral is tomorrow morning, you know, at ten o'clock in the chapel. You'll come, I hope?"

"So soon?" shrilled Adele. "I haven't done a thing about flowers. God, I wonder if Harry the Ghoul is answering his business phone? Maybe he can wake up the florist or something. It would have to be a Sunday! Why didn't you let me know earlier?"

"Cool it, Dell," said her husband. "They'll be around. Those guys would never miss out on a chance to make a buck. You can count on us, Pete. Adele's got a new black mink coat Santa Claus brought her, and she's itching to show it off. Think you can find the door?"

"I expect likely. Thanks for the drink."

"Thanks for the cowpats. See you tomorrow."

Chapter 7

Shandy walked thoughtfully down the path to the short cut. This was the way Jemima had come. It would be. Jemima was a great taker of short cuts. He tried to picture her in front of him as Dysart had described her, a great mass of purple wool weaving and flapping.

It wouldn't work. The path was neatly shoveled since Adele was a great one for getting male students to do odd jobs around the place, although she had to be circumspect in her requests because Mrs. Svenson set a high standard in student-faculty relationships. Still, the shoveler hadn't exerted himself to dig any wider than he had to. There simply was not room for a big woman to weave and flap without toppling into the piled-up snow at either side, and Shandy could find no spot where the smooth bank was disturbed.

She couldn't have been so far gone as Bob made out. That didn't mean anything in particular. It was typical of the assistant professor in electrical engineering to make believe his parties always turned into orgies. In fact, they tended to be rather circumspect affairs, all things considered, including Mrs. Svenson's principles and the president's temper.

At any rate, Jemima had indeed left the Dysarts' under

60

her own power just before half past nine with the avowed intention of vandalizing Shandy's house. He ought to have asked whether anybody else left with her, but thought that was unlikely. Grimble would have mentioned the fact, and Bob wouldn't have missed a chance to drag a second reveler into his story.

Besides, if the killer was also a guest at the party, he or she must surely have had sense enough to hang back long enough to allay any possible suspicion. Jemima would need a fair amount of time to unlock the door and make her way through the different rooms, and it wouldn't take more than three minutes or so to get over to the brick house after her, using the crowd for cover. One would only have to say, "I came to help," wait till her back was turned and strike her down, then set the stage and go away. Somebody primed on tequila and cherry brandy might easily think it a clever touch to spill the marbles but forget to leave the telltale key with the corpse.

Still, he couldn't figure out how anybody could have got away with juggling that outsize body around his living room with the blinds up and tourists glued to the window-panes, or why anybody would want to try. It would be so much easier to kill her right here in the shrubbery.

His path led straight into an enormous hedge between the Dysarts' and the house that actually was first on the Crescent. Old Dr. Enderble never liked to cut down the bushes because many birds and little animals nested and fed in what had, over many years, become a dense tangle. Once in a while, Mrs. Enderble sneaked out with her sewing scissors in her apron pocket and snipped off a few really bothersome twigs. When the Dysarts bought the adjoining property a few years ago, Bob had made savage attacks on the overgrown shrubs, heedless of his neighbors' protests. Then he found out the Enderbles were adored by everybody in town and decided he'd only been pruning out dead wood to encourage new growth. Sure enough, he had. One would have no trouble hiding a corpse in that copse, Shandy thought, and was immediately appalled at himself for the frivolity.

Perhaps it wouldn't have been all that easy, not if you didn't want the body found right away. Quite a few of the guests at the party must have used this short cut both coming and going. So, most likely, had some of the visitors and even perhaps one or two of those obnoxious sled-pulling elves, although they were enjoined to keep off private grounds. It was never completely dark, even in here, with the white snow reflecting hundreds and hundreds of multicolored lights all around the Crescent. In any event, John Enderble couldn't have helped spotting that garish purple cloak when he came out at dawn to check his bird feeders.

Furthermore, how could a plausible accident be staged out here? There was no large boulder or stump or fence post along the path on which she might seem to have struck her head in falling. She couldn't be dragged into the bushes without leaving a trail and giving the show away.

Shandy still couldn't tell whether somebody had slain Jemima on impulse and then arranged the cover-up, but he was more and more inclined to think the crime had been planned in advance. But why kill Jemima Ames? True, everybody in Balaclava Junction except perhaps Mary Enderble must have entertained the notion at one time or other, but would it actually be possible to stay furious with the woman long enough to do her in? Her methods could drive anybody to exasperation, but her motives were always benevolent enough. Even the Illumination was a worthy cause, as the professor had to keep reminding himself. The agony would be over soon, but the money it earned would continue doing good work for months to come.

Now, there was an angle to consider. Had Jemima found out that somebody was helping himself to more than a fair share of the Illumination funds? The setup was supposed to be reasonably foolproof, but with so many people involved in such a freewheeling operation, there had to be loopholes. Ben Cadwall would know, being the comptroller. So would Hannah Cadwall, no doubt, and Hannah was Jemima's bosom buddy. Could one of them have spotted a fiddle and not told the other?

That might depend on who was doing the fiddling. If it should happen to be the comptroller's wife, friendship wouldn't keep Jemima from ripping her to shreds as a matter of principle. It was Jemima, as everybody but Tim himself knew, who'd ratted to Ottermole that her husband's failing eyesight made him incompetent to drive any longer, regardless of the fact that the car was one of Ames's few pleasures outside his work. If she'd do that to Tim, she'd do anything to anybody.

It would be interesting to know where Hannah Cadwall was at half past nine on the night of December 22. Bob had said she and Ben weren't at the party, and Shandy wouldn't have expected them to be. The comptroller did not approve of the way Professor Dysart flung his wife's money around.

Of course the Dysarts' personal finances were none of the comptroller's business. A great many of the things Ben poked his nose into were none of his business, but that fact never stopped him from wanting to know, nor from preaching from whatever text he considered relevant to the circumstance. People listened to Cadwall because he was in a position that made him dangerous to ignore, but his holier-than-anybody manner had not endeared him to his neighbors and colleagues.

Was it in fact possible to be as righteous as Ben Cadwall acted? If he was, could any woman endure that much respectability without at last feeling something snap? Shandy wasn't prepared to believe that Hannah had embarked on a life of crime just to spite her husband, but he wondered if she mightn't be building up a private nest egg as a step toward striking out on her own.

As to killing Jemima, Hannah would certainly have had the best chance. It wasn't possible that Jemima Ames hadn't sounded off to her best friend, as she had to the Dysarts' guests, about going over and ripping down Shandy's decorations. They might even have planned to do it together, Mrs. Cadwall being appointed to get hold of a key while Mrs. Ames put in her appearance at the Dysarts'.

It would be quite within Cadwall's character to own a personal set of keys to all the houses on the Crescent. Although these were owned by the people who lived in them, the land they sat on belonged to the college and they couldn't be resold except to other faculty or staff. That, and the fact that they all got their power from the college plant, was sufficient reason for the Svensonian fiat that each householder must leave a door key with the security office. It would be no problem for Grimble to make duplicates, and he'd do it if Cadwall asked him to. Grimble would not disoblige the man who signed his pay checks.

Grimble was, in fact, altogether too co-operative for Shandy's taste. He was pretty sure the key that let Jemima in must have come from the security chief, either directly or indirectly. The only alternative was Mrs. Lomax, and she was not only pea-green incorruptible but out of town. Besides, she'd talk. The professor had a hunch that Grimble, if suitably compensated, would not.

It wasn't fair to make such a judgment, however, without checking out the office first and finding out whether it was possible simply to steal a key. There were a lot of things that had to be found out. He'd start tomorrow. Right now, he was feeling too abominably tired. Was it that lethal drink of Dysart's, or the fact that he was fifty-six years old?

Why did he have to keep brooding on his age all of a sudden? He and Jemima were born in the same year. Jemmy had organized a joint birthday party for him and her mother while she was still living at home. He'd been pleased at being included, even though he had to wear a paper crown and blow out a lot of candles that kept relighting themselves. Jemmy had a regrettable taste for practical jokes. That baby of hers would probably be born wearing a false nose and celluloid buck teeth. Shandy was glad Tim would be with her when it happened. The poor old coot needed a laugh to cheer him up.

Getting Tim to the airport, that was another chore for his list. Either of the Dysarts would no doubt be glad to take Ames in the Porsche, but they both drove like maniacs and smoked like fiends. Tim would be a wheezing hulk by the time they arrived. He was in no great shape now. Shandy would rent a car from the garage downtown and make the trip as comfortable as possible for his old friend. It was the least he could do, after what's he'd done.

But what the flaming perdition had he, in fact, done? That was the crux and quite likely the nexus of the entire situation. Did his misbegotten whimsy precipitate this outrage, or only provide a handy cover for something that was going to happen anyway?

Shandy got little time to ponder. He was barely inside the brick house, contemplating a spot of badly needed relaxation with Robert W. Service, when the front door buckled slightly. Only one person could knock like that.

Now he knew how Rome felt when the Visigoths arrived.

"Come in, President," he said.

The invitation was superfluous. President Svenson was already in, filling the tiny hall from side to side and from floor to ceiling. If the hall had been large, the effect would have been the same. No space ever seemed big enough to contain Thorkjeld Svenson. Wearing a sweater and cap of untreated gray sheep's wool knitted for him by his wife, Sieglinde, probably with an assist from the Norns, he looked like a mountain gone astray from its bedrock.

"Shandy, what are you up to?"

"I've been wondering that myself." There was no use trying to beat around the bush with Svenson. "Sit down, won't you?"

"No. Grimble tells me you've killed Mrs. Ames."

"Does he, now? I wonder why."

"Because he's a jackass, I suppose," the president replied thoughtfully. "What happened?"

"She's presumed to have broken in here to remove my— er—decorations on the way home from the Dysarts' Christmas party, and had a fatal fall."

"Why presumed?"

"I think somebody murdered her."

"Why?"

"If you mean why was she killed, I don't know. If you mean why do I think so, I have sound reason."

Shandy told of the spilled marbles, the superfluous ladder, and the key that should have been with her body but was not. Svenson ruminated awhile.

"Police didn't notice?"

"They didn't want to notice. Grimble and Ottermole are both scared to death of offending you."

"Damn well better be. You told Ames?"

"Yes. He agrees with me, particularly about that step stool. He says his wife would have stood on the sofa."

"Urgh."

The president pondered some more.

"My wife would never stand on a sofa," he pronounced finally.

Shandy wondered what sofa could hold her, but thought it wiser not to ask. "Mrs. Svenson is a lady of great dignity," he said.

"Yes, and she's going to bean me with a skillet if I'm

not back in time for supper. Mrs. Svenson is not going to like this, Shandy. I don't like it either."

His voice rose to a full gale. "Damn you, Shandy, you've already tried to sabotage the Grand Illumination. If you involve the college in a public scandal over Jemima Ames, I'll personally shove a Balaclava Buster straight down your throat and out your other end."

Professor Shandy had to stand on tiptoe and lean over backward to look his superior square in the eyes, but he managed.

"As far as I'm concerned," he roared back, "you can take the Balaclava Buster and squat on it till you both rot. There's been murder done in my house and I'm not going to stand for it. If you didn't carry your brains in your backside, you'd realize you can't afford to either. Didn't your grandmother ever tell you about the rotten apple in the barrel? Don't you know the meaning of the expression 'moral decay'? You let one member of your faculty get away with a thing like this, and you know what's going to happen to the whole college?"

Svenson's jaw dropped. "How do you know it's a member of the faculty?"

"I don't. It could be a student or someone from Buildings and Grounds or your own secretary, but I don't think so. It has to be somebody who knows the Crescent and the people well enough to have heard Jemima planning to enter my house. I assume it's somebody who could find a way to steal a key from Grimble, unless he's in on the deal, too, which wouldn't surprise me because I think he's a sneak and a liar as well as a jackass, as you so rightly pointed out."

"Urgh. I'll have to think this over. And you can damn well watch your step. All right, Shandy, since you started this mess, you can just go ahead and clean it up. You get it done fast, with no embarrassment to the college, or you'll wish to God you'd never come back. I may carry my brains in my backside, but I also pack one hell of a clout in my fist. Happy New Year."

The president went away. After a while, the walls stopped reverberating. Shandy fixed himself a nightcap and sat down with Robert W. Service, but "The Shooting of Dan McGrew" was pallid stuff compared to what he'd been through this day. To cap it off, he had defied Thor-kjeld Svenson and was still alive.

For how long? That aspersion on the president's intellect was not only uncouth and unworthy of a man of letters, but also damnably ill judged. The insult had been adroitly turned against himself. Svenson knew perfectly well that the team of Ames and Shandy could never misread the available evidence so egregiously as to think Jemima had been murdered if she hadn't, and that it would be morally indefensible as well as administratively irresponsible to let such a crime go unpunished. But Svenson would have handled the dirty work himself if Shandy hadn't given him a glorious excuse to dump the responsibility.

Sitting here hoping Mrs. Svenson had in fact crowned her husband with a griddle would avail nothing. Shandy put down his book and tried to organize his thoughts. His brain had turned to mush. He went to bed.

Chapter 8

Jemima Ames's funeral made a gloomy anticlimax to a festive weekend. People were huffed at the short notice. They acted flustered and hustled and impatient to get on with their planned activities. Since they couldn't very well take out their resentment on the corpse, they pinned it to Peter Shandy. Only the fact that Tim stuck to him like a leech averted a mass cold-shouldering. The widower was fully aware of what was happening and displayed a Machiavellian streak in getting around it.

"Don't know how I'd have managed without old Pete here," he was telling Sieglinde Svenson. "Rotten thing for him, coming home and finding her like that."

"It is a terrible loss for us all." The president's wife knew better than to commit herself. "Your wife was a truly dedicated woman."

She did not try to expand on what Jemima was dedicated to, but gave the widower a sad, ineffable smile, barely touched Shandy's hand with two fingers of her woolly gray glove, and sailed on like a majestic ship of the line. She was wearing a plain blue tweed coat, a blue Angora beret, and enormous black leather boots. Glittering armor would not have been appropriate to the occasion, though it was generally supposed she had a suit at home.

Hannah Cadwall, as mistress of ceremonies, had prepared a collation to which a chosen group were invited directly after the obsequies. Shandy went perforce, hoping for a drinkable cup of coffee to take away the chill that had gripped him ever since he happened to catch the president's eye.

To his surprise, he found not only coffee but a pitcher of bloody marys and a cold buffet that stopped not far short of being lavish. Ben Cadwall was dispensing refreshment with an unwontedly free hand, in the happy knowledge that Timothy Ames would have to foot the bill. Bob and Adele Dysart were munching and sipping along with the rest.

That they'd accepted an invitation was not remarkable. The Dysarts would say yes to anything that in any way resembled a social event. What was astonishing was that Ben had let Hannah invite them. Shandy thought it over and came to the conclusion that the Cadwalls must feel some sense of obligation for all those invitations they'd declined. This was a way to pay back the Dysarts at no cost to themselves.

Unfortunately, the idea struck him as funny. Shandy made the appalling blunder of laughing aloud, then had to pretend he was choking on a crumb. There seemed a general decision to let him choke, but Mirelle Feldster's motherly impulses got the better of her.

"Here, Peter, drink this. We don't want any more accidents around here."

The professor couldn't think of anything to say to that, so he drank the coffee she'd brought without speaking. Mirelle was not one to tolerate a silence for long.

"I must say, Peter, I'm surprised you popped into the house long enough to find poor Jemima, you're such a gadabout lately. I'm also just a bit puzzled as to why you haven't thought fit to tell your old friends about getting engaged to that woman in Baltimore."

Shandy set down his cup. "You haven't heard who she is, by any chance?"

"I'm waiting for you to tell me."

"They say the—er—husband is always the last to know.

Would you mind passing on any further information that comes your way?"

"Are you trying to tell me it isn't true?"

"Mirelle, I cannot imagine how that yarn got started," said Shandy with a glance at Adele Dysart, who was carefully avoiding his eyes, "but I assure you that I am not going to marry any lady from Baltimore."

"Maybe it isn't Baltimore," said Mrs. Feldster archly.

"And maybe she ain't no lady," yelled Bob Dysart, who could generally be counted on to make an awkward situation worse. "Eh, Pete, you old rip?"

"Tim," said Shandy, "don't you think it's time we got started? You mustn't miss that plane."

That set off a chorus of "Who's going to drive him to the airport?"

"I am," said Shandy.

"But you don't have a car," Adele Dysart protested.

"I'm renting one from Charlie Ross. It's all arranged."

"I didn't even know you could drive. I'm beginning to think there's quite a lot I don't know about you."

"Aren't we all?" murmured Mirelle Feldster. "Tim, who's going to look after your house while you're gone? I'd be glad to run over once or twice a day."

"No need," said Ames. "Some relative of my daughter's husband is—oh, my God! Pete, I forgot to tell you, Jemmy phoned again last night. That woman's coming in at twelve forty-two and we're supposed to meet her."

"It's 'way after eleven now," said Hannah Cadwall. "You'll never make it."

"That," Shandy replied, "remains to be seen. Come on, Tim."

"I'll get your coat," said Ben. "It's in the guest room."

"Don't bother, I can find it."

Shandy raced upstairs. His coat was somewhere in a heap on the bed, along with everybody else's including Hannah's own unmistakable red-and-green plaid and the ratty brown ulster Ben had worn for as long as anyone could remember. As the professor fished among the garments, something rolled to the floor and bounced under the bed. Muttering, he stooped to pick it up. The object was a yellow glass marble with brown streaks, oddly crackled inside. He'd have known it anywhere.

There was no telling whose cuff or pocket the marble

had fallen out of, nor was there any sense in stopping to ask. He grabbed his overcoat, tucked the marble carefully into the inside pocket, and thrust his arms through the sleeves. When he got downstairs, Tim was already on the doorstep and Ben was ready to usher him out. They shouted words of thanks, wrung a few hands, and sped down to the garage.

Neither of the men spoke until they were safely in the rented car, headed for the turnpike. Then Timothy Ames heaved a long sigh and fumbled for his pipe.

"Thank God that's over. I'm just as well pleased the kids couldn't come. Lot of damn foolishness, but she'd no doubt have come back to haunt me if she didn't get a proper send-off."

He made loathsome noises with his pipestem and commenced stuffing tobacco into the burned-out bowl. "What the hell were they saying about you and some woman? I couldn't catch it."

"You didn't miss much. Another of my asinine jokes backfired."

Shandy explained his evil impulse and its embarrassing consequences. Ames was unsympathetic.

"Christ Almighty, Pete, when you set out to cook your own goose, you sure do it up brown. You know what's going to happen to you?"

"No, but I daresay I'll find out fast enough."

"Too right you will! They're probably back there tossing coins to see who gets first whack at warming your bed."

"What?" Shandy narrowly missed climbing up a Volvo. "You're out of your mind."

"Wait and see, old buddy. You're going to get propositioned at least six times between now and New Year's. As to what's going to happen when the holidays are over and the women have time to concentrate on tracking you down, all I can say is—" Ames gave way to unseemly mirth.

"I'm glad you're able to enjoy your own joke," said his friend austerely. "In all my eighteen years at Balaclava, I can assure you that none of those women has so much as— er—dropped her handkerchief in my direction."

"That's because they figured you for a sweet, innocent guy. From now on, they'll be dropping a damn sight more than handkerchiefs. Pete, you don't know what's in store for you. If you don't want to take warning, that's your funeral."

"Well, Tim, we won't argue. Time will settle the matter, one way or another."

"I just don't want to come back and find you a shattered hulk."

"On that, at any rate, we're in perfect agreement. Now if you can get your mind off—er—whatever it's on, I have something more important to tell you. I've found the marble."

"You've what? Where?"

"When I went upstairs to get my coat at the Cadwalls' just now. It rolled off the bed." He explained about the jumble of wraps.

"You couldn't tell whose it came out of?"

"Not possibly."

"At least I'm out of it," said Ames. "Now you see why it pays not to bother with an overcoat."

"Good Lord, Tim, I never thought of you."

"Why not? You can damn well bet Ottermole would have, if he could think. Anyway, it looks as though we've narrowed the field."

"That was my first thought. I only hope I can remember who was at the Cadwalls' till I get a chance to write down the names."

"What about the Cadwalls themselves? Are they out of it?"

"They're in. Ben and Hannah didn't hang up their coats, just tossed them with the rest. We all arrived in a bunch, you know, and I expect they were in a hurry to get the party rolling. Anyway, I've been rather wondering about that pair."

He told Ames why. The widower nodded.

"You may have something there, Pete. Ben must be hell on wheels to live with, and Hannah has plenty of chances to get at the cash. For one thing, she goes around and collects from the kids with the sleds. They're not supposed to keep more than a couple of bucks in change on them, and you'd be surprised how much they pull in."

He grinned at his unintended pun and made more noises on the pipe. "Hannah also takes the money from the parking lot and those misbegotten gingerbread houses, which comes to a hell of a lot more than you might think.

There's an elaborate system of cross-checking that's supposed to keep everybody honest, but Ben was the guy who drew it up. You know, old buddy, this is turning into quite an interesting problem. I sort of wish I weren't going away."

"Nonsense! Jemmy would be heartbroken."

Shandy stepped on the gas and concentrated on reaching the airport before Ames had a chance to talk himself out of the trip. They were going to be late for the incoming flight from California, as it was.

In fact, they were not. That plane was overdue. However, it turned out Tim hadn't heard Jemmy properly about his own time of departure. He had to be hustled madly past the reservation desk and down to the boarding gate, with loudspeakers blaring his name. Only when Ames was safely airborne did Shandy realize he'd forgotten to ask the name of the woman he was supposed to meet.

He was having wild thoughts about phoning Jemmy when more bleatings from the public address system sent impatient friends and relatives surging toward a gate far distant from the one they'd been told to wait at. Shandy surged with the rest, deciding he'd just have to hang around until only one person was left, then introduce himself and hope for the best.

It didn't work that smoothly. Outgoing passengers mingled with incomers. He had no way of knowing which was which. At last he drew a bow at a venture, choosing a middle-aged woman in a red wig and six-inch Wedgies as the likeliest prospect.

"Er—I'm Professor Shandy from Balaclava College."

"Whoopee for you. Beat it, Tyrone, I'm not open for business."

He was trying to get up nerve enough to make a second attempt when a gentle voice from somewhere around his left collarbone spoke.

"Excuse me. I believe I heard you say you're Professor Shandy?"

The speaker was a small woman of forty or so. Shandy's first reaction was that she seemed extremely well put together. Her pale blue coat sat on her compact figure as though it enjoyed being there. Her light blue hat showed just the right amount of fair, curling hair and made an agreeable frame for a peach-petal complexion. Her eyes were hidden behind dark glasses, but it stood to reason they would match her costume. Those features which he could see were in delicate harmony with the rounded oval of her face. He felt better for being able to look at her.

"I am," he said gratefully. "I'm supposed to be meeting a relative by marriage of the former Jemmy Ames. Dare I hope that you are she?"

"I'm Helen Marsh. I thought Professor Ames was coming. I expected to recognize him from pictures Jemmy showed me." She held out a small hand.

"You've missed Ames by about ten minutes," Shandy told her. "There was a mix-up in scheduling and his plane left before yours got in. We were in such a state of confusion that I forgot to ask him your name. Mine is Peter Shandy."

"Oh yes, the turnip man." Miss Marsh flushed most becomingly. "I'm sorry. Jemmy has told me so much about you and her father and the giant turnip—"

"Actually it's a rutabaga, *Brassica napobrassica,* as opposed to the—er—common turnip, or *Brassica rapa.* The difference is rather interesting if you—er—happen to be interested in that sort of thing."

"I'm sure it is. Have you any idea where I'm supposed to pick up my luggage?"

"This way, I believe."

Shandy started down the apparently endless strip of light brown terrazzo, feeling exhausted and futile. Strangely, Helen Marsh seemed to sense his mood.

"I do hope you're going to tell me about the *Brassicae.*"

He stopped in his tracks. "Did you say *Brassicae?*"

"Oh, dear, should it be *Brassicidiae* or something? I'm so stupid about botanical names."

"My dear madam, I was merely overwhelmed with joy at hearing a simple Latin noun pluralized correctly. It was like seeing a familiar face in a foreign land. You—er—wouldn't care for a bite of lunch, or a drink or something?"

"They served lunch on the plane, such as it was, but I wouldn't say no to a small glass of sherry, unless you're just being polite."

"There are those who will tell you I'm never polite. We have a longish drive ahead of us, and probably at least half an hour's wait before they finish jumping up and down on your suitcases. I thought we might spend the interval to better advantage in this—er—grotto than standing around the luggage counter."

"Grotto is a lovely word." Miss Marsh took off her sunglasses, confirming Shandy's hypothesis that her eyes would turn out to be a particularly attractive shade of blue, and accompanied him into the murky recesses with every appearance of pleasurable anticipation. A waitress loomed out of the smoky black-and-red like one of Persephone's handmaidens.

"You did say sherry?" he asked his guest. "Dry or—er —otherwise?"

"Amontillado, if they have it."

"Amontillado by all means. Two, please, miss. I suppose everybody drinks sherry in California."

"No, pink Chablis."

"Is that why you decided to come back East?"

"That among other things. I never adjusted. I can't do yoga and I blush terribly at the movies, and I think too much citrus fruit acidifies the system. At least something soured mine."

She ate five kernels of stale popcorn as Shandy counted them in silence, then laughed. She had a clear, small, gurgling laugh that went well with her smile.

"Did Jemmy tell you why I got fired?"

"I didn't talk with Jemmy myself. Tim only said you're a librarian, which was pleasant news to me, I may say. Er —why did you get fired?"

"The president of the college where I was working brought me in a manuscript and asked if I thought the university press ought to publish it. I sent it back with a note saying I'd found the work a lot of pompous nonsense, abominably written. It turned out he was the author. We had what might be called a confrontation scene, after which he said, 'Perhaps you may now wish to alter your opinion?' So I picked up the note and wrote, 'The author is an illiterate windbag,' and that's why I had to skip town."

They both laughed and drank their sherry in a pleasant glow of companionship.

Then Shandy said, "President Svenson is a remarkably intelligent man. I hope you won't make the mistake of— er—not thinking so."

"Am I likely to?"

"Probably not, but people have. The results are usually disastrous and sometimes fatal. Would you care for more sherry?"

"No, I think they must have got me unloaded by now."

She adjusted her scarf and picked up her gloves. Shandy paid the check and added a tip that would have brought a scolding from Ben Cadwall. He'd enjoyed standing Helen Marsh a drink. He even enjoyed shepherding her back along the terrazzo to where two matching blue suitcases were standing like orphans in the storm.

"Goodness, they were prompt," she said. "No, please, let me take one."

"Nonsense."

Shandy picked up both the bags, managing not to stagger. He was fully aware that he was showing off, and that such behavior was silly in a man of his age. Perhaps he might entertain Miss Marsh at a later time by swinging from tree to tree in his leopard skin. He pondered the notion and found it not wholly without merit.

Chapter 9

"We'll have to walk the last bit," Shandy apologized. "Cars can't get up the Crescent during the—er—revels."

Helen Marsh knew all about the Grand Illumination. Jemmy had given her the highlights back in California, and Shandy had perforce filled in the blanks on their drive back, including as much about Jemima's alleged fatal accident as the neighbors knew. He thought it would be injudicious to tell her the truth.

He did confess his own part in precipitating the tragedy. To his unutterable relief, she laughed almost as heartily as Tim had done, though in a more seemly manner, and said she'd probably have done the same, if she'd been clever enough to think of it. By the time he opened the trunk to fish out her luggage, Shandy was in better spirits than he would have thought possible.

"Now, you're not going to carry both those heavy cases up that great, steep hill," she insisted, reaching for a handle.

"My dear lady, I have no intention of carrying either one, nor shall you. Here, Hanson!"

Shandy beckoned to a sophomore student who was lounging about the parking lot across the way. "Would you care to earn a surreptitious stipend?"

77

"If that means money, sure."

The strapping youth picked up the bags like a couple of pretzels, and was halfway up the hill before the others got fairly started.

"We have an unwritten law here at Balaclava," the professor explained. "Never do anything for yourself that you can wheedle a student into doing for you."

"How much is this particular wheedle going to cost?" asked Miss Marsh, opening her handbag.

"You must allow me, please. I don't get to play the gay gallant very often. Gay in the—er—formerly accepted sense, that is."

She laughed again, even more delightfully than before. "I can't imagine why not, when you do it so well. You've been awfully kind, Professor Shandy."

"Er—my given name is Peter."

"It suits you."

"Do you think so? Er—Helen has always been a favorite name of mine." He hadn't realized it until just then, however.

"Why?" she teased. "Did you have a Helen for your childhood sweetheart?"

"No, actually she was a Guernsey—" Shandy's voice died.

The student, making what was perhaps a natural mistake, had dumped the suitcases on the short walk in front of the brick house, and was studying the porch with gleeful interest. A few steps more, and Shandy could see why.

He had quite forgotten the plastic Santa Claus. One of the decorators' more perverted whimsies had been a life-size articulated mannequin of Old Saint Nick. The last time Shandy had seen the thing, on his way to catch the *Singapore Susie,* it had been standing beside the front door, as though about to climb up and feed the reindeer on the roof. Now the thing was back. Its back was turned to the passer-by, its hands were engaged at the front of the body, its red flannel trousers were down around its boot tops, and across the plastic buttocks somebody had printed with a Magic Marker: "Santa Claus is a dirty old man."

"Helen, I do apologize," he said stiffly. "Another of my —er—aesthetic sins has come back to haunt me. Hanson, would you happen to know anything about this?"

The student shrugged. Shandy pulled up the dummy's trousers and laid it on the porch floor.

"I'll put this abomination in the cellar as soon as we've got you settled, Helen. No doubt the students have been carting it all over the campus ever since I left. I should have known better than to have it around in the first place. Hanson, Miss Marsh is a relative of the Ameses and will be staying in their house."

"Oh. Hey, Professor, what happened to Mrs. Ames?"

"She is presumed to have fallen and fractured her skull while—er—checking on my Christmas trimmings while I was away on holiday. Chief Ottermole made that deduction from the available evidence, just as I deduce from that silly grin on your face that you know perfectly well who's been horsing around with my Santa Claus but don't intend to tell me."

Red-faced, Hanson picked up the bags. "Aw, you know how it is. The stiffs expect us guys to be doing crazy stuff all the time. It's part of the act. Somebody got the bright idea of kidnaping Santa Claus and holding him for ransom, but you weren't around so the gag fell kind of flat."

"And where has the dummy been all this time?"

"Oh, around."

"Last seen in the company of Till Eulenspiegel, I presume?"

"Who's she?"

Shandy sighed and drew a bill from his wallet. "Thank you, Hanson. We'll—er—take it from here."

"Okay, Professor. Enjoy your stay, Miss Marsh."

The student leaped off down the hill. Shandy fished out the bunch of keys that Timothy Ames, for a wonder, had remembered to leave with him.

"You'd better brace yourself for a shock, Helen. Jemima liked to think she had a soul above housekeeping."

"Jemmy warned me what to expect."

As they got inside she added with a brave little laugh, "My goodness, it was all true, wasn't it?"

"All and then some," said Shandy. "Wait till you see the kitchen. Look, Helen, if it's too awful, I have a reasonably comfortable guest room ready and waiting."

"Thank you, Peter. I'll remember that. However, I did come to house-sit this place, so I expect I ought to grit my teeth and give it a try. May I come over and borrow mops and things if I need them?"

"Anything you like. And—er—the college runs an excellent faculty dining room. Tim and Jemima generally ate there, and so do I. Perhaps you'd give me the pleasure of your company a bit later?"

"The pleasure would be mine, I assure you. When shall I be ready?"

"They serve dinner from half past five to half past seven. We keep farmers' hours here, you know."

"Then shall we make it half past six? That ought to give me time to blast a path 'twixt bed and bath. Heavens, I've made a rhyme."

"And a very neat one," he told her fatuously. "Then I'll —er—leave you to it."

With reluctance, he did. She was probably glad to get rid of so inept an escort. What madness had come over him, inviting that agreeable woman to stay in his house after that disgusting episode with the plastic Santa Claus? The insult was a direct reference to the reputation he'd so recently and so undeservedly acquired, he had no doubt about that. If Helen spent a night under his roof, she'd be tarred with the same stick.

Halfway across the Crescent, Shandy stopped dead in his tracks. It was the students who'd kidnaped his dummy, but the faculty who were fabricating the gossip. How in Sam Hill had the story got from one group to the other so fast?

The college community had an unwritten law: What the students don't know can't hurt us. While gossip circulated freely around the Crescent and over the hill to the upper reaches where President Svenson and some of the other faculty and administrative people lived, it was understood that nobody ever passed on a word to the undergraduates. Since these young folk thought their seniors a dull lot anyway, the code was seldom broken and then only by gradual osmosis. There had been some unusually fast leakage here, and he wondered who was responsible.

Instead of going into the brick house as he'd intended, Shandy marched up to the Feldsters' front door and thumped the knocker. Mirelle came. He wasted no time on chitchat.

"Did you see who put that thing on my front porch this afternoon?"

"What thing?" Mirelle emitted a self-conscious titter. "Oh, you mean *that* thing. Honestly, Peter, I did think that was going a bit too far."

"So did I. That's why I'm asking you who's responsible. And also why you or somebody else didn't go over and do something about it."

"If you'll remember," said his neighbor nastily, "the last person who tried to do something about those ghastly decorations of yours got herself killed for her pains. Besides, how were we to know this wasn't just another of your quaint little whimsies?"

Shandy managed to control his temper. "All right, Mirelle. I deserved that. Now, since you've got it off your chest, perhaps you can answer my question. Who did it?"

"How am I supposed to know? Do you think I spend all my time gawking out the windows?"

The professor didn't answer. After a moment, Mirelle admitted, "I don't know who they were. They had on those knitted elf masks."

"Males or females?"

"Either or neither. You know as well as I do that all the students and half the faculty wear blue jeans and work boots and those padded, down parkas that make you completely shapeless. It could have been anybody."

"How did they get the dummy here?"

"Carried it between them, wrapped in a sheet of black plastic. Honestly, the thing looked just like a corpse. That's what attracted my attention." Mirelle was voluble now. "I had the impression they were simply going to dump it and run, but then one of them got a better idea."

"I'm intrigued that you think so."

"It's just an expression. I don't know what's got into you all of a sudden, Peter. You used to be such a quiet person. Now you're"—she paused, thought it over, and sidled a step closer—"interesting."

Mirelle's lips were slightly parted, her breath coming hard, her eyes hot and moist as a spaniel's at feeding time. "If I remember anything else," she murmured, "I might drop over later on and tell you. Jim has a lodge meeting, so I'll be alone and lonely."

Good God! This was worse than finding the body. Shandy backed hastily down the steps.

"I—er—expect to be out most of the evening. Thank you for the information, Mirelle."

"Any time, Peter."

In a cold sweat, he fled to his own place, only to be confronted by Mrs. Lomax in a state of righteous indignation.

"I must say, Professor, I didn't expect to come back here and find there'd been a death in the house."

"Neither did I," he retorted. "Do you have any idea how Mrs. Ames might have got hold of a key?"

"If you think she got it from me, you've got another think coming. I wouldn't have given that woman the time of day, always running the roads and laying down the law to everybody with dust on their furniture so thick you could write your name in it anywhere you'd a mind to. Not but what she was an upstanding, civic-minded woman," the housekeeper added hastily, mindful that it was rude to speak ill of the demised. "Did a lot for the college, you can't deny that."

"Ah," said the professor. "There you—er—strike at the heart of the matter. As you so rightly point out, Mrs. Ames was a woman of certain abilities, but she lacked your talents as a—er—homemaker. That fact has created a most unfortunate situation."

"Oh?" Mrs. Lomax perked up her ears.

"Young Jemmy—er—the daughter—"

"I know Jemmy Ames, for heaven's sake. She was in my Bluebirds."

"Well, then," Shandy beamed, "you're the very person to solve the problem. You see, Professor Ames has flown out to be with Jemmy during her—er—impending confinement and a lady who is a connection of Jemmy's husband has come to—er—help out. I brought her from the airport a while back," he added with a touch of complacency.

"Do tell! You mean she's traveled all the way from—"

"California. I was hoping to introduce you to Miss Marsh, but you—er—weren't around."

"You needn't rub it in. I know I'm late. Got home around noontime and found a busted pipe under my kitchen sink. Couldn't expect me to leave before the plumber got there, could you?"

"Er—no, of course not. And—er—plumbers being what they are—"

"I could tell you a thing or two about plumbers, Professor."

Mrs. Lomax seemed disposed to do so, but Shandy knew from experience that it was folly not to head her off.

"So, Mrs. Lomax, the lady is now over at the Ames place trying, as she puts it, to blast a channel. Perhaps you could go over and—er—lend a hand."

"You mean right now?"

"That was the general idea."

"What makes you think I want to take on another job?"

"That's for you to decide, of course. I was merely equating the need with your—er—exceptional qualifications. You might cut down on the time you spend here if you find the work load too heavy. But one cannot expect a woman like her to live in a mess like that."

"What's she like?" asked Mrs. Lomax abruptly.

"Miss Marsh seems pleasant enough," Shandy replied with due caution.

The housekeeper snorted. "You better watch your step, Professor. Those old maids are man-hungry, every one of 'em. Man-hungry," she repeated with a speculative gleam in her eye that her employer had never noticed before.

Shandy realized he was sweating again. "Good, then I'll —er—leave you to it. You needn't bother discussing salary with Miss Marsh. Let me know what's owed and we'll just add the amount to your usual weekly check. I can square up with Professor Ames when he returns."

Knowing he intended to do nothing of the sort, he fled to the bathroom and lurked there until Mrs. Lomax left the house. While waiting, he studied his face in the mirror. It was the same undistinguished, middle-aged countenance he'd seen yesterday, the same one he'd been shaving so meticulously for so long without untoward result. Why, all of a sudden, was it having this peculiar effect on the most unlikely women?

The sky was almost dark now, and had the weighted look that promised more snow. A storm would put no damper on the revels, unfortunately; but would only lead to joyous wallowings, snowball fights, and no doubt the erection of obscene snowmen on his front lawn. He must be sure to get up early and knock down any such artifact. He wouldn't want Helen offended again.

There was still a full hour to kill before he could drop over and pick her up. Actually there was an hour and three quarters, but he thought it might be a courteous gesture to arrive early with a bottle of amontillado and suggest a prandial drink, since no liquor was served in the dining room. He ought to make sure Mrs. Lomax had left by then, however. Shandy was still feeling a bit nervous about that look she'd given him.

In the meantime, he supposed he ought to pop next door and find out whether they could give him any information either about the night of the murder or about the recent embarrassment. He didn't suppose they would. The Jackmans were a family with young children, so involved in their own manifold doings that they barely noticed what was happening around the neighborhood.

This was probably the worst possible time to burst in on them, but so was any other time. Groaning, for he was weary in body as well as mind, Shandy bundled himself up and went out again.

Chapter 10

The Jackmans were at home, no question about that. Even over the babble of the crowd and the peals of the college carillon, the sounds of "Sesame Street" and the shrieks of a child getting its hair pulled were only too audible. Shandy clutched the packet of gingerbread men he had procured from the convenient though ruinously expensive stand on the Common, and began a fusillade on the knocker. After a while, he succeeded in making himself heard.

"Mum! Mum, somebody's at the front door," shrilled infant voices.

"Well, answer it, Dickie," replied one tired adult. "You're door monitor today."

"No, I'm not. Wendy is."

"I am not!"

"You are, too!"

"Stop it, both of you!"

Mrs. Jackman came herself, looking determinedly bright and motherly, with a moppet clinging to each leg of her blue jeans. Mrs. Jackman always wore blue jeans. She had jeans of blue denim patchwork and jeans with her children's handprints embroidered on them and rhinestone-studded jeans for evening wear. Shandy tried to recall whether she had worn jeans edged in black to the funeral, but couldn't remember seeing her there at all. That was as good an opening gambit as any.

"Er—good evening, Sheila."

"Why, Peter Shandy, what a surprise! Wendy and Dickie, say good evening to Professor Shandy."

Dickie howled, "I don't want to," and Wendy began to sniffle. Shandy made the mistake of trying to placate them with gingerbread men. Their mother's firm "After dinner, darlings" brought wails of protestation. At last she managed to herd the children back into the playroom and shut the door against the din.

"They're overtired," she apologized. "We only got home a little while ago. Do sit down, Peter. Where have you been keeping yourself? We haven't seen you in ages."

"I know. I was hoping we might—er—meet at the funeral this morning."

"Oh, heavens, was it today? I completely forgot. We'd planned this tobogganing trip, you see, and then Roger and the two older boys are sleeping out overnight at the shelter, which meant bundling up the sleeping bags and getting gas for the camp stove, and generally running around and back and forth like crazy. Then at the last minute we couldn't find the batteries for JoJo's electric socks, which meant a rush to the Sporte Shoppe. I couldn't disappoint the children by staying home, but I did mean to pop over and leave a note in Professor Ames's mailbox. Do explain for me when you see him."

"He's gone to California."

"How nice."

Sheila Jackman would have made the same response, Shandy thought, if he'd told her that Timothy Ames was being lowered inch by inch into a vat of boiling quicklime. She had one ear cocked toward the playroom and her mind on whatever was about to boil over on the kitchen stove. He might as well have saved the price of those controversial gingerbread men.

"I'm afraid I've come at a bad time," he ventured.

"Oh, not at all. I'm letting the children watch television an extra half hour as a special treat, so there's no rush about dinner. We're having things they specially like, baloneywoppers on French toast and cocoa with extra marshmallows. I don't suppose you'd care to stay?"

"Er—thank you, but I have another engagement."

"Then let me give you a drink. Just one second till I turn down the gas. I'm making mulligan stew to take up to the shelter tomorrow. The boys are having a cookeroo."

She went out before the professor could tell her he didn't want a drink, and returned with two very large and dark bourbon old-fashioneds.

"Hope you like the specialty of the house. Rog and I always keep a jug mixed in the fridge. We tell the kids it's Geritol."

She flopped into a modular arrangement of sofas and ottomans that bore the imprint of tiny feet on its cushions, and took a long, grateful swig.

"I suppose you think it's terrible to deceive a child, but honestly, sometimes you simply have to."

"Er—what might be called survival tactics," said Shandy.

"How nice of you to understand."

Sheila gulped some more of her vitamin compound and began giving the visitor her undivided attention. "You are nice, Peter. Come on over here where I can see you better."

She patted the squashy cushions, and the hairs on the back of his neck began to prickle.

"Thank you, but I'm afraid my—er—old bones require a straight chair."

"Don't be silly. You'll never be old."

This was getting worse by the second. He could swear she was batting her eyelashes at him. Shandy gulped and hastened to get on with his business.

"Sheila, I came to ask if you or Roger had seen anything unusual at my house on the night of the twenty-second."

" 'Way back then? How could I possibly remember?"

"That was the night of the Dysarts' party. And also the day I—er—had my decorations put up."

"Oh, now you're ringing my bell. Wendy came home with her eyes like saucers. She still hasn't stopped talking about those reindeer on your roof. She blows kisses to them every night. Like this."

Shandy flinched. "Did you go to the Dysarts'?"

"Yes," Sheila pouted, "but we couldn't stay long. We had a problem getting a sitter. Everybody was either off holidaying or working at the Illumination."

Shandy wasn't interested in sitters. "What time did you leave?" he prodded.

"About a quarter past nine."

"Then Jemima Ames was still there when you left?"

"I believe so. I know she came in right after we did, making a big entrance in that goofy purple cape of hers. Rog calls her the Batmobile. Oh, gosh, that doesn't sound so funny now, does it? Let me fix your drink, Peter."

"No, really, I have to be going. Just tell me one more thing, Sheila. Did you happen to see her after the party?"

"How could I? Wasn't it that same night she was killed?"

"I meant that same night, on her way to my house. She'd have come past your house, wouldn't she?"

"Probably." Sheila didn't sound very interested.

"And she left only a few minutes after you did. Adele Dysart says it was shortly before half past nine."

"Peter, that is odd." Young Mrs. Jackman bounced herself upright against the back of the sofa. "You see, we were stuck for a sitter, as I mentioned before. I was moaning to dear old Mary Enderble about missing the party, so she very sweetly offered to come over for a while. They never go to the Dysarts' for more than five minutes, you know. It's just not their kind of thing. But that's why we had to rush off, because it wouldn't have been very nice to keep her up past her bedtime. They sack in with the titmice, you know. Besides, she might not have been so ready to help me out another time. Survival tactics."

Mrs. Jackman chewed the orange peel from her drink. "So I started nagging Rog at nine o'clock sharp, and maybe fifteen minutes later I managed to pry him away. But by the time we'd stood chatting with Mary about the party and she'd told us this perfectly fantastic thing Dickie said—"

Shandy didn't want to know what Dickie said. Sheila went on with her tale. "Anyway, it must have been pretty close to half past when Roger started walking Mary home, and I stood right over there at the window watching to see if they made it. Frankly, I didn't think Rog could hold himself up, much less an elderly woman, but he managed somehow. He'd been drinking that God-awful punch Bob made. I swear it was radioactive. I took one sip and snuck out to the kitchen and fixed myself a bourbon when nobody was looking. Sure you won't have another?"

"Positive. But you say you stood there watching."

"For ten or fifteen minutes, anyway. They weren't making much headway against the crowd, then Rog had to stop in and say hi to John and pat the rabbit. He always gets silly when he's plastered. It must have been close to a quarter of ten by the time he got back in the house."

"And you didn't see Mrs. Ames at all?"

"Not for one itty-bitty teentsy-weentsy second. The first thing I said to Rog when we heard yesterday that she was dead was that we didn't even say good-by to her at the party and now we'd never see her again, which should be a lesson to us all," Sheila concluded somewhat owlishly.

"Yet according to the Dysarts, Jemima walked through the short cut straight into the Enderbles' yard. It seems most peculiar that she didn't meet Roger and Mary."

"Well, she didn't. Rog would have said so. You know Rog. Golly whiskers, it's going to be lonesome around here tonight. Peter, couldn't you possibly—"

At that moment the playroom door burst open and Wendy, pursued by Dickie with a rubber snake, hurled herself yowling into her mother's arms. Shandy took advantage of the incident to escape.

He was an extremely puzzled man. How was it possible neither of the Jackmans had spotted that magenta bulk in the Crescent? He must check with the Enderbles. Not now, though. It was getting close to six and the couple tended to be gently garrulous as no doubt he himself would when he was their age.

Why was he thinking so much about age all of a sudden? Annoyed with himself for no reason he could put his finger on, Shandy went back to the brick house, got a bottle of his best sherry, camouflaged it inside a folded newspaper, and battled his way over to the Ames house.

Already Tim's place, if not yet transformed, was beginning to resemble a human habitation. It was possible to walk through the vestibule without stumbling over fallen objects. The living room was almost tidy and the fire in the grate, for once, burned clear. Helen remained dissatisfied.

"I'm afraid everything's still in a terrible mess. Mrs.

Lomax did wonders, but she couldn't stay long. She had to go home and feed her cat."

"The beast has a delicate stomach, I understand."

"So she told me. However, she's coming back to-morrow."

"Good."

Shandy unwrapped his present. "I thought you might like a drink before dinner. The college doesn't serve anything stronger than rose-hip tea."

"Peter, you are a kind man. I'll get us some glasses."

"Just a small one for me. I've already been dragooned into having a cocktail with one of the neighbors."

"Yes, Mrs. Lomax saw you going into the house next door to yours. She mentioned ever so casually that the husband's away."

"Good Lord."

"I gather there's not much around here she doesn't know."

"She often knows a good deal more than the facts warrant," said Shandy crossly. "Can I help with the wine?"

"No, sit still. You must be exhausted."

"So must you."

"I suppose I am, but I don't feel it yet."

Miss Marsh handed him a glass and sat down on the other side of the fireplace. "It's too late for Merry Christmas and a bit soon for Happy New Year. And Cheers doesn't sound particularly appropriate under the circumstances, does it? Poor Jemmy was dreadfully cut up about losing her mother. I'm so glad Professor Ames decided to go."

"So am I," said Shandy. "To your good health, then. That seems decorous enough, don't you think? I hope you're going to like Balaclava, Helen."

"So do I. I'm getting too old to keep moving. California was the worst mistake I ever made. I used to have nightmares about standing smack on top of the San Andreas Fault when it finally made up its mind to let go."

"It's just too bad you had to find chaos in this house and a carnival on your doorstep."

"But the chaos isn't permanent, I hope, and compared to what goes on out there, the Grand Illumination could pass for tranquillity. Peter, I don't want to rush you, but do you think we might go to dinner pretty soon? I've worked up a ravenous appetite and there's not one solitary thing to eat in this house except a box of Triscuits the mice have been at."

"Whenever you like," he replied, making no move to rise. "I'll take you grocery shopping afterward."

"If you're sure it won't be putting you out."

"Not at all. I'm down to three stale doughnuts myself."

"Poor Peter."

Helen picked up the empty glasses and carried them out to the kitchen. "I'll get my coat."

Shandy rather wished they didn't have to rush off. He was comfortable here in the tidied room beside the bright fire. It was the first time he'd ever been inside the Ames house and not wanted to leave.

Still, the anticipation of taking Helen Marsh to dinner was pleasing, too. Perhaps she'd invite him back afterward. He caught himself wondering if she'd pat the sofa cushions.

No such luck. Helen wasn't that sort of person. But then, he hadn't thought the others were either. Life was full of surprises lately. Surely one of them must turn out to his liking.

Chapter 11

"Watch it, Professor!"

"Drat it, I told you to keep that sled off the walkway!"

Needless to say, the girl charged on unheeding. Helen Marsh turned to look after her.

"What a gorgeous creature! Who is she?"

"A student named Heidi Hayhoe."

"Peter, you're making that up."

"Not I."

"Well, I suppose anything is possible. I went to school with a girl named Ethel Gasse. Is Heidi in any of your classes?"

"I wish she were," snarled Shandy. "I'd take great pleasure in flunking her out."

"Really? I should think you'd prefer to keep her after school."

"What for? My reputation as a—er—dirty old man is, I assure you, newly acquired and totally unfounded. In any event, President Svenson has strong views on the subject of—er—extracurricular fraternization between faculty and students."

"I'll bet Heidi Hayhoe hasn't. Somehow, I hadn't expected to find a girl of that type at an agricultural college. I don't know why. They're common enough. Sorry about that. I don't know if it's your sherry or my empty stomach. How far is the dining room?"

"First building on the right at the top of the Crescent. Think you can hold out that far?"

"I'll try. I do feel like a lady salmon at spawning time. Will it be as mobbed as this walkway?"

"Oh no. The public's not allowed and I don't expect many faculty people will be around. Monday's dinner is apt to be a warmed-over version of Sunday's, I'm afraid."

"It can't possibly be any worse than the lukewarm cardboard I had for lunch."

"As a matter of fact, we think the food is generally not bad. The dining room's operated as part of the course in restaurant management and the cooks get graded on their biscuits." He explained a bit of the college's unique workstudy program as they topped the rise and entered the restaurant.

"I'm beginning to have a good deal of respect for this place," said Helen. "It doesn't sound like any institute of learning I've ever been at, but it certainly seems to fit students for the ways they're no doubt going to live."

"President Svenson would be pleased to hear you say so."

"I am pleased," boomed a voice in their ears. "Who is this perspicacious lady and why have I not met her?"

"She's only been in town since about half past three."

Shandy performed the introductions. "She's the relative of Timothy Ames's son-in-law who's come to—er—thrust a finger in the dike."

"Decent of you to come on such short notice. Mrs. Svenson's going to have you to tea some time or other."

"Thorkjeld, what a way to give an invitation," chided Sieglinde. "We shall expect you at half past four on Thursday afternoon, Miss Marsh, and you must bring this bad Peter Shandy with you to keep him out of mischief for a little while. Peter, I did not find your latest decoration amusing."

"Neither did I," he replied grimly. "I'm trying to find out who was responsible."

"Thorkjeld, don't you know?"

"I do not," snapped the president. "There seem to be quite a few things around here I don't know."

"How very remarkable."

Mrs. Svenson's handsome face actually lost its serenity for an instant. "Well, shall be find our tables? At least we shall learn who is responsible for giving us a good dinner tonight. *Smaklig måltid, Fröken Marsh.*"

"*Tack, Fru Svenson,*" Helen replied without batting an eye.

Shandy was impressed. "Are you Swedish, too, Helen?"

"No, but I worked for a while in South Dakota."

"What did you get fired from there for?"

"Peter, that's unkind."

Helen settled herself in the same chair Timothy Ames had occupied the day before and studied the menu for a moment. "Actually, it was on account of an irreconcilable difference between myself and the head of the English Department."

"On what subject did you differ?"

"I'd prefer not to say," she replied demurely. "Would I be safe in ordering the turkey divan?"

"There's only one way to find out. Two turkey divans, please, miss."

"Yes, Professor. Will you have the cranberry mousse suprême with it?"

"Who made the mousse?"

"I did. We're shorthanded on account of the Illumination."

"Then we must have some, by all means."

The girl flushed with pleasure. "I'll bring your soup right away."

She was back in no time flat with an armload of salads, hot breads, and two steaming bowls of, inevitably, turkey soup. The Svensons, who still had not been served, looked somewhat taken aback. Shandy noticed, and gave Helen a wry smile.

"As if I weren't in enough trouble with the boss already."

"What are you in trouble about?"

"Partly those idiotic Christmas trimmings, of course. Mrs. Svenson is not amused. Neither was poor Jemima."

"Peter, you mustn't dwell on that. You don't honestly hold yourself responsible for her death, do you?"

"I think we'd better discuss that later," Shandy murmured with an eye to the other tables. Leftovers notwithstanding, the dining room was doing a fair business.

Helen looked surprised, but changed the subject. "You were right about the food, Peter, it's excellent. And you say the whole operation is run by students?"

"Under supervision, of course."

He went on explaining the college's innovative curriculum. His companion began viewing President Svenson with such an approving eye that the great man motioned them over to his own table for coffee.

"Miss Marsh thinks you're fascinating," Shandy told him.

"So does Mrs. Svenson," said the president. "Don't you, Sieglinde?"

"Yes, Thorkjeld. Eat your good rice pudding. Is it his looks or his mind you admire, Miss Marsh?"

"I think it's his common sense," Helen replied. "I've worked at colleges all over the country, but this is the first I've struck where everybody seems to know what he's doing, and why."

"Ah. Now that, Thorkjeld, is a compliment worth having. You are right, Miss Marsh, my husband is a sensible man. Some would think that makes him a dull man, but never in twenty-seven years have I found him so. No, Thorkjeld, no cream in your coffee. You had cream on your pudding. And what is it you work at, Miss Marsh?"

"I'm a librarian."

"*Ja?* Then you will be able to take over the position that Mrs. Ames did not leave. I say did not leave because she never began."

Mrs. Svenson playfully slapped the president's hand away from the sugar bowl. "She was a good worker only if she was minding somebody else's business. What you should have done with her, Thorkjeld, was appoint somebody else assistant for the Buggins Collection. Then she would have stolen the job out from under his nose and it would be done in no time. You will remember that if you ever strike another like her. My husband is like an elephant, Miss Marsh. He never forgets. He would also look like an elephant if I let him. No, Thorkjeld, you must not have more coffee. It gives you bad dreams. Explain to Miss Marsh what she ought to do and come home."

"Show up tomorrow morning at the library and ask for the key to the Buggins Room. I'll tell Porble you're coming."

"But don't you want to know about my background or training?" Helen gasped.

President Svenson rose and pulled out the chair for his wife. "I'll find out fast enough. Peter, you take her over. And remember, I've got my eye on you."

"They're quite a pair," said Helen when the Svensons were out of earshot.

"They're all that and then some. You watch your step, young woman. Is this coat really warm enough for you?"

"No, but I have my South Dakota woollies on underneath. Where are we going?"

"I think we'd better stop in and break the news to Porble that he has a new assistant before somebody else gets to him. Porble's inclined to be touchy."

"But Dr. Svenson is going to let him know."

"The tom-toms will be beating long before the president gets around to it."

Shandy took Helen's elbow and steered her toward the door. They didn't get far before somebody said, "Who's your friend, Peter?"

"Oh, hello, ladies. Pam Waggoner and Shirley Wrenne, this is Helen Marsh, who's just been made assistant librarian."

"So we heard," replied Ms. Waggoner, a thin, dark assistant in Animal Husbandry. "You're Jemmy Ames's mother-in-law or something, aren't you?"

"Just a sort of courtesy aunt. Jemmy tossed me into the breach when she found out her father was going to need a housekeeper."

"He always did," said Ms. Wrenne, a long-faced blonde clad in a great deal of hand-weaving; she specialized in native crafts. "Are you a real librarian or another phony like Ames?"

"For God's sake, Wrenne," snapped her companion, "we all knew you hated Jemima's guts, but you needn't strew them around and stamp on them now that she's gone."

"Now that she's got what was coming to her for poking her nose in where it didn't belong, you mean," amended Ms. Wrenne, champing down hard on a radish.

"Oh, shove it," said Pam. "Enjoy your stay, Marsh, for however short it may be. I can't imagine you'll stand Balaclava long."

"I'm a qualified librarian," Helen replied, "and I think

Balaclava is marvelous. Do come and see me at the library. If I find any Faith Baldwins in the Buggins Collection, I'll save them for you."

Before either of the women could form a reply, she moved on, a polite smile barely curving her rose-petal lips. Shandy bowed and went after her, wondering if Shirley Wrenne had in fact loathed Jemima as heartily as she claimed. If she did, it was stupid to keep saying so since Tim's wife was murdered.

But nobody but himself and Ames and President Svenson knew that. So her bitchiness ought to be a proof of innocence.

On the other hand, it could be a clever defense. Later on, when the facts leaked out as they surely must, she could say, "If I'd known it wasn't an accident, do you think I'd have been idiotic enough to talk about her the way I did?" President Svenson did not hire unintelligent instructors.

Pam Waggoner was no dimwit either. Shandy wondered, not for the first time, what precisely was the relationship between the two women. The fact that they shared a house and went about together a lot didn't necessarily mean they enjoyed each other's company, let alone any other close tie. Doubling up was probably a fiscal necessity on assistants' salaries, and unmarried females in this overwhelmingly uxorious society, denied any personal relationship with the male students, must often be hard put for companionship.

Pondering, he almost snubbed the Dysarts. Adele was having none of that.

"Peter, don't you speak to your friends any more? Aren't you going to introduce us?"

"Oh, sorry. Adele and Bob Dysart, this is Helen Marsh. Bob is the one with the mustache."

"Helen?" Mrs. Dysart laughed merrily. "I was sure you were going to say Susie."

"Miss Marsh is here from California," Shandy reminded her severely. "As you may recall, Timothy Ames and I spoke of her coming this morning after the funeral."

"Oh, of course. Do forgive me, Miss Marsh. It's just so difficult to keep up with Peter and his women. I hope you're going to enjoy your stay at Balaclava."

"We'll make damn sure she does," said Bob, pumping

Helen's hand with unnecessary vigor for far too long a time. "Have to plan a little get-together as soon as we've recovered from the last one. Too bad you missed our Christmas party, Helen. Old Pete here did, too. You watch out for that guy. If he starts giving you a hard time, come and tell me."

"Thank you," said Helen, managing at last to extricate her fingers from his grasp. "I'm sure he won't. Good evening."

She was out the door before Shandy could effect any more introductions. He didn't blame her for wanting to escape.

"Perhaps you'd rather put off meeting Porble until tomorrow?"

"Oh no. People do run in types, don't they? Who's Susie?"

"Another of the petards by which I've been hoist."

As they threaded their way among the wandering sightseers, he confessed his latest awfulness and its appalling repercussions.

"So of course Adele started dropping hints right and left, with the result that I'm now regarded as a—er—wolf."

"Oh, Peter! I shouldn't laugh because I'm sure you're in hot water up to the eyebrows already, but you must admit it's funny."

"I'm glad you think so. Tim would, if he were here. He predicted—er—dire consequences."

"Have they begun to happen, and is it really that dire?"

"Yes to the first question. As to the second, not yet but I expect it soon will be. I suppose I ought to have warned you, Helen. Being seen in public with me is probably going to—er—"

"Blacken my honest name? I'll just have to take that chance, won't I? Which is the Porbles' house?"

"Right down there. First on the Crescent, as you see. Porble doesn't care to walk any farther than he has to."

"Why? Is he handicapped or just lazy?"

"Neither. He doesn't believe in wasted motion. That's why he's let the Buggins Collection gather dust for so long. He says the books have no practical value."

"What are they?"

"Nobody knows. The books aren't even listed, much

less catalogued. And because they're not, we mustn't go in and disturb them."

"You mustn't blame the librarian too much," said Helen. "He's probably overworked and underpaid, like the rest of us. Most librarians have a bunch of old books stuck away somewhere that they're afraid to dump and haven't time to bother about. They're always meaning to get around to cataloguing them but usually don't unless somebody pesters them into it. Who got on Mr. Porble's back? Mrs. Svenson?"

"No, me," said Shandy unhappily.

"What made you get interested in the Buggins Collection?"

"I just thought there might be some things I'd like to read. That's a concept Porble doesn't understand. Neither did Jemima. Svenson gave her the job for the sole purpose of shutting me up and she used it to keep me out."

"Was that easy to do?"

"Yes, very. You'll see. Watch your step here. He hasn't wasted any extra motion sanding the path."

Shandy rang the librarian's bell. A girl of about fourteen answered.

"Good evening, Lizanne. Is your father in?"

"He's just sitting down to dinner," said the child doubtfully.

"This won't take a moment. I merely want to introduce Miss Marsh, who's going to take Mrs. Ames's place at the library."

"Oh." Lizanne gave Helen a sort of frightened bob and ran off, calling, "Daddy! Professor Shandy wants you to meet a lady."

"What lady?"

Not the librarian but his wife appeared. "Well, Peter, this is a surprise. I was just putting the food on the table. I'm afraid I can't ask you to join us at such short notice."

"No, no, we ate up at the college. That's why we stopped at such an inconvenient time. The president was there and suggested Miss Marsh take over the Buggins Collection assistantship. I thought Phil ought to meet her before he heard about it on the grapevine, out of—er—respect for his position. Helen's come to hold the fort for Timothy

Ames. You remember we spoke of it at the Cadwalls' this morning."

"Oh yes. I must say not many women could pick up stakes and fly across country at a moment's notice." She emitted a particularly nasty little laugh.

Helen refused to be annoyed. "Actually, I was all set to come back anyway. I've given Buck and Jemmy my plants and furniture and they're keeping my books and whatnot till I decide where I'm going to settle."

"Oh, then you won't stay with Tim indefinitely?"

"I have no idea. I'm only trying to be useful in an emergency. Jemmy's such a love and she was tearing herself to pieces with the baby coming and her mother dead, wanting her father and being afraid of what would happen if he left the house empty during the Illumination, that I just said I'd come and I did."

Mrs. Porble began to thaw. "I always say families should stick together in time of trouble. Jemima's death was a terrible shock to us all. I said to Phil—"

They never did get to hear what she'd said, as Phil himself came bustling into the hallway.

"Well, Peter. Nice of you to do my work for me. I understand I've hired a new assistant for the Buggins Collection. Miss Marsh, is it? Would it be rude to ask if you've had anything in the way of library experience? Or perhaps a library card? You have at least been inside a library?"

"Fairly often," Helen replied calmly. "I got my doctorate in library science from Simmons College in Boston." She mentioned a few of the positions she'd held and Porble's sneer changed to awe.

"My God," he gulped. "I feel as if I've swallowed an oyster and choked on a pearl. And Svenson hired you to work on the Buggins Collection. The Buggins Collection!"

For the first time in their eighteen years' acquaintance, Shandy saw Porble crack up. "The Buggins Collection! Grace, did you hear that? The president's got me a DLS for the Buggins Collection."

His wife managed a dutiful giggle, though she was obviously more puzzled than amused. "But, Miss Marsh, since you're so well qualified, whatever possessed you to take such a ridiculous job?"

"I didn't exactly take it, I was given it. You know Dr.

Svenson better than I. His wife asked me what I do and I said I was a librarian, and there we were. I might as well fill in until you can get someone else, if you want me. I'm supposed to see you tomorrow morning, but Peter thought we should just stop in and say hello. Now I think we ought to run along before your dinner gets cold."

They were back in the Crescent before Porble could recover from his paroxysm. Shandy was chuckling, too.

"You've brightened their evening."

"His, not hers," Helen corrected. "Mrs. Porble's probably feeling threatened just now. She's a nice woman, don't you think?"

"I thought she went out of her way to be nasty to you."

"I might be, too, if somebody barged into my house just at dinnertime waving a strange woman in my husband's face. As soon as she's got over the shock, she's going to arrange a little dinner for us. It will be a buffet with two different casseroles, a molded salad, and a fancy dessert she got out of *Better Homes and Gardens.* She'll wear a long plaid skirt and a black nylon blouse because it's dressy and doesn't show the dirt. They'll invite three other couples. We'll have a much pleasanter time than we expect."

"Tell me more."

"No, I won't. You're being snide. But you just wait and see."

"With pleasure." He liked the sound of that "three other couples."

"Where do we go next?"

"Groceries. There's a sort of general store down on Main Street that keeps open all hours. You can do your shopping, then invite me over for breakfast."

"Peter Shandy, you fox! Don't tell me that fish-eyed blonde was right about you, after all?"

"Adele is never right. She only thinks she is."

"She's the one with the money, I suppose?"

"Have you ever considered getting yourself burned as a witch? How do you know these things about people you've barely met?"

"I meet them everywhere. He's the sort who marries money and she's the sort who falls for men like him because she doesn't really know anything about people except that one needs them for an audience. I expect nobody cares much for either one of them, but everybody pretends to because they play so hard for notice that they make you feel guilty."

Shandy laughed ruefully. "I'd never thought of that. I always leave their parties wondering why everybody else is having so much more fun than I. Perhaps the others wonder, too."

"I know. Lots of noise, loaded drinks, and Adele's wearing a jellaba she picked up on a guided tour of Morocco. I am being bitchy. What do you eat for breakfast?"

"Whatever you choose to give me."

A latter-day Antaeus, renewing his strength with every rib he elbowed, Shandy plowed a path for himself and Helen through the crowd.

Chapter 12

They threaded their way back up the hill carrying brown paper bags. Shandy had tried to take her groceries along with his own, but she wouldn't let him.

"No, really, Peter. I'd feel like an old woman."

"Not possible. I suspect you're just trying to keep me from feeling like an old man. Speaking of longevity, would you mind if we dropped in for a few minutes on an elderly couple who are your neighbors, the Enderbles? He's professor emeritus of local fauna. Quite a distinguished scholar in his field."

"Not the Enderble who wrote *How to Live with the Burrowing Mammals* and *Never Dam a Beaver?* I'd be thrilled!"

"He has a new one coming called *Socializing Among the Snakes*. Mrs. Enderble believes it the crowning achievement of a long and distinguished career. She is—er—perhaps more broad-minded on the subject of reptiles than most ladies."

"I love the way you say ladies, Peter. You're so Victorian. You ought to wear lavender spats and carry a cane to twirl."

"Whatever you say. A cane would be a fine idea, actually. I could lay about me savagely when these confounded—Miss Hayhoe, if I catch you in the Crescent with that disgusting vehicle one more time—"

"Don't sweat it, Professor."

With a jolly laugh, the Amazon charged on.

"Drat the wench! She flouts me."

Shandy pulled off his glove and scratched his nose. "That's rather odd, come to think of it."

"Why? Have you never been flouted before?"

"I wasn't referring to any—er—personal chagrin, but to the young woman's flagrant indifference to a sensible rule. She could run over a gawker and lose the Illumination some business. I'm surprised the other students haven't cracked down on her."

"She's the type who gets away with things," said Helen. "With a name like Heidi Hayhoe, the girl's a natural for the role of campus cutup. She's here for laughs and men, and she doesn't make any bones about it."

"Then why in heaven's name did she choose Balaclava?"

"Oh, I expect she has some relative who's a rich and generous alumnus. Isn't there a Hayhoe who makes threshing machines?"

"Hayhoe Havesters! Good Lord, of course. They donated one a while back. The school raises a lot of grain, you know. Tim and I have been working on a strain of super drought-resistant millet. Millet is a very underappreciated crop in this country. Except by canaries."

"But much of the world lives on millet. Peter, that's breathtaking! May I see what you're doing sometime?"

"Of course, not that there's much to see. Agrostology is not the most—er—flamboyant of professions. That's my proper field."

"I see. Rutabagas are just a sideline. But think of all the cows you've made happy. Poor things, eating's about all they have to look forward to nowadays. I'll bet Professor Dysart's field is artificial insemination. He looks like a male chauvinist pig. Probably a terror among the undergraduate women."

"Wrong this time, madam. Dysart's an engineer and Dr. Svenson is very strict about the student-teacher relationship."

"Dr. Svenson says himself that there's a lot going on around here he doesn't know about."

"That's only what he said. What he meant was that

there is one particular thing he doesn't know about and God help me if I don't provide him with an answer."

"What will he do?"

"I don't know."

"Is it about Jemmy's mother?"

"Yes."

"But surely he's not blaming you?"

"Helen, could we talk in a less public place?"

"I'm sorry, Peter. Is this where the Enderbles live? I thought he'd have a hobbit-hole."

"Perhaps John would prefer that, but I doubt Mary would. I can't visualize Mrs. Enderble living anywhere but here. She's like the little woman in the weather house, never far from her own front door."

His description was apt. Mrs. Enderble did pop out on signal. She did look like a quaint folk figure, hair in a bun, face round and rosy, eyes rounded in perpetual wonderment, and lips curved in a merry smile. Even the maroon wool skirt and hand-knitted pink cardigan she wore contrived somehow to look like a peasant costume.

"Peter Shandy! I hadn't expected to see you again so soon. That was a lovely funeral, wasn't it? Exactly as Jemima would have wanted, though I daresay she'd as soon have put it off a few years, like the rest of us. Come in, both of you. John's in the study, wondering where he put something or other as usual."

"I've brought an admirer of his. This is Helen Marsh."

"Oh, you're the lady from California. How nice! I saw you and Mrs. Lomax out shaking rugs this afternoon. Jemima had many enthusiasms, but she always used to say housekeeping wasn't one of them. She was always scolding me for spending so much time puttering around the house when so many worthwhile things were happening outside. But I've never been one for committees and such. You have to let a place know you love it so it will love you back, don't you?"

"I expect so," said Helen. "I've never had a house of my own."

"Ah, but you're a nest builder at heart, like me," said Mrs. Enderble. "I can tell by the way you shake a rug. John, we have company. Here, let me put those bundles down for you. What a pretty coat, Miss Marsh! Is that what they're wearing in California? I had a notion they didn't wear much of anything, from what you see in the papers. Come into the study, if you can stand the clutter."

The clutter consisted of a scattering of papers on a flat-topped golden oak desk and a basketful of pine cones spilled over the hearth. Two tiger-striped kittens were batting the cones around while the mother cat, a large dog of indeterminable breed, a vast white Belgian hare, and a man not much bigger than the hare observed their frolickings with benign indulgence.

"Peter, my boy, good to see you. What do you think of these little rascals, eh?"

One kitten abandoned its pine cone and started up Shandy's trouser leg. He reached down and gently disengaged needle-sharp claws from his left shin.

"That will do, young sir or madam. I am not a tree. I'm sure, John, that the error was due to youthful inexperience rather than perversity of nature. No, puss, don't eat my necktie."

"Animals always go straight to Peter," Mary Enderble explained to Helen. "They even like the way he tastes. Oh, John, this is Helen Marsh from California. Peter says she's a fan of yours."

"Glad to hear it." Enderble shook hands not without difficulty, as he was now in possession of the other kitten. "Mary, do we have anything to give these nice people?"

"Never mind us," said Shandy, who was trying to count the first kitten's whiskers while it sucked on his tie. "You'd better get a nursing bottle for this deluded infant. It thinks I'm its mother."

"Oh, dear, he's getting that lovely silk all wet. Go to mummy, Eugene."

Mrs. Enderble placed the tiny creature under his dam's stomach and waited until he was blissfully kneading fur before she nodded and started toward the kitchen.

"You two sit and warm yourselves. The Dysarts brought over some kind of fancy cordial and we've been wondering what it tastes like, but it didn't seem right to open the bottle just for ourselves."

She was back in the speed of light, bearing thimble-sized glasses, a small decanter, and a plateful of sugar cookies.

"Ouzo, they call it. Smells like paregoric to me."

"Good," said Helen. "I was raised on paregoric."

"So was I, my dear. Now you can't buy any without a prescription. I don't know what we're coming to. Well, happy days, though I suppose that's not a very kind thing to say considering what brought you here."

"What did bring her here?" asked Dr. Enderble.

"Why, she's that relative of the Ameses', come to keep house for Tim."

"How can she keep house for Tim when he's out with Jemmy?"

"Oh, John, you'll be a tease to your dying day. You know what I mean. I expect it must have been an awful shock to you, Helen. You don't mind my calling you Helen? I haven't got over it myself, Jemima here one day and gone the next and nobody the wiser. That was the awful part, nobody missing her for so long. We were so used to her being here, there, and everywhere that everybody just thought she must be somewhere else. Do try one of these cookies, dear, though I'm afraid I got in a speck too much vanilla."

"Not a bit. They're perfect. I'd love to have you call me Helen, and I don't deserve your sympathy. I'm only a cousin of Jemmy's husband's mother, and I'd never even met either of the Ameses."

"Then that makes it all the nicer of you to come and help out," said Mrs. Enderble. "Don't you think so, Peter?"

"Indeed I do. Er—speaking of Jemima's habit of not being where you thought she was, I've run into a bit of a puzzle."

"Tell John. He's good at puzzles."

Mary took the daintiest possible sip from her minuscule glass. "There, I knew it would taste like paregoric."

"What's this about Jemima, Peter?" John Enderble broke in.

"She doesn't seem to have come out where she went in. According to the Dysarts, she left their party just a couple of minutes before half past nine and walked down the path to the shrubbery. Several of the guests watched her out the window. However, Sheila Jackman claims her husband was walking Mary home at that same time, and that she herself stood looking out the window the whole time he was gone, which was perhaps ten or fifteen minutes because he stopped to say hello to you, John. And she insists Jemima never came out of the shrubbery."

"You don't suppose she stopped to listen for the screech owl?"

"Oh, John," his wife protested. "With all the yelling and hollering and carryings-on up and down the Crescent, she couldn't have heard a calliope under full steam, let alone a poor little bird too scared to open its beak. Anyway, Jemima never stopped for anything, you know that as well as I do. You always said Jemima didn't know whether she was coming or going half the time, but at least she never loitered along the way."

"Did I? Wasn't very charitable of me, was it?"

"It was the truth," said Shandy. "Jemima was not the woman to hang around in a cold, dark shrubbery when she had something on her mind. She'd been telling everybody at the party she was going over to rip down those—er—ill-chosen decorations of mine. She was found in my living room with one of the things beside her, but how did she get from here to there without being seen?"

"Blessed if I know," said Professor Enderble, "unless the Dysarts got the time wrong. I'm sure Sheila didn't because young Jackman did bring Mary home right about half past nine. I'd been watching out the window myself, worrying that they might keep her out late and wondering if I should go over there, when I saw them coming across the Crescent. I don't recall seeing Jemima go by during that time either. She'd be wearing that purple cape, wouldn't she?"

"So far as anybody knows. She had it on when she left the Dysarts' and was still wearing it when I found her."

"Well, all I can say is, if she'd come through our yard then, I'd have seen her," said Mrs. Enderble, "and so would John. We both have good eyesight, and we're both trained observers and we're neither of us afflicted with softening of the brain, though you might think so from the way we let these critters boss us around. Peter, I'm afraid Algernon is eating your shoelaces."

Shandy lifted his foot away from the nibbling hare. "I hope he doesn't choke on the tips."

"No fear. He may be naughty, but he isn't stupid. Here they are."

Mrs. Enderble pounced on the tiny cylinders, though they must have been almost invisible against the dark rug in the flickering firelight. She did have exceptional eyesight.

"Perhaps she went by while you were in here talking to Mr. Jackman," Helen suggested.

"Mercy on us, child, we know better than to ask Roger Jackman in when he's been celebrating. Roger's a lovely boy, but he gets to showing you how to throw forward passes with your best china vase. We just stood around the door till it got so cold we had an excuse to shut it and get rid of him. Jemima wouldn't have passed without at least saying hello."

"Oh. Well, that does leave one possibility, though I'm shy of mentioning it in mixed company."

John Enderble chuckled. "You mean that she got taken short? I thought of that myself, but I'd say it's hardly likely. She could have gone back to the Dysarts' or knocked and asked to use our bathroom. It's not as though we were strangers. She was only a couple of minutes from her own house, for that matter. I hardly think Jemima would take a chance on being surprised in an undignified position unless she couldn't help it. And then she'd have left sign in the snow and I'd have noticed. Mary and I visit the shrubbery every day to fill the bird feeders, and we're always on the lookout for animal tracks and owl casts."

"What about human footprints?"

"None in the deep snow. The path is well trodden, of course."

"Speaking of treading," said Helen, "don't you think we ought to, Peter? I don't want to wear out my welcome on my first visit."

"No fear of that," Mary Enderble assured her. "You drop over any time you take the notion. John and I don't go out much, and we're always glad of pleasant company. You won't mind sleeping over there all alone?"

"Oh no. I've been sleeping alone for more years than I care to count."

"Then you lock your doors and windows. This is a peaceable village ordinarily, but you never know who might be hanging around during the Illumination. Lately I've had a sort of feeling, like you get in the woods when there's an animal watching you. John knows what I mean."

"Yes, I do," said her husband, "and while I haven't felt

it myself, I don't discount it. Mary's more intuitive than
I. We're not trying to scare you, Helen, but you just
remember there are neighbors handy and a spare room if
you get edgy."

"Thank you. I won't try to be brave."

"We'd lend you old Rex here, but he's deaf as a post
and no earthly use for a watchdog. Besides, he'd probably
keep you awake all night fussing about Imogene and the
kittens."

Mary Enderble bundled them into their wraps, reminded
them about their groceries, and was still waving from the
doorstep when Shandy saw Helen to her new abode.

Chapter 13

"Peter, that's bizarre! More coffee?"

"Thank you, Helen, I couldn't. That was a superb breakfast. Then you don't think Tim and I are deluding ourselves about Jemima's having been murdered?"

"I don't see how you could think anything else, especially since that marble turned up at the Cadwalls'."

Miss Marsh began stacking dishes. "Is there any chance they might be involved themselves?"

"At the moment, I can't think of anybody more likely."

Shandy told her why. "Of course the motive is pure conjecture."

"Yes, but it makes sense, and they did have the best opportunity. The obvious answer is most apt to be the right one. Where do they live?"

"Right there." He pointed out the window at the house next door.

"Then that could be why nobody saw Jemima come out of the shrubbery. Mrs. Cadwall was waiting for her at home. They'd planned to go over to your house together. To avoid the crowds on the Crescent, Jemima cut through the back yards."

"Wallowing in snowdrifts all the way? I'm not much up

111

on ladies' finery, but I shouldn't think even Jemima would
show that much disregard for her party clothes."

"Even when she was on a cloak-and-dagger mission?"

"Which she'd announced at the top of her voice all over
the Dysarts' living room. Anyway, she'd have left a trail
like a herd of elephants."

"It could have snowed and covered her tracks."

"It could have, but apparently it didn't. I can still see
the tracks the workmen made putting up those accursed
lights on my spruce trees, and that happened on the afternoon before she was killed."

"Oh, Peter, you do make things difficult. I'll have to
think up a different theory. Right now, I suppose I'd better go brighten Dr. Porble's day. Are you going to walk
me up to the library, or have you something else on tap?"

"Yes to both. I'll leave you to your job, and collect you
for lunch about half past twelve, if that's agreeable?"

"Are you sure you want to?"

"Of course." He'd never been surer of anything in his
life. "Why, would you rather not?"

"I'd adore to have lunch with you, but people might
begin to think things."

"That would be a refreshing novelty, which we as edu-
cators have a duty to encourage. If you mean they might
begin to talk scandal about us. I expect they already have,
so we might as well be hanged for sheep as for lambs. Is
this the coat you're going to wear? I do wish you had
something warmer."

Helen gave him a wicked smile. "Go shopping with me.
That should rattle a few eyeballs."

"It should, indeed. We must add that to our list of things
to do."

"Don't you love making lists? It always gives me such a
self-righteous glow to scratch things off."

Shandy hoped she wasn't planning to scratch him off,
once she got the urge to move on again as she apparently
was wont to do, but he didn't dare ask. He must make
do with what he could get. The walk to the library was
far too short, and Porble altogether too eager in welcom-
ing his new assistant.

"Well, Helen. Don't mind if I call you Helen? We're one
happy family here. I've been thinking how we might best
use you."

"But I'm supposed to catalogue the Buggins Collection."

"Balderdash! Can't waste a person with your qualifications on that old junk. Now, I thought we'd start by—"

"Couldn't I at least see where the books are kept?" she pleaded. "I'm invited to tea with the Svensons on Thursday afternoon, and they'll be sure to ask for a progress report. The president seemed insistent that I get started on the collection right away. Didn't you think so, Professor Shandy?"

"Very insistent," Shandy replied.

Porble scowled. "Then I suppose you'll have to make some show of effort. It's a complete waste of time, but we don't want to get Svenson roaring in here chucking the desks around."

He fished in his top middle drawer for a key that had got tangled up in a wad of elastic bands and paper clips.

"This way." He opened a door that led into a rear corridor lined with doors, one to the mop room, one to the staff toilet, one to the basement, and finally to a room at the very end. This one, he attempted to unlock but couldn't.

"Drat! I seem to have brought the wrong key. Funny, I thought that was the only key I kept in that drawer. Usually I'm pretty careful about leaving them around, but this one wasn't worth—well, I'll have to go back and look again."

"Wait a second," said Helen. "I have Mrs. Ames's key ring. Maybe there's one on here."

After a couple of tries, they found it. The door opened on a smallish room that looked to be one solid jumble of books.

"God, what a mess!" said the librarian. "As you can see, Helen, your predecessor didn't get much done. She might at least have stacked the books in piles, instead of pawing them into one big mess. I can't imagine how the room got into this state."

"Neatness wasn't Mrs. Ames's thing," Miss Marsh agreed. "Are you sure a few freshmen haven't been in here having a book fight?"

"Not possible. Nobody except staff and cleaners is allowed into this corridor. As a rule, we keep that door out of the main reading room locked. You need a key to get to the bathroom. No doubt you'll find that on Mrs.

Ames's key ring, too. She was big on prerogatives, though short on performance. I believe that's a desk over there among the debris."

"I'll fight my way to it in time," said Helen. "First, I'm going to need some more shelving and an armload of dustrags."

"We've got some old bookcases in the basement. I'll assign a couple of student helpers to move them up here and start tidying, in case the president should take a notion to check on you. He prides himself on running a tight ship. His grandfather was third mate of a New Bedford whaler or something. I suspect his grandmother was one of the whales."

"*Balaena mysticetus?*"

"*Grampus orca,* I should say," Porble replied gloomily. "They say it doesn't kill for sport, but we take no chances. Right, Shandy?"

"Entirely so, Porble. I think you're showing great acumen in—er—ordering full speed ahead on the Buggins Collection just now. Mrs. Ames's death is bound to raise questions at the next general meeting. I know you don't play campus politics, but it can't hurt to have the jump on those who do."

Having tossed his golden apple, Shandy judged it was time to leave, and did so. He looked into the Germination Laboratory, smiled fondly at the flats of vermiculite under whose misted plastic roofs lay the promise of Portulaca Purple Passion, then went to call on the security chief.

Grimble was in his office, yelling through the telephone about some matter that sounded remarkably trivial in proportion to the fuss he was making about it. Shandy learned a good deal about the fine art of fulmination before he got to state his business.

"I've been wondering how Mrs. Ames got into my house."

Grimble stared. "Through the door, I s'pose. How else?"

"That's precisely my point. To get in, she'd need a key. To lock the door after her, she'd also need a key. The doors were locked when I got home, but no key was found on or near her body. Where did it go?"

The security chief puffed out his cheeks and scratched his head. After a while, he replied, "So? Somebody else must have unlocked the door for her and taken the key away."

"Yes, but who?"

"How the hell do I know? Whoever had a key."

"Nobody had a key except myself and you and Mrs. Lomax, my housekeeper. Mrs. Lomax was visiting her daughter in Portland and took her key along with her."

"What for?"

"I suppose because it was in her pocketbook and she didn't bother to take it out."

"How they lug them trunks along is beyond me. And they claim women are the weaker sex."

Grimble showed an inclination to expand on this outmoded theme, but Shandy was having none of that.

"Grimble, I'm not a careless man by nature, neither am I a forgetful one. You told Ottermole that people around the Crescent are always leaving keys with their neighbors, and I daresay some of them do. I myself have never once, in all the eighteen years I've lived here, done so. I have no pets to feed or valuables to guard, so there's no need for somebody to keep running in. Mrs. Lomax is paid to take care of the place and she'd always been willing to adjust her holiday plans to mine. This was the first instance I can recall when we've both been out of town at the same time. As far as I can see, that key had to come from here."

"Well, it damn sure didn't," yelled Grimble. "Look here, Professor, I know my job. Nobody gets at those keys except me personally. Come in here."

He led Shandy to his private sanctum, a tiny office whose main feature was in fact a huge keyboard that ran all around the room. One wall was given over to faculty residences, with each hook marked by a neat sticker bearing one family's name and address. Each key on the hook bore a tag stating whose it was and what door it fit.

"See that?" Grimble pointed at the board with totally justifiable pride. "Nobody takes a key off there but me. Anybody wants their own, they have to come to the outer office and ask for it. Anybody wants somebody else's, they have to give me a damn good reason or they don't get it. I can tell at a glance who's in and who's out. That board gets checked every day and if your key was missing, I'd damn well know it. And see this?"

He dragged out an immense ledger and dumped it on the

desk. "Everybody's listed here. Every time the key gets taken out it has to be entered on the right page with the time written down, and when you bring it back I enter that time, too. Look, here's your page. One key, front door. Not one damn entry on it since the day you turned it over to this office. So the key didn't get taken. See, there it is, right where it's hung for the past eighteen years."

Shandy glanced at the tarnished bit of brass and shook his head. "That's not my key."

"The hell it ain't! It's got your name on it."

"That doesn't mean anything. Look here."

Shandy fished his key ring out of his pocket. "This is my front door, this is the back, and this is the cellar. The key on your board doesn't match any one of them."

"Could you have changed a lock, maybe?"

The professor didn't answer right away. He was counting keys. "Sixty-seven. And how many are listed in your book?"

"I never thought to count 'em," Grimble mumbled.

Shandy thumbed pages like a hound on the scent. "Sixty-eight. There's your answer. Somebody just lifted my key, switched tags, and put another in its place."

"Whose, for instance?"

"How should I know? Check your list and find out which hook is a key short."

The security chief was a shaken man. "But how could it happen? Nobody gets to these keys but me. Nobody."

"Are you sure of that?"

"Of course I am! My guys know the rules. They wouldn't dare set foot in here without me saying it was okay."

"But you have visitors coming and going all the time, don't you? Students getting keys to the labs, faculty people who've locked themselves out and whatnot?"

"Sure, that's what we're here for. But nobody gets past the outer office."

"What happens when you go on vacation?"

"I give Sam, my head assistant, a set of master keys that unlocks all the doors in the college, and I make damn sure nobody gets it away from him because I lock it on a chain around his waist. Cripes, his wife is glad to see me come back! Then I send around a notice that campus residents have to make their own arrangements about spare keys.

You ought to know that. You get one, same as everybody else."

"I suppose I do. I've never paid much attention, since I make my own arrangements in any case. Then what it boils down to is that my key could have been stolen any time these past eighteen years."

"No, it couldn't! I keep telling you." Grimble was thoroughly demoralized now, scarlet-faced and bellowing. "Nobody touches these keys but me."

"Don't be a jackass," Shandy snapped back. "The damned key's gone, therefore somebody took it. Since nobody's ever broken into my house before, it's probably safe to assume either Mrs. Ames or somebody who let her in stole the key for that specific purpose. If you'd stop yelling and use your head, we might be able to determine how it happened. Who cleans up in here, for instance?"

"I do, damn you!"

"All right. Now, when you say nobody ever comes into this office, precisely how literally do you mean that? Suppose, for instance, that President Svenson was locked out and came to get his house key. If he happened to follow you, chatting as people do, would you slam the door in his face?"

"Well, no, but—"

"Or Mrs. Svenson, or one of the trustees, or anybody in a position to make things hot for you if you gave him or her a hard time?"

"I suppose not," the security chief mumbled, "but—"

"Of course you wouldn't. Neither would I. Let's take it a step further. Suppose this person asked for a key that was on the opposite board. Since the hooks are so admirably well marked, how long would it take him to lift my key and put another in its place? The name tags would have to be switched, but these clever little clip things you use don't seem to present much difficulty. Time me."

Shandy plucked two keys from different hooks, whipped the tags off, put one on its opposite, and hung that key back on the board.

"How long?"

" 'Bout a second and a half. Okay, Professor, have it your way."

"I'm not trying to score off you, man, I'm trying to make some sense of what happened. It's a great deal more important than you seem to realize. Who was in here late on the afternoon of the twenty-second? Have you some way of knowing that?"

"Of course I know," said Grimble sulkily. "It's in the daybook."

He led the professor back to the outer office and pointed to a dog-eared binder lying open on the counter that barred entrance to his private office. "See, everybody that takes a key has to sign out when they take it and in when they bring it back, no matter if it's college or residence. If it's college keys, I make damn sure they bring 'em in by the end of the day, even if one of my boys has to track 'em down in the girls' shower rooms. If it's residential, there's not much I can do but call up and remind 'em. That's why I keep a special ledger for the house keys, so if somebody comes in here wantin' a key some other member of the family took out and didn't return, I've got a comeback. We don't run into that kind of trouble very often, I must say. Got 'em pretty well trained. It's a good system. At least I thought it was."

"Nothing is perfect," Shandy mumbled absent-mindedly. He was running his finger down the list of entries for the twenty-second. "Seventy-two. Good Lord, this place must have been a madhouse."

"It's like that sometimes. Then some days you don't get hardly anybody for hours at a time. Comes in bunches."

"Mrs. Jackman locked herself out, I see."

"She generally does. Sends the kids to get the key and we have a big fight about whose turn it is to sign the book."

"This time she seems to have signed it herself."

"Christmas shopping. Went by herself so the kids wouldn't see her dragging home the loot."

"Half past four," Shandy mused. "I rather had the impression she'd been at home with her children that afternoon, watching the men put up my decorations. Probably I misunderstood. Did she happen to follow you into the private office, do you remember?"

The security chief's eye became a thought less fishlike. "Can't say I'd mind if she did, them tight pants she wears."

"What ought I to infer from that?"

"Oh hell, I was only kiddin'. You know the rules around here, same as me."

Shandy also knew equivocation when he met it. Yesterday, he would never have entertained the possibility that pretty young Mrs. Jackman might look twice at a randy old goat with a paunch. Still, her name was only one among many.

"Who are all these people I don't know? Students, I suppose. You wouldn't let any of them past the counter?"

"Damn right I wouldn't."

"What's this name?"

Shandy pointed at a scrawl that spread itself across four spaces. Grimble hitched up his eyeglasses.

"Looks like Heidi somethin'. Oh, I know. Big blond kid. Took the key to the sled shed."

"Heidi Hayhoe? It would be, with a handwriting like that. But she's put down the time as a quarter past five. I should have thought the sleds would all be out by then."

The security chief smirked. "Maybe that's why she wanted the key."

"I see. You certainly are a stickler for morality on campus."

"What the hell am I expected to do, follow every damn kid on campus around to make sure nobody don't get screwed but the bunny rabbits in the animal lab? She brought the key back, see? That's all I have to know."

The man was starting to yell again. Shandy changed the subject.

"Why do you suppose Dr. Cadwall wanted the key to the weaving shop at two minutes before six? Why should he want it at any time, for that matter?"

"Because he's a goddamned Nosy Parker is why! Comes in here just when I'm ready to shut up an' go out to supper, follows me into my office chewin' my ear about—"

Grimble stopped short. "Followed me into my office, sure enough. And I was so damned mad I turned my back on him and took my own sweet time pickin' out the key."

"That key being on the board opposite the residential keys?"

"You bet your life it was. I ain't accusin' nobody of nothin', you understand. I'm just tellin' you what happened."

"Then do me a favor and don't tell anybody else. I'll take it from here."

Shandy left the security office. He didn't particularly

want to confront Ben Cadwall right away. He ought first
to think out a line of approach. Nevertheless, he found
himself climbing the broad granite stairs of the yellow
brick building that had housed the administrative offices
since Balaclava College was hardly more than a few clapboard sheds and one small herd of Guernseys.

There was hardly anybody in the building today, not a
telephone nor a typewriter to be heard. Those few secretaries who hadn't called in sick must be taking late coffee
breaks or early lunches, or both combined. It was an unwritten rule that while the wheels of administration must
be kept turning during the Illumination, nobody was to
push any harder than necessary. Most of the bosses, including President Svenson, would be off skiing or otherwise
holidaying. Cadwall, however, would probably be holding
the fort. Shandy pushed open the golden oak door with
"Comptroller" stenciled in black on its frosted glass panel,
and went in.

Sure enough, Cadwall was at his desk. His mouth hung
open. His eyes were staring, the pupils dilated. Nobody
could look like that, and be alive.

Chapter 14

Very carefully and deliberately, Shandy backed out of the comptroller's office and shut the door behind him. There was a telephone in the outside cubbyhole where Cadwall's secretary ought to have been sitting, but he did not use it. Instead, he walked down the corridor to Registrations, where Miss Tibbett was also absent from her post. He sat down at her desk because he suddenly realized his knees were wobbling, and reached for the local directory.

"Police station. Officer Dorkin speaking."

Shandy recognized the voice. A few years back, Budge Dorkin had been the guiding force behind his lawn mower.

"Hello, Budge," he said. "This is Peter Shandy. Is Chief Ottermole there?"

"Oh, hi, Professor. Gee, no, there's nobody here but me. Some guy in a sixty-six blue Stingray held up the liquor store, ran the red light on Main Street and totaled Mrs. Guptill's Dodge, fled the scene of the accident and skidded off the Cat Creek bridge. The chief's down at the scene, waiting for the fire department to fish the guy out so's he can throw the book at him."

"Well, you'll have to get hold of your chief somehow and tell him to come up to the college fast. I've just found Dr. Cadwall dead in his office."

"What from?"

"I don't know. That's why I want Ottermole. Hurry him along, will you, Budge?"

"I'll do my best, Professor. I'd go myself, only we can't leave the office unmanned. Say, doesn't it strike you sort of funny, Dr. Cadwall dying right after Mrs. Ames, them being next-door neighbors and all?"

"Funny is hardly the word," said Shandy grimly.

"Hey, I tell you what. If the chief doesn't show pretty soon, how about if I get on to the state police? They take over when something comes up we can't handle."

"That would be an excellent thing to do. Good thinking, Budge."

He hung up and searched the phone book again. The president would have to know, not that Shandy relished the prospect of telling him. After many rings had produced no result, he concluded the Svensons must have gone off on one of their family cross-country ski treks, no doubt toting knapsacks crammed with smorgasbord and extra socks. They'd be lost in the frozen wastes until sunset.

Who else? Melchett. The doctor could do nothing for Ben now, but he must be called anyway. Doctor was on his way back from the hospital and couldn't be reached at this time, but would be given Professor Shandy's message the second he walked through the front door. In a pig's eye he would. Shandy slammed down the receiver, sat brooding a moment, then switched to the interoffice line and rang Security.

"Grimble, this is Shandy. I'm over at Administration. Dr. Cadwall's dead."

"He's what?"

"Dead. Deceased. Defunct. I walked into his office a few minutes ago and found him. You'd better get over here. No, I won't touch anything."

Having done his best to sound the alarm, Shandy decided he'd better look for any sign of life in the building. At last a babble of voices led him to the mail room, where four or five secretaries and assistants were gathered around the sorting table sharing a spread of Christmas pastries. They were only mildly abashed at being caught.

"Come in, Professor. Care for some coffee?"

"Er—yes, thank you. Black. I've—er—" he stalled, wondering what line to take. Direct questioning might be less productive than shock tactics.

"Ladies and gentlemen, something terrible has happened. Dr. Cadwall—"

Kindly Miss Tibbett spoiled the effect he was trying to make by thrusting a paper cup full of boiling hot coffee at him. "Here, drink this right up. It's good for shock."

"Miss Tibbett, I am not in shock." Nevertheless, he took a sip of the scalding liquid. "Dr. Cadwell—"

"What's wrong? Is it his heart? Did he fall on the ice? Don't tell me he—" they were all talking at once. Shandy had to raise his voice to make himself heard.

"Dr. Cadwall has died. He is in his office. Just—sitting there." Shandy drank more coffee. "I've notified Security and Grimble is on his way over. Perhaps I shouldn't have left him alone, but the building seemed strangely empty, and I was wondering if any of you—"

"Bumped him off?" the mail boy suggested.

"That's not funny, Charles," snapped Miss Tibbett. "Professor Shandy means did we see him looking ill or—or anything?"

From a further confusion of tongues, Shandy gleaned that the comptroller's secretary was out with a cold, that nobody had seen Dr. Cadwall enter the building, and that in truth those present had spent most of the morning doing precisely what they were doing now. He finished his coffee and went back to the main corridor, with the lot of them tiptoeing after him like the chorus in an operetta. Nobody was putting on much show of grief. Cadwall had not been a liked man. Still, he was one of their own. As they neared his office, the chatter died and the faces turned somber.

"Who's going to tell his wife?" whispered one of the clerks.

"I'm sure I don't want to," sighed the professor. "Twice in three days would be a bit much."

"Oh, that's right! You're the one who found Mrs. Ames. What a strange coincidence. I wonder who's going to be next. These things always go in threes, my mother used to say."

"Thank you for those words of cheer and comfort, Miss Baxter."

"Professor, I didn't mean—"

Miss Baxter's protestation was cut off by the arrival of the security chief. He was not happy.

"For Christ's sake, Professor, what have you done now?"

"I haven't done anything," Shandy snarled back, "except to open the comptroller's office door and close it again."

"You didn't touch nothing?"

"Only the doorknob."

"Why the hell not? I'd have thought you'd take his pulse or something. Maybe he's just havin' a fit."

"He is not having a fit. Dr. Cadwall is dead. Go and look for yourself."

Grimble showed a not surprising inclination to stall. "What did he die of?"

"How should I know? I'm no doctor."

"Doctor. That's what what we got to do, call the doctor."

"I've already called him," said Shandy.

Grimble sighed and decided he ought to look in on the corpse to make sure there really was one.

"I guess we better not get any more fingerprints on this doorknob. Anybody got a clean handkerchief?"

"There's a box of Kleenex on Charlene's desk," somebody suggested.

Grimble took a couple of tissues and made a great performance of wrapping them around the handle. "Don't none of you come in here. Is that how you left him, Professor?"

"Exactly."

The man was making an ass of himself, of course, but to call him one in front of office personnel would be an act of gratuitous cruelty. Two corpses in three days, as Shandy himself had remarked only a few minutes before, were a bit much for anybody. Perhaps this was harder on the security chief since he had to at least put on a show of coping, while Shandy need only dither on the sidelines.

Except, of course, that President Svenson had dumped the responsibility flat on his shoulders. That Cadwall's sudden death could be unrelated to Jemima Ames's was just not possible.

Now that he was mercifully numbed by shock, the professor found he could study the body quite objectively. There was no sign of a wound or a weapon. The color of the skin was bad, but Ben had always had an unhealthy complexion. There was a pen lying on the desk, and a pile of checks were scattered around, as though he'd been in the act of signing them when the final spasm occurred.

"Just—sitting there working." Miss Tibbett, whose thoughts must have been running parallel to Shandy's, craned her neck through the door. "I'll bet he never knew what hit him. Was it his heart, I wonder?"

"It was an embolism," pronounced another. "My aunt had one. Popped off in the midst of peeling potatoes."

"Ugh, stop it! You're giving me the creeps," cried the youngest of the group. "Professor Shandy, what do you think?"

"I think we ought to abandon futile speculation and wait for the doctor," he said. "In the meantime, perhaps it would be wise for you people to—er—resume your customary functions. Don't you agree, Grimble?"

"Yeah, that's right. You folks get back to work. Don't nobody leave the building till we find out what the doctor says."

"But what about lunch?" protested the boy from the mail room. "It's almost noontime."

"If I know you, buster, you been eatin' ever since you got here. Don't worry, you ain't goin' to starve. When did he say he was comin', Professor?"

"His wife said she'd give him the message as soon as he gets in, for what that's worth. He's alleged to be on his way home from the hospital."

"Means he's goin' to eat his lunch and take a nap, most likely," Grimble moaned. "We won't see him for another hour. I don't s'pose there's a spare cup o' coffee around anywheres?"

"I'll bring you some," said Miss Tibbett. "Cream and three sugars, isn't it?"

She headed back toward the mail room. The others straggled after her, some looking relieved, some disappointed.

"At any rate, the police should be here soon," Shandy said hopefully.

"You called them, too?"

"Of course."

"What the hell for? Look, Professor, I don't bust into your lab an' tell you how to grow your turnips, do I? I already caught hell for bringin' Ottermole up to the Crescent when we found Mrs. Ames. Dr. Svenson says he don't want no police called in for anything short of murder."

"What makes you think this isn't one?"

"Oh, Jesus! Why should anybody want to kill the comptroller? He's the guy who signs the checks."

"Very funny. Then why did you go through that performance about not touching anything?"

"Oh hell, that was just part o' the act. Got to show I'm on my toes, ain't I?"

They sat scowling silently for a moment. Then Shandy remarked, "It's interesting that you mentioned Mrs. Ames."

"You tryin' to make out there's some connection here?"

"We have to look at the facts."

"What facts? Mrs. Ames falls off a stool an' busts her head. Dr. Cadwall takes a fit or somethin'."

Miss Tibbett appeared with coffee and cake. Shandy gave up the struggle. Grimble would admit to nothing he didn't have to. They'd just sit here glaring at one another until somebody came to take over the responsibility. He might as well call Helen and cancel their luncheon. Sighing, he got up and moved toward the door.

"Hey, Professor, you ain't leavin'?"

"I'm going down the hall to use Miss Tibbett's phone. I was supposed to meet someone for lunch."

"Come to think of it, with all that telephonin' you been doin', you got hold of Mrs. Cadwall yet?"

"No, I haven't," Shandy was forced to admit.

"Should o' thought you'd call her first off the bat. Better do it now, hadn't you?"

"Grimble, why can't you tell her? I got stuck the last time."

"What the hell, we takin' turns? I wouldn't know what to say. Anyway, you found him."

"God, yes! After this, people will run when they see me coming."

Like it or not, he couldn't decently postpone the task any longer. To his intense relief, Hannah Cadwall didn't answer her phone. She was probably out hectoring somebody, in her new role as Jemima's successor. How would she react when she found out she was a widow? Ben had not seemed a lovable man, but one never knew.

Shandy made a couple more calls, to the commissary and other places where she might possibly show up, leaving messages for her to get in touch with her husband's office. Then he called Mary Enderble, who sensibly didn't waste his time asking questions he couldn't answer but said she'd look for Hannah around the Crescent and down at the supermarket.

Lastly, with extreme reluctance, he dialed the library and asked for Miss Marsh.

"Helen, you'd better go along to lunch without me. I'm in another mess."

"Poor Peter! What is it this time?"

Grimble appeared at his elbow all of a sudden, mouthing, "Is that her? What's she sayin'?"

Shandy fought down an urge to belt him over the head with the telephone.

"I regret having to break our appointment, Miss Marsh," he said severely, "but unforeseen circumstances have—er —circumstanced. I'll look for you in the faculty dining room if I manage to get out of here any time soon. If not, I'll get back to you when I can."

He hung up and turned around to scowl at Grimble. "No, I haven't been able to reach Mrs. Cadwall. Mrs. Enderble's out looking for her. Why don't you send one of your men to help?"

"Who, for instance? They're all on their lunch break but Ned an' he can't leave the office. She'll show up sooner or later."

They wandered back into the dead man's office, hideously fascinated by that waxwork figure in the high-backed leather swivel chair.

"Don't look much different dead than alive," the security chief grunted. "Old Smiley, that's what the kids called him. Don't expect he'll be much missed."

"I think he will, you know," Shandy contradicted. "He was an able and hard-working administrator. I only wish—"

"Wish what?"

"If you want the truth, I wish I knew whether he was also honest."

"Why shouldn't he be?"

"Why should he be dead?"

"Will you quit harpin' on that? He died, that's all. He just died!"

"Grimble, for God's sake, I'm not deaf. What's the matter with you?"

Well might Shandy ask. The man's face was purple, his hands trembled, his eyes were staring wider than the corpse's. Still he insisted, "Nothin's the matter with me! It's just—oh, what the hell? Havin' my routine upset, hangin' around here with a dead body while the work piles up—Svenson on my ear about one damn thing after another—now you tryin' to make out—oh, the hell with it! I'm goin' down the hall to see if they got any more coffee. If the doctor shows up, tell him I'll be right back."

Shandy didn't care. Being alone with Cadwall was less disagreeable than having Grimble there with him. Besides, it gave him a chance to look around. He knew he ought not to touch anything, but surely there was no harm in using his eyes.

He was sure Cadwall had been poisoned. As an agriculturist, the professor knew altogether too much about pesticides and their effects. Though he and Tim had for years been waging a ferocious battle against such toxins, there was still no dearth of lethal substances around Balaclava. But what poison would kill in just that way, and how was it got into the victim?

There was nothing on the desk to give a clue, only a clean blotter, the pile of checks, a few pens on a tray, and two baskets marked "in" and "out," both of them empty. There was no disarrangement of the victim's garments. Ben had always dressed like Calvin Coolidge, with starched collars and tightly knotted neckties and a buttoned-up vest under a buttoned-up suit coat. Even in summer, his only concession to the thermometer was to shed his vest. Presumably somebody could have sneaked up behind him and thrust a hypodermic needle through those several layers of clothing, but Shandy could see no indication that anybody had.

A person entering this office on evil intent during Ilumination Week would be taking a special risk, simply because the normally busy Administration Building was so quiet. Should any of the staff happen by chance to be at his or her rightful post, the chance of being both observed and remembered was extremely high. It would make far greater sense to administer a slow-acting substance like arsenic and be far away when the stuff began to work.

Arsenic, being tasteless, was easy to give but Shandy didn't think it had been used in this case. He couldn't force himself to sniff at those slack lips but thought he could detect the disagreeable odor of gastric upset. Vomiting would be consistent with arsenic poisoning, but wouldn't it keep on until the victim died in agony, since nobody had been around to get help? Shouldn't Ben have been found on the floor in the men's room, not sitting here at his desk? It looked more as if the comptroller had got hold of something that made him sick, then put him permanently to sleep.

Ben wouldn't necessarily be alarmed at a sudden attack of nausea. He always welcomed a new symptom. If it took the form of cramps and diarrhea, he'd credit the laxative he'd no doubt dosed himself with the night before. If he vomited, he'd assume he was coming down with one of the viral bugs that were always around. Anticipating a stay in bed, he'd make a valiant stab at finishing up his work before he went home.

What sort of poison might give you a bellyache, then make you helpless and comatose before you realized how sick you were? Since plants were his business, Shandy's thoughts naturally turned to vegetable poisons. Why not? Why should a killer stick his neck out to buy or steal a lethal compound when plenty of local windowsills offered death for the picking, even in midwinter?

Poinsettias and mistletoe, for instance, were far less innocent than most people supposed, but Shandy wasn't sure how they'd act. For guaranteed results, a murderer would be wiser to stick with the alkaloids. Trusty old *Conium maculatum* would leave Ben's mind clear enough to keep signing checks while his lungs were gradually paralyzed, but where could one find poison hemlock in December?

Solanine produced narcosis and paralysis. All you needed for that was a green potato, or the eyes of one that had begun to sprout. Then there were the simple heart depressants such as *Cannabis sativa*. A concentrated dose of pot could take a person so high he'd never come back. People weren't supposed to grow the stuff around campus, but there were always a few who thought it cute to do so.

All at once, Shandy could stand the sight of the dead man no longer. He went out and stood by the window in the corridor, hoping to catch sight of Dr. Melchett's car. However, nothing was to be seen but trodden snow and leaden sky and trees with bare branches moving in the raw December wind: maples silvery and slim-looking even when their trunks could hardly be spanned with outstretched arms, oaks rugged and stubborn as Thorkjeld Svenson with brown leaves still clinging to their boughs, a few graceful streaks of white bark where the birch-leaf miner hadn't yet managed to complete its dirty work; all silhouetted against the welcome emerald of pine and the deeper green of yews grown tall and knock-kneed in the many years since they were planted. There was a lot of yew around Balaclava. It made a goodly show at small expense and could be counted on to come safely through hard New England winters, though new students always had to be cautioned against eating the translucent red berries and animals kept from grazing on the foliage.

In fact, a decoction of taxine distilled from the omnipresent yew needles could also function as a heart depressant, working unfelt in the system until it brought just such a death as Ben's, if he remembered correctly. Shandy was pondering the various possibilities, wishing he could get hold of Professor Muencher's book on plant poisons or some other reliable text, when a four-year-old maroon Oldsmobile pulled up in front of the building and a shortish man in a dapper camel's hair car coat got out, pulling a pigskin satchel off the seat. Shandy hurried to open the door for him.

"Dr. Melchett, I'm relieved to see you. You got the message about Dr. Cadwall?"

"Only that I was supposed to get over here as fast as possible. I haven't even eaten lunch yet. Where is he? Why haven't you taken him to the hospital? Or the infirmary? What's the matter with him?"

"Er—he's dead. I called in on a—er—matter of business and found him sitting in his chair, exactly as he is now."

"Well, well."

Melchett set down his satchel on the comptroller's desk and hung his coat very carefully over the back of a wooden chair. "You never know, do you? I'd have said Ben was good for another fifty. Told him so at his last check-up. He didn't believe me, of course. Ben always liked to think he was on his last leg. Apparently he was right and I was wrong. Just goes to show we doctors aren't infallible, much as we'd like to think we are."

He bent over and rolled back one of the dead man's eyelids. "Where's Hannah?"

"We've been trying to get hold of her."

"Ah. Gone shopping, no doubt. It's amazing the amount of time women can spend in stores. I'd like to ask her what Ben's been dosing himself with."

"I've been wondering about the vegetable alkaloids," Shandy ventured.

"Why?"

"Because they're so easy to get hold of, I suppose, and because I've seen farm animals poisoned by feeding on them. They may remain in the body for some time with no symptoms, you know, then cramp and coma—"

"You don't have to teach me my profession," Melchett snapped. He studied the corpse a moment longer, then asked in a less belligerent tone, "Did you have anything particular in mind?"

"Coniine, cannabinine, sloanine, taxine. I could give you a complete list, I expect, if I sat down and thought awhile. Toxicity in plants is something we agrologists have to concern ourselves with, you know."

"But how would the poison get into his system? Nobody with a grain of sense would ingest that muck."

"Not on purpose, certainly."

Melchett looked startled and began rubbing his chin. "Still, Ben was one of those health food freaks. Sprinkled wheat germ on his corn flakes, that sort of thing."

"I grant you that, but don't you think he'd make sure it was in fact wheat germ he sprinkled? Unless someone—er —switched the boxes."

The doctor quit rubbing his chin. "Shandy," he said primly, "that strikes me as a somewhat irresponsible statement. In view of your recent peculiar behavior, don't you think you'd better tone down your remarks?"

"In view of the present circumstances, don't you think you'd be well advised to request an autopsy?"

"I suppose so," the doctor sighed. "Damn it, my wife's nagged me for months about taking her to Florida over the holidays. This is what I get for staying home. Where's Grimble?"

"He said to tell you he'd be right back. That was about half an hour ago. I'd better go see if he's—er—finished interrogating the staff."

"He's probably interrogating some stenographer in the broom closet, if I know that old goat. Tell him to get the hell out here and call the county coroner's office. I'm not writing a certificate on this one."

There was a little stress on "this one" that prompted Shandy to retort, "Then you weren't entirely satisfied with the way Mrs. Ames died either."

Dr. Melchett stared. He opened his mouth, then snapped it shut, which was probably a wise thing to do under the circumstances. Shandy, knowing there was no use in pressing the issue, went to fetch the security chief. He found Grimble engaged in no more lascivious pastime than eating fruitcake.

The man rose with a fair show of alacrity, cramming the last bite into his mouth. "Thanks, folks. See you later."

"You will let us know what happened to poor Dr. Cadwall, won't you?" begged Miss Tippett.

"Yeah, and when we can split for lunch," added the mail boy.

"I think they'd better have some sandwiches brought in," said Shandy when the two men were out in the corridor. "Dr. Melchett isn't going to sign a death certificate."

"Huh?" Grimble sprayed fruitcake crumbs. "Why not?"

"I expect he'll explain that to you himself. He says you're to phone the county coroner."

"Oh, Christ on a crutch!"

Grimble managed to get rid of his mouthful in order to vent his feelings. "Professor, if you talked him into this, I'll—"

"He didn't talk me into anything," snapped the doctor, who had got tired of waiting and come to meet them. "The evidence speaks for itself. Where have you been, man? Get on that telephone and make it fast. In my professional opinion, you people have one sweet mess on your hands here, and I want no part of it."

Although he still had on his overcoat and galoshes, Professor Shandy began to feel cold. He walked over to one of the big old-fashioned steam radiators that ran the length of the corridor and pressed his hands against the grids. They were hot to the touch, almost too hot for flesh to bear, but they didn't convey any warmth to his body.

"I'm in shock," he thought dispassionately. "I ought to get some coffee."

He didn't go back to the mail room. Grimble had probably emptied the pot. Miss Tippett would be glad to make him some more, but he didn't want to stand waiting among that gabbling crew. He wanted to go get Helen Marsh and take her someplace where nobody had ever heard of Balaclava College.

Dr. Melchett was talking to the coroner's office. Shandy didn't bother trying to understand what he was saying. It was what the doctor had not said, that little flicker of his eyelid when Jemima Ames was mentioned, that told the most. Something must have struck him wrong the morning she was found, but since Ottermole and Grimble were so determined to call her death an accident, that same caution which was causing him to pass the buck now had prompted him to sign the death certificate without which Harry the Ghoul wouldn't have dared commence his gruesome rites.

One couldn't blame him, Shandy supposed. Murder, at least this kind of murder, just didn't happen in respectable little college towns. Even if a country GP did suspect there was something fishy about a sudden death, he'd think a long, long time before he risked his practice by starting a scandal.

If someone other than Shandy had happened to find Dr. Cadwall dead in his office, the normal reaction would be to call Security, just as he himself had done when he discovered Jemima Ames's body behind his sofa. Grimble would not have got the police, he'd have sent for Dr. Melchett. It was entirely possible that the pair of them would have managed to convince each other there was no need for further investigation, not because they were either wicked or incompetent but because anything other than natural death would be outside their customary frame of reference.

And also because they knew Thorkjeld Svenson would tear them apart if they raised a stink and couldn't produce a villain. As the affair now stood, if Miss Baxter's prediction ever came true, the third body found on campus might well be Peter Shandy's.

Chapter 15

Was there any outside possibility that Melchett could have wanted a cover-up for more urgent personal reasons? But doctors didn't kill people, at least not on purpose. Shocked by this outlandish idea, Shandy studied the man at the telephone more closely than he ever had before. The adjective that came to mind was "respectable."

Dr. Melchett had been part of the background ever since Shandy came to Balaclava. As official physician-on-call, he showed up at most of the bigger social affairs with his wife, a woman who, as Shirley Wrenne once remarked, had a new dress and an old cliché for every occasion.

The Melchetts' brand of respectability must cost them a pretty penny. Had the doctor found income not up to outgo, and started padding his bills to the college? If so, Cadwall would surely have found him out; but would that be sufficient motive for murder, and where would Jemima Ames come in?

What, in fact, did she and Ben Cadwall have in common, other than being faculty folk and next-door neighbors? They were both on intimate terms with Hannah, and they'd both had a hobby of finding out other people's business. Whether or not they ever got together and compared gossip was beside the point, since Hannah would surely pass along to her husband any tidbit Jemima let fall.

Jemima would tell, there was no doubt about that. Shandy had never once been able to visit Tim in her presence without having to listen to some story he'd far rather not hear. He couldn't imagine her getting hold of any piece of news and not confiding it to her best friend's ear.

During these past several weeks, Jemima had been closely involved with many of the students. What if she'd got wind that Melchett could be bribed to perform an abortion without going through channels and disturbing Balaclava's high moral tone, or that he was supplying drugs to undergraduates? Neither she nor Ben would be shy about confronting him with the rumor, or about cooking his goose in short order if he failed to convince them of his innocence. The moral tone at Balaclava being what it was, even a hint of malpractice could finish him with the Svensons, hence with the college, the town, and perhaps with Mrs. Melchett and all else he presumably held dear.

Poisoning a dedicated hypochondriac like Ben should be no hard task for the physician who for years had been hearing his complaints and doling out his placebos. Choosing taxine as the vehicle would be a clever touch indeed, since the stuff was not in the pharmacopoeia but available for the plucking to anybody who knew how to prepare a simple decoction; and Shandy could think of nobody on campus who didn't.

The fact that Melchett was at present engaged in passing the buck meant nothing one way or the other. No respectable doctor would care to be mixed up in a murder case. Shandy wasn't even thinking about that. He was thinking that if Melchett had in fact killed both Ben and Jemima, he'd be a fool not to kill Hannah, too.

Maybe he already had. Maybe that was why Mrs. Cadwall wasn't responding to any of the messages that had been left for her. Maybe she and her husband had shared a lethal breakfast and she was still sitting back in their house on the Crescent with an empty coffee cup in front of her, staring into infinity. Shandy found a chair, pulled it close to the radiator, and sat down, drawing his overcoat tight around him.

Melchett got through talking to the coroner's office,

fetched his natty car coat from the comptroller's office, and came over to Shandy, satchel in hand.

"No sense in my hanging around here any longer. My wife's got lunch waiting. You and Grimble can hold the fort until the police get here."

"Are they sending another unmarked van?"

The doctor didn't seem to catch the allusion. "Are you feeling all right, Shandy?"

"No. I think I've caught a chill."

"Take some aspirin and go to bed."

"How can I, if I'm supposed to sit tending a corpse while you weasel out?"

Shandy was talking to the air. Melchett was already out the door. Grimble stared morosely at the departing Oldsmobile.

"The president sure ain't goin' to like this."

"The president will have to lump it," Shandy snarled.

He was sick of the lot of them. Two people murdered, and all they could think about was filling their guts and keeping their noses clean. He stayed huddled inside his good gray tweed, not responding to any of Grimble's observations, until a small procession drove up, headed by Ottermole in the village's one police car, then a state police vehicle and an ambulance.

"Here they are." Grimble swallowed noisily. "What are you goin' to tell 'em?"

"The truth, of course. I came to see Dr. Cadwall and found him dead at his desk."

"Yeah, but what about the key an'—an' the rest of it?"

"I don't know."

"Jesus, Professor, watch it, will you? Svenson's goin' to be—"

He shut up fast as the door opened and the law arrived. Shandy, realizing that the security chief was having an attack of mental paralysis, stood up.

"Thank you for coming, gentlemen."

Ottermole, who might have been expected to make the introductions, wasn't saying anything either, so Shandy took them upon himself.

"My name is Shandy. I'm a member of the faculty. This is Mr. Grimble, head of campus security. The—er—deceased, Dr. Cadwall, our comptroller, is in his office, through that door."

Grimble suddenly found his voice. "Yeah, see, Professor Shandy here was in my office and he says, 'I'm goin' over to see the comptroller,' an' the next thing I know, he's on the intercom tellin' me—"

"Whoa, back up," said the state policeman. "Ottermole, do you want to take notes, or shall I?"

"You better," mumbled Balaclava's chief.

"Right. My name's Olivetti. Now, Professor Shandy, suppose you do the talking."

He whipped out a small black notebook and a dashing gold pen just like Cadwall's. "When did you get here?"

"Well, as Grimble told you, I left the security office about half past eleven."

"Eleven thirty-two," Grimble put in. "It's right on the record."

"My God! I had no idea you were so thorough."

"Sure. Everybody gets checked in an' out, even if they only stop by to use the john."

Olivetti cleared his throat. "So you came straight here?"

"Yes, I did."

"Why?"

"I wanted to speak to Dr. Cadwall."

"What about?"

Now was the moment of truth. Shandy was pondering what to say when he felt a small, involuntary tightening of his body muscles. It was the same instinctive drawing-away that had kept him from dousing the embryo Balaclava Buster with an improperly mixed solution of liquid fertilizer which would surely have cremated the infant sprouts.

"A key," he replied cautiously. "I thought he might have —er—taken one that belonged to me."

"Happens all the time," Grimble butted in. "Not that I'm makin' cracks about absent-minded professors or nothin'—"

"Sure," said Olivetti. "So you came in and then what? Did you speak to his secretary?"

"She was not at her desk. I subsequently learned that she called in sick this morning. We always have some kind of mysterious epidemic among the administrative staff during the holiday season."

"Sure. Did you knock, or what?"

"I believe I merely opened his door and poked my head in. That's the—er—accepted custom around here. One asks, 'Are you busy?' or something of the sort, then either enters or goes away."

"Kind of dangerous, isn't it?" asked a cheeky youngster in whites who was carrying a folding aluminum stretcher. "What if he was taking a little time out with his secretary?"

"At Balaclava? That would seem a remote contingency. Although," Shandy added nastily, "no doubt Grimble would know better than I."

"Could we stick to the point?" asked Olivetti patiently. "How did you find him?"

"Do you mean in what position?"

"I do."

"Exactly as he is now. I realized at once that he was dead, so I shut the door and called for help."

"Where from? The secretary's phone?"

"No, I came back down the hall and used Miss Tibbett's. In the registrations office, right over there."

"Why?"

"I'm sure I can't tell you. Instinct, I suppose."

"Okay, so then what?"

"I started wondering where everyone had got to. The building appeared empty as a tomb, if you'll forgive the ill-chosen simile. I went along the corridor until the sound of voices attracted me to the mail room. There I found several staff members having their—er—coffee break."

"Probably been having it ever since they got in," said the young stretcher-bearer.

"That was my impression," Shandy conceded. "They looked—er—comfortably entrenched. All expressed surprise and dismay at my news. Miss Tibbett suggested that I drink some coffee, which I accepted most gratefully, I must say, then they accompanied me *en masse* back here."

"Did any of them go into the office?"

"No. Grimble arrived just about at that same moment. He and I went in together. The rest remained outside—er—looking through the door."

"No doubt," said Olivetti. "All right, Grimble, you take it from there."

"Well, I took a look at him an' decided the first thing to do was call the doctor an' find out what he died of. Looked to me as if he'd had a heart attack or somethin'. He was just sittin' there. See for yourself."

He marched them all into the comptroller's domain, took a tissue from the secretary's desk, and used it to protect the doorknob.

"This is what I done before. Bein' careful about fingerprints, see."

"Must have wiped them all off, if there were any," grunted Olivetti.

"Mine would be there," said Shandy.

"Right. Did you touch anything else?"

"No, I'm quite sure I didn't. Not on this—er—visit, at any rate," the professor amended. "Of course I've been in Cadwall's office on various other occasions. Most of us have, for one reason or another. Cadwall paid all the bills, you know, signed the salary checks, made the bank deposits, handled our insurance and tax deductions and so forth, took in the proceeds from the Grand Illumination—"

"You mean he was like the business manager?"

"Exactly."

"Then what does the treasurer do?"

"Very little, in my opinion. He would negotiate large bank loans or head fund-raising drives, say, if money were ever needed. But at Balaclava, money never is needed."

"You've got to be kidding. How come?"

"President Svenson runs a taut ship. Read our catalogue. Copies are available at the registration office, and I'm sure Miss Tibbett will be able to explain the fine points if you can—er—coax her back to her desk."

"I'll talk to the staff soon as we get squared away here," said Olivetti. "Okay, guys, let's take some pictures. What did you say his name was, Professor?"

"Benjamin Cadwall."

"Address?"

"Balaclava Crescent. We never bother with house numbers. It's that brown shingled house with the light tan trimming, next to the last on the right as you're coming up toward College Row."

"Married?"

"Yes. His wife's name is Hannah. We've been trying to reach her. She's apparently out somewhere."

"Shopping, most likely. They always are. Okay, Professor, I guess we don't need you any more at the moment. Weren't planning to leave town, by any chance?"

"Oh no. I'll be around. Grimble will know where to find me."

Shandy grabbed his hat and sped from the building. It was probably too late to catch Helen at the dining room, but he might as well try.

Chapter 16

Luck of a sort was with him. He met Helen just outside the dining room door. However, she was on her way back to the library.

"I don't dare go back in with you, Peter. I got a stiff little lecture on punctuality. Dr. Porble expects me to set an example."

She studied his face. "It's something bad, isn't it?"

"Very bad. I went to accuse Ben Cadwall of pinching the key to my house from the security office, and found him dead at his desk."

"Oh no! Was it—?"

"I believe so. So does Dr. Melchett, although I have a hunch he wouldn't have refused to sign a death certificate if I hadn't forced his hand. My personal guess is taxine poisoning."

"Taxine? That's from yew, isn't it?" Helen instinctively drew the skirt of her light blue coat away from the shrubs that flanked the path. "How does it work?"

"Ben would think he was coming down with an intestinal bug. He might have to go to the men's room and vomit. Then, being Ben, he'd crawl back to clean up his desk before he went home. By the time he realized how sick he was, he'd be too weak and short of breath to call for help. Then he'd go into coma and that would be that."

"You do have a tidy way of putting things." She shivered and tried to bundle the thin coat more closely around her body. "What's happening now?"

"They've got the state police in, thank God. They're taking pictures. Hannah Cadwall's off shopping or something. At least, I hope to God she is. We haven't been able to reach her."

"I shouldn't worry. She's probably doing the after-Christmas sales. You'd better go have some hot soup or something." Helen hesitated. "Peter, would you know the taste of taxine?"

"In case somebody laced my soup with it, you mean?" He tried to smile. "Oh yes, I think so. It's very bitter, I believe. Not the sort of thing you or I would swallow willingly."

"Then how did this Cadwall man get it?"

"Ben was a dedicated hypochondriac. He was always dosing himself with one thing or another. He'd assume that if something tasted ghastly, it must be good for him."

"I suppose everybody around here knew that."

"Oh yes. The neighborly aspect does rather intrude itself."

Shandy rubbed at his eyes. Helen put a hand on his coat sleeve.

"Go get some food now, Peter. Come over and have some of your sherry after I get through work, if you feel like it."

"I shall feel like it. How are you getting on?"

"Awful. He's got two kids slamming things around in the Buggins Room and me lashed to the reference desk copying out statistics on hog production. I'm so frustrated I could spit."

"Make sure you spit in Porble's direction, then. Will you be out by five, do you think?"

"Make it a quarter past. I'd hate to have you standing out in the cold, after all you've been through."

Feeling somewhat better than he had a few minutes ago, Shandy went in to lunch. It was late for Balaclava faculty people to be lunching. Hardly anybody was in the dining room except Professor Stott, the pig expert for whom Helen must be performing her distasteful task, and a somewhat boisterous gathering at one of the big round tables in the center of the room, made up of engineering teachers and aides from the power plant. Dysart was among them and, as usual, was doing most of the talking in a technical jargon that might as well have been Choctaw as far as anybody outside the group was concerned, and gave Shandy a legitimate excuse not to join them.

Stott was no threat to anybody's privacy. He was an agreeable man in his way, but wrapped heart, soul, and mind in swine culture. He even looked like a pig, with a large, pale face, turned-up snout, and small eyes set in deep circles of firm, healthy fat. He was eating a great deal, slowly and with concentration, and was doubtless unaware that a colleague had entered the room. Shandy was about to slide gratefully into a chair near him when Dysart happened to notice a chance to increase his audience.

"Hey, Pete, why so unsociable? Come over here and park the carcass. What's new among the rutabagas?"

"I haven't had time to notice."

Perforce, the agrologist jointed the engineers. He debated whether to refrain from mentioning Cadwall's death, then decided there was no use in trying to keep it quiet. Dysart would be mortally offended, for one thing, and he'd already done enough to antagonize his neighbors.

"Actually, Bob," he began, "I've had quite a morning. I dropped in to see Ben Cadwall and found him sitting at his desk, stiff as a poker."

Dysart was startled, but not silenced. "Jesus, Pete, what are you, some kind of Typhoid Mary?"

"I'm beginning to wonder."

"You mean Dr. Cadwall's dead?" exclaimed one of the teaching fellows. "What happened to him?"

"That I'm afraid I can't tell you. Nothing—er—spectacular, at any rate. He was just sitting there."

"Didn't you call the doctor or something?"

"Oh yes. I called Dr. Melchett, who in turn called the county coroner, who sent over a delegation from the state police."

"The police? What for?"

"I suppose because that's the way it's done. I'll have the soup, miss."

"Tomato bisque or corn chowder?"

"Er—chowder."

"And something to drink? Coffee?"

"Tea," said Shandy firmly.

"Hey, coffee." Dysart slammed down his own almost-empty cup with a strange expression on his face. "That reminds me. Ned, you were here this morning, when Cadwall spilled his coffee."

"Was I?"

"Sure, you were."

"If you say so. Why, do you think he'd begun to feel faint or something?"

"Faint, hell! He was strong as a horse. You know what a health freak he was. Took better care of himself than Sieglinde does of Thorkjeld."

At this *lèse-majesté*, some of the younger men looked alarmed, but nobody contradicted Professor Dysart.

"Exactly what happened, Bob?" Shandy prodded.

"Well, Pete, you know what it's like around here in the mornings. People wait on themselves cafeteria-style, and there's apt to be a lot of confusion. Tom stops to talk with Dick while Harry's trying to get at the cheese buns or whatever. It's a nuisance, but they will do it."

Shandy nodded. The one who did it most often was Dysart.

"Anyway," the engineer went on, "I was at my usual table here with a few of the guys. Ned here needed a second cup of coffee to wake him up, obviously since he can't even remember what happened, so he took his mug and went back to the counter. I decided maybe that wasn't such a bad idea, so I yelled after him, 'Get me one, too.' Got that? In the meantime, Cadwall had collected his All-bran and prune juice or whatever he was currently poisoning his guts with, and headed for a table. Somebody joggled his elbow, and his coffee went flying. Ben was plenty teed off, as you might expect. So to make a long story tedious, I told Ned to give him mine. Had to keep in with the bloke who signs the checks, you know."

"Sure, Bob, we know all about it," said one of his satellites. "Did you get those cuff links in a Cracker Jack box?"

Dysart flashed the massive new gold jewelry with more than a touch of smugness. "Adele gave them to me for Christmas."

"Nice of her," snapped Professor Shandy. "So what it

boils down to is that Cadwall drank a cup of coffee meant for you."

"That's the kernel in the filbert, Pete. Does it make you wonder a bit?"

"Yes." Shandy took a spoonful of chowder and chewed thoughtfully. "Yes, it does."

"Say, Ned," Dysart went on with a half-laugh to demonstrate that he wasn't really taking the matter seriously, "I suppose it's useless to ask if you remember who was standing next to you when you poured the coffee?"

"Oddly enough, I do, now that you mention it. It was Shirley Wrenne. I was trying to decide whether to be a gentleman and let her go first, thus risking a poke in the eye for sexist discrimination, or stay where I was and be a chauvinist pig. I opted for piggery, with all due respect to our learned colleague," he added with a dutiful bow toward the oblivious Professor Stott.

"Anybody else?"

"Professor Feldster annoyed me by grabbing over my shoulder for the cream. You know that boardinghouse reach of his. I'm sure there were others close by, because there always are, but I couldn't tell you who."

"Did anybody say anything to you, distract your attention in any way?"

"I suppose so. Somebody always does. Asks for the sugar or whatever. Honestly, Bob, I just can't remember. You know I'm never what you'd call brisk first thing in the morning."

"Yes, I know it, and I shouldn't be surprised if other people did, too. Pete, am I making something of nothing?"

The young assistant broke in. "Bob, you can't think there was something in that coffee I poured for you?"

"I'm not thinking anything, Ned. I'm only stating certain facts. Cadwall's dead all of a sudden for no apparent reason. I gave him my coffee. Or rather, you did."

"Are you accusing me?"

"God, no! That's the last thing I'd ever think. If you'd meant to kill me, thus scuttling your chances for promotion as well you know, you sure as hell would have managed to drop that cup rather than give it to Cadwall. And you couldn't have intended it for him because you didn't know you were going to be asked to leave it at his table until you were heading back here with both hands full. But think it out, Ned. There was a crush at the coffee urn. People were reaching for things. Everybody was either half asleep or talking to his neighbor. Who the hell would notice if something was dropped into a cup? I'm not saying it happened. I'm just saying it's possible."

"But what if they got the wrong cup? My God, I could have drunk the stuff myself!"

"Use your head. Yours was stained around the rim. Naturally the clean one had to be for me. It was foolproof, and damned clever." Dysart scribbled on the check, threw money on the table, and stood up. "Only of course it's all damned nonsense. See you, Pete."

Left alone, Shandy went on eating chowder for which he had no appetite. Was there any validity to Dysart's theory? It was typical of the man to grab any chance of putting himself in the limelight. Nevertheless, it was not an impossible supposition.

Most of the college people, even those like Jackman who made a point of breakfasting with their families, were in the habit of dropping in at the faculty dining room on their way to work. From half past seven until almost nine, the place was sure to be crowded, especially during this holiday season when those who might otherwise be rushing to early classes had a chance to linger and chat. This was where all the news and much of the gossip got circulated. Cadwall the busybody and Dysart the social lion never missed a morning. If somebody wanted to feed either one of them a slow-acting poison, this was as likely a place as any.

Shandy didn't know whether strong black coffee could mask the bitter taste of taxine. It might, he supposed, if the coffee was worse than usual, and that also could have happened with waitresses doing double duty as cooks during the Illumination. If he hadn't breakfasted with Helen, he'd know. A conscientious investigator ought, perhaps, to feel regret.

Had somebody in fact gone to the dining room with poison in his or her pocket, spilled Cadwall's coffee on purpose, and snatched at a fortuitous chance to dose the cup Ned had poured for Dysart after it had been rerouted to the comptroller? Preposterous as it sounded, the scenario was yet less inconceivable than that somebody had meant to poison Dysart, then sat and watched another man drink the lethal potion. Could any of their colleagues be so inhuman?

Possibly, Shandy supposed, if the murderer could see no way to take the substitute cup from Cadwall without attracting undue notice to himself. If he'd already killed Mrs. Ames, he might have suffered a dulling of the moral sensibilities, to the point where one corpse more or less wouldn't seem to matter.

On what grounds could Dysart be associated with Jemima's death? She'd been at his party and he'd watched her leave. Was that all? There was still the unexplained circumstance of her going into the shrubbery and not being seen to come out. Might Bob in fact have noticed something odd about her departure, and kept quiet about it?

Shandy couldn't imagine the engineer's ever keeping quiet about anything. It must be borne in mind, however, that none of the Crescent folk except himself and Timothy Ames and now Helen Marsh knew Jemima had died by design instead of accident. Maybe Bob wasn't talking simply because he didn't yet realize he had something to tell. That, from the murderer's point of view, would make him a walking time bomb.

By Professor Dysart's own account, though, he'd been too drunk to make a reliable witness by the time Jemima started her fatal walk. Ben Cadwall, who'd boycotted the Dysart punch bowl and was probably snooping as usual, would be far more apt to observe and remember.

Hannah wasn't at the party either. She was making her rounds of the Crescent. What if Ben had caught her where she wasn't supposed to be, doing something not even the most devoted husband could condone?

Hannah knew, of course, that her husband always got something to eat at the dining room on his way to the office. If she were to feed him a slow-acting poison before he left the house, show reasonable intelligence about getting rid of the evidence, and stick to her guns on questioning that she'd done nothing of the sort, attention would have to focus on the possibility that he'd got it here. By the time he died, whatever dishes he'd used must have been passed through the kitchen's efficient sterilizers and stacked with dozens just like them. Dysart's grandstand play would be an extra stroke of luck for her, but she really wouldn't need it. Any good lawyer could get her off on the ground of legitimate doubt, assuming she was ever brought to trial.

Did Hannah really have the brains or the enterprise to commit a double murder and not get caught? People tended to write her off as negligible because she was always in the shadow of two domineering personalities. Yet Jemima and Ben were both dead now, and Hannah had at least shown no lack of confidence stepping into Mrs. Ames's shoes.

Thinking of the Buggins Collection and the house Helen was still trying to make habitable, Shandy wondered. Could a woman who left her private affairs in total chaos have been, in fact, the great organizer she was cracked up to be? Might not the faithful henchwoman have done most of the real work on those many public projects for which Jemima snatched credit?

Ben couldn't have been any picnic to live with either, with his complaints and crotchets and his personal vendettas and his smarmy, know-it-all air. Maybe Hannah was plain sick and tired of being bullied.

Still, it did seem that an apparently sane and sensible woman could find some way of getting her friend and her husband off her back without having to kill them both.

Chapter 17

Shandy was still brooding over half a bowlful of corn chowder when, to his intense astonishment, Hannah Cadwall entered the dining room alone and looking frazzled but not upset.

"Hannah, what are you doing here? Didn't Mary Enderble find you?"

"She was yoo-hooing to me across the Crescent, but I just waved and came on. I'm famished. Jackie, bring me a bowl of whatever Professor Shandy's eating and make it snappy, will you? If I don't get something inside me pronto, I'm going to faint."

She plumped herself down opposite Peter, snatched a stick of celery from his untouched hors d'oeuvre tray, and began to chomp. "Been over to the shopping mall," she told him with her mouth full. "What a madhouse! Had to fight my way every step. Thanks, Jackie. That was quick."

She picked up the spoon and began to bail chowder into her mouth at an incredible rate. Shandy watched, stupefied. Obviously Mrs. Cadwall still didn't know she was a widow, but how was a man to tell her while she was stuffing herself like a starved wolverine? When she paused to slap butter on a roll, he plucked up his nerve.

"Er—Hannah?"

"What, Peter? Why are you goggling at me like a fish out of water? Honestly, you're getting more peculiar every day of your life. What did Mary Enderble want?"

"To tell you that the police are looking for you."

"About that stupid permit for the extra parking facilities, I suppose. Why I ever let myself get sucked into taking over Jemima's job—"

"It's about Ben," Shandy fairly shouted.

"Well, what about him?" She took a giant bite of her roll. "Has he robbed a bank, or kidnaped the president?"

"He's dead, Hannah."

Incredibly, she kept on eating her roll. Then the impact of his words reached her. She gulped and shoved her plate away.

"Peter, is this another of your little games?"

"It's the truth, Hannah. I found him myself. I went over to see him a while back and found him sitting at his desk. He was just—gone. It must have happened quite suddenly, with no pain."

"But Ben wouldn't die! He's so darned careful of himself, he'll— I always thought he'd live to be a hundred."

"Hadn't you better drink your tea?"

"I don't want tea! I want my husband." Burying her face in a paper napkin, Hannah began to sob.

The young waitress ran over to the table. "What's the matter? Did you choke? Mrs. Cadwall, are you all right?"

"My husband's dead!"

"I'm sorry," Shandy told the bewildered girl. "The comptroller died suddenly this morning in his office, while Mrs. Cadwall was out shopping. This is the first chance anyone's had to tell her. I ought to have managed it more tactfully."

"How could you be tactful about a thing like that? My gosh, Dr. Cadwall, of all people! Shall I bring some more hot tea?"

"I don't know."

Shandy was experiencing the normal discomfiture of a man in the company of a hysterical woman. "Hannah, would you like more tea?"

"No."

"Shall I take you home?"

The widow blew her nose into the soggy napkin. "I suppose so."

"I'll get her coat," offered the waitress.

"You'd better give me the check first," said Shandy.

"Oh no! I couldn't make you pay, at a time like this."

"My dear young woman, you're going to make a fine wife and mother."

"Professor Shandy!"

Nevertheless, the girl helped him on with his overcoat and gave him a friendly pat on the arm. "You take good care of her, now. See if you can get a neighbor to come in. I'd go with you myself, but we're so shorthanded on account of the Illumination."

"Thank you. I daresay we'll manage."

At the moment, Shandy didn't see how. Hannah was a dead weight on his arm, not seeming to notice where she put her feet. If he managed to get her down the perilous walk without at least one sprained ankle between them, it would be an agreeable surprise.

"Peter, what am I going to do?" Hannah wailed.

He took a firmer grip on her arm. "The best you can, Hannah. You'll manage."

"But I'm alone. I've never been alone, not once in my life. First I lived with my folks, then I went away to school and lived in a dorm, then I moved to the sorority house, then I got married right after graduation and had the two children and now they're gone and Ben's gone, too. Peter, I don't think I can stand it."

"Of course you can." Dear God, this was awful. "Your friends will stand by you."

"What friends? Jemima was the only one who ever gave a hoot about me, and she's gone like the rest."

For a wonder, she didn't start to cry again. Realizing her complete bereavement seemed to have a calming effect.

"I'm on my own. On my own."

Hannah didn't say another word until they were inside the house she had shared with Ben Cadwall for so many years. Shandy got her coat off and led her to the biggest armchair in the neat, characterless, somewhat bleak parlor.

"This was Ben's chair. The kids got it for him one Father's Day. They had them on special down at the Emporium. Now it's mine, I guess."

She rubbed her hands over the slick brown vinyl arms, as though to make sure the furniture was there.

"Ben left everything to me, you know, for as long as I

live. I can keep it or sell it, just as I please. That's one thing you have to give him credit for. He could be hell on wheels to live with, but he never went back on a promise. He said he'd take care of me, and he did. I get the insurance and the savings accounts and the securities and the money from the house. I'll sell as soon as I can. I couldn't go on living here by myself, even if the college would allow it. Anyway, I'm sick of Balaclava and everybody in it. Turn up the thermostat, Peter. Ben always insisted on keeping it down to sixty-two. I'm going some place where I won't have to freeze to death all winter long. How much will I get out of the pension fund? There'll be something, won't there, even if it's not as if he'd lived to sixty-five? But who's going to give it to me? Ben was always the one to sign the pension checks, and he's gone. Peter, you'll have to stick up for my rights."

"I'm sure there won't be any problem, Hannah. The treasurer will simply take over until a new comptroller can be found."

"Oh, that old fool. Ben always said he was about as much good as an old wet hen, though he'd kill me if he ever knew I repeated it. Ben always thought the post should have gone to him, though he wouldn't have been happy in it. Ben was a detail man. He liked having a finger in all the pies, and he got a kick out of knowing everything that went on. Not much got by my Bennie, I can tell you."

"That was my impression," said Shandy cautiously. "Tell me, Hannah, was Ben in the habit of discussing these —er—goings-on with you?"

She shrugged. "Yes and no. Of course we discussed things. What do you think? We couldn't sit around staring at each other like a couple of dummies. The trouble was, he always cautioned me against repeating anything and of course I wouldn't dare because it would surely get straight back to him. Then when gossip did get started, as it always does sooner or later, which you well know, he'd blame me when I hadn't said a word to anybody."

"Not even to Jemima?"

"She'd be the last person. I'm not one to talk against my own dead friend, but if they'd ever run a contest for the biggest mouth in Balaclava Junction, she'd have won hands down. Ben wasn't like her. He could talk your hind leg off, but he never said anything he didn't want you to know. Even with me, he'd clam up sometimes and get that mysterious smirk on his face. He'd be sitting right here in this chair, hugging some new secret to himself, and I swear to God, Peter, there were times when I could have taken that poker and wrapped it around his neck. He did that with everybody. In a way, I'm surprised he got to die a natural death."

Hannah blinked. "Come to think of it, you still haven't told me what he died of. Was it a heart attack? Peter, why are you goggling at me like that? What was it?"

"I can't tell you, Hannah. There were no—er—external indications."

"Didn't you call the doctor?"

"Of course. Dr. Melchett was unable to form an opinion."

"What's that supposed to mean? Wouldn't he sign the death certificate? Dr. Melchett, of all people? Peter Shandy, you quit beating around the bush and tell me what happened to my husband."

"Hannah, I do not know. My personal opinion, for what it's worth, is that he may somehow have been poisoned."

"Oh, my God! They'll say I did it for the money."

Ashen-faced, Mrs. Cadwall cowered back into the vinyl armchair. "Peter, what am I going to do?"

Damn it, woman, how should I know? was the retort that sprang to his lips. Mercifully, he managed not to say it.

"Now, Hannah, there's no sense in borrowing trouble. Wait and see what they find."

"What who find?"

"They—er—took him to the county coroner's, I believe. It's a routine procedure in cases of sudden death. Oh, Lord, that reminds me. I must get in touch with Grimble and let him know you're here."

"Peter, don't! I'm scared."

"Why? You didn't poison Ben, did you?"

"Jemima said you had a rotten, vicious streak in you. She said you put up those awful lights and things on purpose to get back at us. I didn't believe her then, but I do now."

"Never mind that. Tell me what you gave Ben for breakfast. I know he stopped at the college dining room, but did he eat anything before he left the house? You'll have to tell the police, you know."

"I'll tell anybody who asks me. I have nothing to be ashamed of, which is more than you can say."

"All right, Hannah. What did Ben eat?"

"We each had a cup of rose-hip tea for the vitamin C, and a little All-bran for our bowels. And we used the same tea bag and the same bran out of the same box and the same milk out of the same carton. Then we had a piece of coffeecake that Sheila Jackman sent over by one of the kids. I suppose she meant well. Anyway, it was a change from All-bran."

"Ben ate some of the cake?"

"A little. He growled about the empty calories, but he ate it, so he wouldn't have to lie and tell Sheila it was good when he hadn't tasted it. Ben was honest, you know. Too damned honest, sometimes."

"Is there any of the cake left?"

"No, I finished it after he'd gone. I made myself some coffee. I always do."

"What was the cake like? I was thinking that if the children made it, they might have gone in for some—er—fancy touches."

"Like putting rat poison on top? You don't have to beat around the bush with me, Peter Shandy. In my opinion, the cake came straight out of a Betty Crocker box, and if there'd been anything wrong with it, I'd be dead instead of Ben because I ate about three times as much as he did. I can ask Sheila for the recipe, if you want."

"Let the police do that if they want. It will give them something to think about. I do think I ought to put in that call, Hannah. If you don't come forward, somebody might start wondering why."

"Oh, go ahead," she sighed. "What difference does it make? I'll have to get word to Benita and Frank, too."

"Yes, your children ought to be with you as soon as possible. Why don't you call them as soon as I've got hold of Grimble?"

"Not now! We always wait till evening, when the rates go down."

Shandy shrugged. "Where's the phone?"

"Right out in the front hall. Oh, Peter, do you have to?"

As it happened, he didn't. Shandy was looking about

him for the instrument when Grimble and Olivetti came up the walk. He opened the door for them.

"I was just about to call you. I found Mrs. Cadwall in the faculty dining room and brought her home."

"We know you did," snarled Grimble. "Why the hell didn't you get in touch with me right away?"

"Because she was upset and wanted to come home. I believe you'll find her able to talk now."

"You been tellin' her what to say, huh?"

"Grimble, have you ever thought of getting yourself stuffed and mounted? What can she say, except the truth?"

"You'd be surprised, Professor," said Olivetti. "Where is she?"

"In here."

Shandy motioned them into the parlor, where Hannah still hunched in the brown vinyl armchair. She looked up at the men, but made no effort to rise, or even to speak.

Grimble lost his truculence. "Well, Miz Cadwall," he began awkwardly, "we kind of hate to bother you at a time like this. Sure was an awful shock, us findin' the comptroller like we did. Gosh, it was only yesterday afternoon he dropped in at my office, friendly as you please. We had a high old time."

At last Hannah broke her silence. "You surprise me, Grimble. Dr. Cadwall told me he was going over to tear your hide off. He said you'd been playing games with your expense account again and he was pretty fed up with trying to keep you honest. I'm glad you took the criticism in such a cordial spirit, though I daresay you have reason to feel you got off more lightly than you deserve. I believe he did put it to you straight that if you ever pulled one more stunt like the last time, he was going to take the evidence to President Svenson and you'd be out on your ear before you knew what struck you. I wasn't supposed to breathe a word to a soul, but I don't suppose it matters now. They can't fire him for breach of confidence, can they?"

Shandy blinked in admiration. The comptroller's widow was going to manage all right. Olivetti was gazing at the security chief with an interested glint in his steel-gray eyes. Grimble was squirming.

"Aw, nothin' like that ever happened. He must o' been jokin'."

"My husband never joked about money."

She made the statement in a flat, uninterested tone that was the ultimate in credibility. "Officer, have they found out what he died of?"

"I don't know, Mrs. Cadwall. I'll check with the lab again right now, if you don't mind my using your phone."

"Not at all. Peter, would you show him, please? I seem to be dreadfully tired all of a sudden. Shopping always exhausts me. Ben said I ought to wait for the final markdowns, but everything gets so picked over."

She started to cry again without sound or stirring, letting the tears run down her face and dampen the front of her sensible tan polyester dress. It was unbearable to watch.

Shandy got up. "Hannah, can I bring you a drink or something?"

She realized what was happening, and snuffled. "There's a box of Kleenex on the kitchen counter, and some of the sherry from Jemima's funeral in the underneath cupboard to the right of the sink. You might bring me a little of that. Maybe it will warm me up. I feel so cold, as if it were myself and not Ben who—"

"Yes, of course. That's perfectly natural."

He hustled out of the room to get away from the sight of those coursing tears. Olivetti was hanging on the phone when he passed through on his way to the kitchen, still waiting when he got back. He paused to ask, "Any news?"

"They're checking now. We can't expect results this fast. They've hardly had time to—yeah? You did? Well, what do you know about that? Sure, I understand. Thanks."

The state policeman hung up. "That doctor of yours is one smart man, Professor, in case you didn't know it. He told the coroner's office to test for the commoner vegetable alkaloids first, and they think they may be on to something already."

"Most interesting," said Shandy demurely. He was betting on taxine himself, but he deemed it prudent not to appear too knowledgeable. "May I pass on the information to Mrs. Cadwall?"

"Thanks, I'll tell her myself, when there's anything to tell. Say, Professor, haven't you got some papers to correct?"

"Or peddle? Certainly, if you'd rather I left. For what

it's worth, Lieutenant, I really don't think Mrs. Cadwall poisoned her husband."

"Am I supposed to take that as an expert opinion?"

"Anybody who's been monitoring exams for a great many years tends to develop a certain sensitivity as to who has the answers taped inside his socks."

"So who's got the answers this time?"

"I don't know yet, but there's a chap named Dysart who has a story you might care to hear. Grimble can track him down for you."

"Thanks. And where do I track you down, just in case?"

"My house is directly across the way, the small red brick one with the—er—reindeer on the roof. Then I'll just give Mrs. Cadwall her drink and explain that I have to leave."

Hannah accepted the sherry, the tissues, and the good-by without comment. Shandy went out feeling guilty for no definable reason. He'd always thought of Ben's wife, when he thought of her at all, as one of life's minor nuisances. Now she was a person in trouble. How much of this trouble had been precipitated by his vicious reaction against her and Jemima's annual pestering?

His cousin's wife, Elizabeth, who was a religious woman, would no doubt say that this horrible turn of events was a judgment upon him for losing his temper. He would not have believed himself capable of entertaining the possibility that Elizabeth could be right.

Chapter 18

Of all the black thoughts surging through Shandy's mind, the blackest was that Helen wouldn't be free for at least another hour and a half. Next most dire was the fact that, although its presiding genius was dead and its acting chairman perhaps even now being arrested for a murder she almost certainly didn't commit, business at the Illumination was brisk as usual.

The master switch for the lights—his own, alas, among them—had already been thrown. The Gingerbread Houses had dropped their plywood fronts. Red-and-green elves cavorted about wearing sandwich boards that announced a Giant Marshmallow Roast with music by the Eskimo Piemen, whoever they might be, to start at half past seven on the lower playing field, admission one dollar. One of them stopped the professor and tried to sell him a ticket. Shuddering, he turned downhill and sought refuge in the Enderbles' shrubbery.

It was curious how the dense growth, caked with hardened-on snow, created a sense of isolation. Even the hubbub he'd found intolerable on the Crescent so few steps away penetrated here only as a blending of happy sounds.

There were plenty of yews here. That didn't mean anything, of course; Balaclava was overgrown with yew. Still, if one wanted to gather the needles in total privacy, this would be a safer place than most. Shandy pottered along, trying to discern in the fading light whether any of the branches showed signs of being stripped. He went too far along the path, and Adele Dysart spied him.

"Peter!" she shrieked from a window. "Thank God you've come. I'm stuck in the house with a lousy cold and ready to climb the walls. Just a second, I'll open the door."

Shandy wanted neither Adele's cold nor her company, but she'd got him trapped and herded into what the Dysarts insisted on calling their family room before he could think up a tactful way to tell her so.

"Now you sit there and don't move. I'm going to fix you a slug of my special cough medicine."

"No, please don't. I'm due at a cocktail party pretty soon," he lied.

He should have known better. She pounced.

"Who's giving it, and how come I wasn't invited?"

"Er—it isn't actually a party, just drinks with a—er—friend."

"Who, for instance?"

"Helen Marsh," he replied unhappily.

"You mean that washed-out old maid librarian you dragged over to the dining room last night? What is she, some poor relation of the Ameses'? Honestly, Peter, can't you do a little better than that? What happened to Susie?"

"Susie who? Oh—er—Susie. She—er—floated out of my life, so to speak."

It would be ludicrous as well as futile to try explaining why Helen was so much the more attractive of the two. Adele was looking, to use a trenchant simile often employed by Mrs. Lomax, like something the cat dragged in. Her hair-do had come unstuck and she'd made no attempt to sort out the resultant tangle of wiry elflocks. The make-up she was wearing must have been applied at least one day ago. Her housecoat could have done with a washing, and so could her neck. She dabbed at her scarlet nose with a wad of tissues and took a swig of her own prescription.

"And what brings you to these parts in the midst of your busy social life?"

An explanation came into his mind, and he uttered it. "I've been trying to figure out how Jemima got through that shrubbery after she left your party without being seen."

She wiped her nose again. "For God's sake, why?"

"I think it's curious. Mary Enderble and Roger Jackman must have been walking straight toward the entrance in one direction at the same time she entered the path from here, yet they didn't meet. Sheila was watching for about fifteen minutes out their front window and says she never saw her come out. Are you positive she didn't change her mind and go around by the street?"

Adele stared at him over her Kleenex. "Why would she do a thing like that? Look, she went out that same door you just came in, right? There's a path shoveled from the door into the short cut, right? And there's no path from that path to any other path, right? The only way she could get from the back to the front would be to come back through the house, which she didn't because a whole bunch of people watched her go down the path, right? Unless she went wallowing through the snow up to her eyeballs which nobody in her right mind would do when she had a path to walk in. Christ, if we ever get out of this lousy climate—" she sneezed again and sought solace in her tumbler.

"Then I suppose the only logical explanation is that somebody mistook the time."

"I don't see how. Sheila Jackman knew what time it was, all right. She'd been eying the clock and making noises at Roger for at least half an hour before they left. Needless to say, she had one hell of a time dragging him away. Rog has the hots for me, in case you hadn't noticed."

Shandy found that a highly improbable statement. It occurred to him that Adele must be twice Roger's age.

"I see, so that made you aware of the time."

"Me and everybody else. That's what got Jemima fussing about having to go and be the boy on the burning deck some more."

"I see. And you had some—er—refreshment of sorts in the oven, I believe."

"Squid puffs. You know me, I have to be different. All they know around here is onion soup dip and potato chips."

That was a flagrant lie. Thanks to Mrs. Mouzouka's gourmet cooking courses, most faculty parties tended to be journeys into the unknown. Adele and her pretensions were a pathetic combination.

"And then of course my loving husband made this big scene about watching Jemima leave and my timer went off and there I was, rushing back and forth like a whirlwind."

"Did you personally see Jemima going down the path?"

"Well, of course. Who could miss that purple burnous? I suppose I oughtn't to talk that way now she's dead."

"But in fact you do know for certain that she left by the short cut almost immediately after the Jackmans."

"Not immediately, because she had to put on a big thing about how she had to rush off and all that garbage. Maybe five or ten minutes. Not longer. I know, because it's always scary when people start leaving one right after the other. Gives the rest ideas, and before you know it your party's died on you. I have a hunch that's why Bob started this big deal about Jemima. After the way he made fun of her, nobody else would dare bug out for fear he'd do the same to them."

She chuckled. "Bob's clever, you know. Plays dirty pool sometimes, but what the hell? You do the best you can with what you've got, right?"

"Er—within legal limits, at any rate."

"Peter, you're a one-man panic. Come on over here so I won't have to strain my throat hollering at you. Unless you're afraid of catching my cold," Mrs. Dysart added with a laugh he could swear was meant to be provocative.

"One can't be too careful this time of year," he replied caddishly. "Miss Tibbett says these things go in threes."

"What things?"

"Good Lord, do you mean to say you haven't heard about Ben Cadwall? Hasn't Bob told you?"

"Soon as he found out I was out of commission, Bob developed urgent business at the power plant. I haven't seen him since some ungodly hour this morning. What happened to Ben? Peter, you don't mean—not Ben?"

"I'm afraid so, Adele."

Shandy was surprised to see the woman looking genuinely disturbed. "I found him myself, in his office. It's getting to be an unpleasant habit of mine."

"My God, two in a row! If I'd known that, I wouldn't have let you in. But Ben, of all people. Look, be a pal and get me some more bourbon. Never mind the ice. I think I'm having a chill."

"Here, put this shawl thing around you."

The professor snatched up a Mexican serape that had been thrown across the top of a sofa, and draped it over her thin shoulders. He was slightly worried lest she take the courtesy for a come-on, but Adele didn't even seem to notice. She was staring into the unlighted fireplace with a look on her face that might almost have been awe. Considering that the Dysarts had barely been on speaking terms with the Cadwalls until Jemima's funeral, her reaction seemed excessive, yet he didn't think she was play-acting this time.

He got her the drink, not without difficulty. The house was a tricky one. A narrow hallway that should logically have led to the kitchen took a sudden turn and wound up at the foot of the back stairs. He wondered if Jemima had come down that way. Bob would remember, perhaps, not that it meant anything one way or the other.

After blundering around awhile, Shandy did in fact locate the kitchen, which was in an unholy mess. The cleaning woman must be off for the holidays. The bourbon was sitting on the counter top, along with a repellent collection of unscraped plates. He slopped a couple of fingers into the glass and got out of there as fast as he could, which still wasn't fast enough for Adele.

"What took you so long?"

"I got lost."

"I wish I could, sometimes. What did Ben die of?"

Shandy had a sudden urge to play his hunch, and see how she reacted.

"Taxine poisoning," he said firmly.

"I don't believe you."

"Then wait for the official autopsy report."

"Peter, how could it be that? Taxine isn't something a grown-up takes by accident. It comes from yew. We had a lecture at the garden club. I remembered that one, because the name sounds like taxi."

Shandy had got roped into speaking at the Balaclava Garden Club once or twice. He knew many faculty ladies belonged. It was one of the few places where town and gown met on an equal footing, though no doubt some were more equal than others. If Adele knew about taxine, probably every woman in town did.

"No," he replied, "I'm sure Ben wouldn't ingest the stuff knowingly unless for some reason he decided to commit suicide."

"Ben kill himself? Never!"

"That's my personal opinion, but I must say I'm surprised to hear you being so definite. I had no idea you were that well acquainted with him."

Adele made a sound that could have been a laugh. She was quite drunk by now.

"There's one hell of a lot you don't know about me, Peter Shandy. I knew Ben Cadwall long before I ever met Bob. We were almost engaged once. Of course he was years and years too old for me," she added hastily.

"I'm sorry," Shandy replied. "I had no idea. Er—where did you know Ben?"

She set her glass down on the sticky coffee table. "Look, do me a favor and don't mention this to Bob. It was all over years ago, but he doesn't like to be reminded. That's why he and Ben always sort of had it in for one another."

"Does Hannah know?"

"I don't suppose so. Ben always got a kick out of keeping secrets. I must say it was a jolt when we moved here and found them on our doorstep. I might have known Ben would wind up in a place like Balaclava."

"I've often wondered what brought you and Bob here," Shandy ventured. "I'd have thought you'd prefer a more —er—urban atmosphere."

Adele shrugged. "Variety's the spice of life, they say. How about it, Pete? Care for a little variety?"

To Shandy's overwhelming relief, Bob Dysart chose that moment to barge in, shouting.

"Dell? Dell? Where the— Oh, hi, Pete. Entertaining the little woman while the old man's out hustling a buck, eh? Nice work if you can get it. How're you feeling, gorgeous?"

"A fat lot you care," sniffled his wife. "Why didn't you tell me Ben Cadwall's dead?"

"Give me time. I just got here."

"You could have come home earlier."

"I was busy."

"Oh yeah? Who with?"

"You mean with whom. What are you drinking, Pete?"

"He's saving his thirst for later," said Adele with a savage laugh. "He has a heavy date with the lady librarian."

"Ah, so? I must check her out. Pause for laugh. Nobody laughs. How about you, pussycat?"

Without waiting for an answer, Dysart went and got what looked to Shandy like a great deal of whiskey.

"Thanks, pal, I needed that. Christ, what a day this has been! Pete, did you tell Adele how somebody tried to murder me this morning?"

"No, I—er—hadn't got to it yet."

"Jesus! Just because you don't give a damn, didn't it occur to you that somebody else might?"

Dysart was furious. He must actually have worked himself around to believing his own story.

"Bob, what are you talking about?" demanded his wife.
"Peter says Ben was poisoned with taxine."

"Yes, and it was meant for me."

Dysart went on about the incident in the dining room. "And what would any intelligent person make of that?" he finished.

A great deal less than you're making of it, Shandy thought.

The second hearing was no more plausible than the first, to his mind. Why choose so risky a way of getting at a man who left himself vulnerable in so many other ways? And what could be the motive? Adele asked that question. Her husband had his answer ready.

"I can't say for sure, but I have a hunch it's something to do with the plant."

"The Skunk Works?" Shandy injudiciously exclaimed, using the inevitable student nickname.

"If you want to call it that," Dysart replied stiffly. "It just happens that we have some very interesting research going on there. I don't want to talk about it, and I don't want to toot my own horn, but just among us three, there's a potential for commercial development that will make your Balaclava Buster look like a worm-eaten radish, and I'm the guy who's pushing it. And if we do what I have in mind, it's going to be a real kick in the guts for the oil companies and the gas companies and the coal mines. I know this sounds like cloak-and-dagger stuff, but I'm talking straight fact, and I'm the only one who sees it. The rest of them down there are dragging their feet and piddling around, while I've been trying to line up ways to exploit the potential. And it's beginning to look as though somebody wants to stop me. Looks as if I'd better make sure my insurance is paid up. Got to keep the little woman in bourbon. Jesus, on second thought, I'd better not. I might be worth more to Dell dead than alive."

"Oh, stop talking like a fool!" his wife exploded. "I never know whether to believe you or not. You can be so damned convincing, then it turns out you're just building up for another of your funnies. Peter, could he possibly be telling the truth?"

Shandy hunched his shoulders. "I trust Bob won't take offense if I say that for his own sake, as well as yours, I sincerely hope he isn't. I don't mean that you're consciously trying to deceive either of us, Bob," he added hastily. "It does seem to me, though, that if somebody were—er—out to get you, he might choose a less chancy method. I can understand that with this—er—tremendous responsibility preying on your mind, you might make the interpretation you did. Being a simple-minded person myself, I'm more inclined to believe that since Ben Cadwall got the poison, it was Ben somebody meant to kill."

Dysart scratched his chin. "I don't know if you're trying to deflate my ego, Pete, or get my mind off my troubles. What the hell would anybody murder Ben Cadwall for?"

"Well, for one thing, he handled all the money around here, which meant that he had a great deal of power. For another, he was a busybody. Let's assume, by way of hypothesis, that somebody was actually plotting to sabotage your research, or your—er—merchandising efforts. Don't you think Ben would get wind of that fact even before you did?"

"My God, Pete, you've hit it! So that's why whoever poisoned my coffee this morning made no effort to get it away from Ben. It didn't matter which of us got killed first, since we'd both have to go anyway."

"Will you stop talking like that?" shrieked Adele. "Why did you drag me here in the first place? I can't stand it any more! We've got to get away."

"I'm not running, Dell."

Shandy reached for his hat. "I am," he said firmly. "I hope your cold is better soon, Adele. And, Bob, I shouldn't dwell on this matter if I were you. The comptroller's death probably has a very prosaic explanation."

He spoke more bravely than he felt. The likelihood that Ben had been killed for some reason less exotic than sabotage didn't preclude the possibility that Dysart was also on the murderer's list, and that the episode of the coffee cups didn't in fact mean exactly what Bob thought it did.

Chapter 19

"Helen, may we skip the faculty dining room tonight?"

"Certainly, Peter, if you're tired."

"I'm not tired, I'm fed up. If I don't get away from here for a while, I'll start to climb the walls and gibber. There's a place about twelve miles out on the Dallow road that serves fairly decent roast beef."

"That sounds delightful. Shall we take the Ameses' car? I presume I have the keys."

"Thank you, no. Can you imagine what shape any vehicle Jemima drove would be in? I'll phone down to Charlie's garage and rent one. That will at least give us a fighting chance of coming back alive."

"Peter, you poor man! You're having a ghastly time, aren't you? Shall we talk now, or wait till we get some food?"

"Food first if you don't mind. Go get your things while I talk to Charlie."

He ought to think about buying a car of his own. Until now, it had never seemed worth the bother. Shandy poured another tiny puddle of sherry into the bottom of his glass, and went to the Ameses' telephone.

After he'd made his arrangements with the garage, he phoned to see how Hannah Cadwall was doing.

"She's asleep," Mary Enderble told him. "Dr. Melchett phoned in a prescription to the drugstore, and John went down to pick it up. Oh, and the police just called. They say it was taxine that killed Ben, of all things! Can you imagine?"

So Shandy's guess had been right. The knowledge gave him no satisfaction.

Helen was upstairs about ten minutes. She came down wearing a long-sleeved, long-skirted dress of flaming scarlet.

"I bought this thing ages ago and have been itching for a chance to wear it. In California, it always looked out of place."

"It's very nice," said Shandy awkwardly. It was a great deal more than that, but he didn't quite know how to tell her so.

"There's a heavy black cape hanging in the closet," Helen went on. "I don't suppose Professor Ames would mind if I wore it."

"Oh, no, I'm sure he'd be delighted. Jemima rather went in for capes."

"So I understand. One of the girls was telling me how she used to come swooping in with yards and yards of purple hand weaving swirling around her, knocking things off the desk and creating general confusion. They used to keep book on how many times a week she'd rush into the place, tell everybody how much she had to do, and rush out again without lifting a finger. They must find me horribly dull by comparison."

"I don't see how they could," said Shandy. "Jemima was a tiresome woman. Speaking of tiresome, how did you manage this afternoon? I hope Porble didn't keep you at hog statistics all day long."

"Not quite. I managed to sneak into the Buggins Room about half past four. The kids had got most of the mess up off the floor. Everything will have to be reshelved eventually, but at least it's possible to read the titles of those few that got put in right side up, or would be if they'd give me more than one forty-watt bulb for that entire room."

"Oh, I expect you won't have any trouble there. We have no energy shortage at Balaclava just now, though we may at any moment. Dysart thinks there's a plot afoot to sabotage the power plant."

"My stars and garters! Never a dull moment around here, is there? Could he possibly be right?"

"Only if you accept the premise that Standard Oil and Exxon are likely to feel threatened by a system that runs on animal droppings. We turn left at the foot of the hill."

"I know. We came this way when you brought me from the airport. Good heavens, was that only yesterday afternoon? It seems a lifetime ago."

"Yes, it does."

Shandy suddenly realized with a sort of horror that he could no longer imagine Balaclava Junction without Helen in it. Would he ever get up courage enough to tell her so? For the moment he must be satisfied to pilot her safely through the jostle of climbing visitors, many of whom stopped them to ask the way to the Giant Marshmallow Roast. At last they got the car and started threading their way through the traffic.

"Good God," he panted when they were clear of the mob and out on the Dallow road, "I hope the prime ribs are worth the struggle."

"I'm sure they will be," said Helen. "You're a very good driver, Peter."

"Do you think so? I learned on a John Deere tractor when I was five years old. Then I worked a lot at farms and field stations where one was always running a bulldozer or combine or something of the sort. I don't believe I've ever quite grasped the concept that a vehicle can be operated solely for pleasure."

"Probably not many of them will be, unless something can be done about the fuel shortage. Too bad your power plant people can't invent one that runs on cowflaps. You don't suppose that's why Professor Dysart's talking about sabotage, do you?"

"Oh, I hardly think so. The project would have to be discussed at faculty meetings before any work got started. Dr. Svenson believes in co-ordinated efforts toward shared goals."

"Do you share?"

"Fairly often. There's always a certain amount of jockeying as to whose project takes precedence, but in general

I'd say the *esprit de corps* is maintained at a tolerable level. At least, I've always thought so."

Helen caught the doubt and despair in his voice.

"I know. It's like having a nail in your shoe, isn't it? No matter where you try to step, you keep landing on that same nasty little sore spot. I am sorry, Peter. Let's really talk about something else for a while. Tell me what you did when you worked at the field stations."

"It's so long ago, I can't remember."

Once started, however, Shandy recalled a great deal, some of it funny enough to set them both laughing. By the time they got to the restaurant, he felt ready to enjoy his meal.

The place was quieter than he'd ever seen it before. Everybody was broke from paying for Christmas presents, the waitress explained, or home eating leftovers or over at the Illumination. She piloted them to a corner booth Shandy had often coveted but never before got to sit in. They had salad and baked potatoes and medium-rare prime ribs and a California Beaujolais that made Helen feel more kindly toward the San Andreas Fault. When he ran out of stories about life among the combines, the professor discovered that he didn't mind telling Helen about Ben Cadwall.

"Don't you think it's logical to assume," he concluded, "that Ben and Jemima were killed by the same person, for the same reason?"

"I think it's lots more logical than to believe there could be two unrelated murders within such a closed community in the space of three days," she replied. "Then there are so many possible connections. That marble you found in the Cadwalls' bedroom, for one thing. You don't know whose coat it fell out of."

"Good Lord, no, I don't. I was thinking of Ben or Hannah, but it could have been anybody. Ben might have seen the thing drop when he was taking someone's coat and not bothered about it because others were crowding in at the same time. Then later downstairs, when I told my little tale about slipping on the marbles—"

"Did you actually tell that?"

"I did. They wanted all the details, you know, about how I found Jemima's body. Somebody asked why I looked behind the sofa, so I explained about finding the marbles scattered over the floor and realizing that somebody must have been in the house."

"There you are! The marble falls. Maybe Dr. Cadwall actually sees what it is. Anyway, he says, 'Oh, you've dropped something,' and the other person says, 'No, I haven't,' because he doesn't know he has the marble on him."

"Or her."

"Of course. Then after you've told your story, he—I do wish somebody would think up a new collective pronoun —realizes it must have been the marble that fell, and sneaks back to hunt for it."

"But it's gone, because I took it. Tim and I rushed out before anybody else because he suddenly remembered we were supposed to meet your plane."

"So the murderer thinks Dr. Cadwall has the marble and will remember his having said he didn't drop anything when he obviously had. But then why hasn't he killed Mrs. Cadwall, too? Wouldn't he be afraid Dr. Cadwall had told his wife?"

"Maybe he tried. The taxine might have been meant for both of them and somehow she missed getting any. Or he might have known Ben's penchant for keeping secrets and gambled on her not knowing."

"Or she might have been the one who dropped the marble," Helen finished.

"She was my first suspect," Shandy admitted. "I figured she'd have had the best chance of killing Jemima because she wasn't at the party and might logically have gone along with Jemima when she broke into my house. I had some notion that Hannah might have been embezzling the Illumination money and was afraid Jemima would expose her. Jemima would do that, you know, even to her best friend. She was great on principle."

"She must really have been a rather awful woman. No wonder Jemmy went to California and her brother to the South Pole. I'm surprised it wasn't Dr. Ames who killed her."

"He might have, I daresay, except that Tim's deaf as a haddock and pretty much wrapped up in his work. In any event, I can assure you he didn't. And I'm fairly well convinced Hannah didn't kill Ben, either. His death came as a total surprise to her, I'll swear. I had the happy task of breaking the news in both instances, you know. However, as you say, I don't know anything about women."

"Poor Peter."

Helen touched his hand lightly. "Do you think we ought to start back? You've had a rough day."

"At least it began and ended pleasantly."

"Cross your fingers. It's not over yet." Helen shrugged Jemima's old black cape around her shoulders and slid out of the booth. "That was a lovely dinner."

"I'm glad you enjoyed it. We must come again soon."

"I'd like to."

After that, they didn't say much. Helen must have been feeling the effects of adjusting to a different climate and her first day on a new job. Shandy had to concentrate on his driving. The snow that had been threatening all day was now beginning to fall, spreading a slippery film over the road. They were almost back to Balaclava Junction before he broke silence.

"I think we'd better go around by the back road. The marshmallow roast must be breaking up about now, and Main Street will be total disaster. At least this will give you a panoramic view of the Skunk Works."

"I'm all anticipation. All but my left foot, at any rate. That's gone to sleep."

Helen slid her foot out of her shoe and rubbed at her toes, gazing out through the now thickening snow.

"How many marshmallows did they roast, for goodness' sake? I can see the bonfire from here."

"You couldn't possibly," said Shandy. "The playing field's in a deep hollow on the far side of the college buildings. What you're seeing—my God!"

He scrambled for the snowbanks as fire engines whooped down the icy road.

"Well, Helen, I guess I own Dysart an apology. That's the power plant."

Chapter 20

"We'll just have to keep going."

Shandy found that he was sweating. Holding a car to this narrow, snaking road was tricky enough in broad daylight under decent conditions. On a night like this, with the snow falling thicker every moment and fire engines crowding past in astonishing numbers, he'd be lucky not to wrap them around a tree, or slide into one of the deep gullies he couldn't see but knew were far too close.

"Where are all these fire engines coming from?"

Helen sounded nervous, as well she might.

"They must have sent out a general alarm to the neighboring towns. Balaclava Junction only has one old ladder truck and a couple of pumpers for grass fires."

"That wouldn't happen unless it's really bad, would it?"

"I don't know, Helen. We've never had a fire before at the college. And why the bloody, flaming hell did it have to be tonight?" he snarled as another siren almost sent them into a bad skid.

"I shouldn't be surprised if Professor Dysart set it himself, just to prove his point."

Shandy grunted, then, to his own relief, began to chuckle.

"Neither should I. He's probably lashed himself to a turbine and vowed to go down with the ship."

"Not unless there's a television news crew around," said Helen. "Why does it make me feel better to be catty, do you suppose?"

"The natural perversity of humankind. If we succeed in getting out of this mess alive, I shall be glad you were with me."

"Peter, that's sweet. I'd give your hand a friendly squeeze, only I don't want to distract you from your driving."

"A wise but regrettable decision. I hope I can get you to reconsider at a more auspicious time."

"Are you flirting with me?"

"Flirtation implies a lack of serious purpose. Good Lord, look at that!"

They had rounded a hairpin turn that brought them out on a rise almost directly above the power plant. Even with snow blurring their view, the spectacle was awesome. From one of the methane storage tanks, a tongue of flame was shooting almost to the level of the ledge they were on. Nearby, a shed was being reduced to crimson embers by crisscrossing streams from fire hoses. Red searchlights cast an eerie glow over the snow, revealing swarms of black-clad figures rushing among the imperiled buildings.

The temptation to stay and watch was almost irresistible, but this was too dangerous a place. Shandy kept going until an auxiliary policeman barred his way.

"You can't go down there, mister!"

"It's Professor Shandy," he shouted back through the rolled-down window. "I'm trying to get home. I live on the Crescent."

"You'll have to ditch the car and walk."

"But this lady has no boots on."

"Oh, Jeez. Wait a second."

The snow-caked vigilante fumbled in a pocket of his parka and hauled out two enormous slabs of gray fuzz. "Always carry spare socks. Never know when you're going to need 'em. If you pull 'em over your shoes, they'll at least keep the snow out."

"What a marvelous idea! You're a lifesaver."

Shandy pulled the car off the road as best he could. Helen pulled on the policeman's socks. They reached to her knees and made her feet look as though they'd got tangled in a bath mat, but the rough knitting would give traction on the slippery road.

"What's happening down there?" Shandy asked the man while Helen was still struggling to coax the clinging wool over her already soggy shoes.

"Darned if I know, Professor. I heard the general alarm and came running. Ottermole sent me up here to direct the engines and stop anybody else from going down. Cripes, there's fire apparatus stretched from hell to breakfast. We thought for a while the whole place would go, but they seem to be making headway now."

"When did it start?"

"Maybe half an hour ago. One of the gas tanks blew first. Then that barn caught fire."

"What caused it? Does anybody know?"

"No, but I can make a mighty shrewd guess. See for yourself. There's the gas tank bang in front of us, and there's the barn 'way the hell and gone over behind the main turbine building. How's a flame supposed to jump that far and not hit anything in between? If you ask me, Fred Ottermole better start looking for a guy with a good pitching arm and a couple of beer bottles full of gasoline."

The man's attention was diverted by a carload of misguided sight-seers. Shandy took Helen by the arm and started the downward trek.

At eye level, the fire was less impressive than it had appeared from above. The two separate blazes were well under control and everything around them encased in protective layers of ice from the fire hoses. Nevertheless, the fire fighters were taking no chances. They had the area so widely cordoned off that spectators were strung out into a thin, straggling line. Most of these seemed to think that the near-disaster, like the marshmallow roast, had been laid on for their entertainment. The only glum faces in the crowd belonged to college folk. Shandy and Miss Marsh had hardly begun to skirt the fire lines when they were hailed by a bundle of fake mink that proved to be Mirelle Feldster.

"Peter! Peter, where have you been? I went looking for you as soon as the sirens started."

"Why?"

"Oh, I don't know. I just did." She giggled self-consciously. "You know me, just being neighborly. Actually, it wasn't quite that soon. Jim and I were over at the Dysarts' playing Scrabble. Adele's got this awful cold, so Bob called and asked us to come over and cheer her up. We couldn't very well say no, though personally I'd rather have—oh, I didn't notice you've got somebody with you." Her voice, like the buildings around them, was abruptly encased in ice.

"This is Helen Marsh," said Shandy. "Mirelle Feldster is one of your new neighbors, Helen."

"Oh, then you must be the woman who's come to stay at the Ameses'. You travel fast, don't you, Miss Marsh?" Mirelle turned her back on Helen and resumed her narrative.

"As I started to say, we were playing Scrabble and having drinks—you know Bob—when the chapel bell started banging away like mad. At first we thought it was some of the students putting on a show. Then we heard fire sirens and thought the marshmallow roast must have got out of hand, but we kept hearing more and all of a sudden Bob jumped up and yelled, 'Christ! It's the power plant.' So then he grabbed his coat and ran. Jim ran straight after him, leaving me in the lurch as usual, but I wasn't about to get stuck alone with Adele and her germs. I said I'd better come along and see if I was needed because I'm in the Civil Defense auxiliary—at least I used to be when we had one—so anyway, here I am."

"Where's Dysart?"

"Around somewhere. I saw him up by the main turbine building a while back, waving his arms and yelling. I think he was trying to make the fire chief let him through the lines, but he didn't make it. I don't see why they should myself. Bob doesn't even have tenure. Honestly, the fuss he's been making, you'd think he owned the plant. Between you and me, he's about half sloshed."

It occurred to Shandy that Mirelle was, too. He tried to break away, but she had no intention of letting him go.

"Were you surprised when they arrested Hannah Cadwall?"

"Good Lord! When did this happen?"

"Around six o'clock. Of course they'd had her under house arrest all afternoon, ever since Grimble found Ben's body. Wasn't that a ghastly thing? Can you imagine just walking into somebody's office and seeing a dead man staring at you?"

"Er—yes," said Shandy.

Mirelle paid no attention. "So they started searching the house and found the poison, as I knew they would. As soon as I heard Ben was murdered I said to Jim, 'You mark my words, she's the one.' Did it for the money, of course. Ben would never let her spend a cent and they say he was absolutely rolling. Much good it's going to do her where she's going. I wonder who the man is."

"What man?"

"Oh, Peter, use your common sense. A woman wouldn't kill one husband unless she thought she had another one lined up. Would she?"

"I wouldn't know, Mirelle. Come on, Helen, we've got to get you home. I don't suppose those socks are doing much good."

"N-not much."

Her teeth were chattering. Shandy looked around, saw a hand sled which one of the elves had injudiciously abandoned, and snatched up the rope.

"Get on."

"Peter, should you—"

"Go ahead. Better to look silly than freeze to death."

Helen was in no shape to argue. She sat down on the sled and drew its plastic protective sheet around her shaking body. Shandy set off at a trot, heedless of amused glances. When they got to the steep incline that led down into the Crescent, he hopped on behind and shoved off, forgetting that these sleds were not made to be steered by the rider. In order to stop, he had to spill them in a snowdrift.

"Sorry about that," he panted, brushing Helen off and helping her to her feet. "If we'd kept going, we'd have been out in the middle of Main Street by now."

"I don't mind. It was fun, once I began to thaw. Are you coming in?"

"Only to see you safe inside. I expect you'll want a hot bath as soon as possible."

"If there is one. The fire may have done something to the power plant."

"Can't have. The lights are still on. Including mine, unfortunately."

"Peter, I do want to thank you for this evening."

"Even though it didn't turn out as I'd hoped."

"What were you hoping for?"

He hadn't kissed a woman for years, but he managed fairly well, all things considered. "Now go get your feet dry."

"If you say so."

Helen turned the key in the Ameses' lock, let them in, and started to hang up the wet cape. Suddenly she burst out laughing.

"Oh, Peter, what a spectacle I must have cut on that sled, with my feet in bags and that silly cape flapping out behind me."

"The sled got you here, didn't it?" Shandy's jaw dropped. "Good Lord, of course it did. How could I be so dense?" He planted one more fast kiss on Helen's startled face, and hurtled back out into the storm.

Chapter 21

The Jackmans had not gone to the fire. Through the unshaded window, Shandy could see the young parents, their offspring presumably tucked away, sprawled on that overstuffed passion pit he'd so narrowly escaped having to share with Sheila. Fatigue was etched on their faces. Each clutched a large tumblerful of grown-up vitamins. It was cruel to get them up, but Shandy kept his finger on the doorbell until, after a short but vicious quarrel, the husband came to let him in.

"Peter Shandy! What brings you here?"

"An ill wind. Why aren't you at the fire with everybody else?"

"Listen, Peter, last night I slept, if you want to call it that, in a lean-to on Old Bareface with the wind howling up my pant legs and damn near freezing my—"

"It better hadn't," Sheila called from the sofa. "Come and have a drink, Peter."

"No, thanks. I just want to ask you one question. And believe me, it's important. Did either of you, or any of your children, see one of those elves dragging a passenger on a sled around my house the night I went away?"

Both Jackmans stared at him, as well they might. "For

180

gosh sake," said Roger, "those kids are around all the time. How should we notice?"

"That's right," said Sheila. "They're supposed to keep the sleds up off the Crescent, but they come just the same."

"I know that. I don't mean on the walkway, I mean actually in my yard. Very late, when they ought to have quit."

"They never quit. Nor rain nor snow nor dark of night. Are you sure you won't join us in a little general anesthetic?" said Roger. "I'll get it. Sheila brought Dickie and Wendy up to the shelter for a cookeroo this morning. She's even more whacked out than I am, or so she claims."

"I know all about the cookeroo and I don't give a damn," snapped the professor. "For God's sake rack your brains. Did you or did you not see anybody with a sled around my house late on the night of the twenty-second?"

"Honestly, Peter, I think you've lost your tiddleywinks," Sheila protested. "With all the pandemonium that's been going on around here over the holidays, how can you expect us to remember one stupid little—"

"Wait a second," her husband interrupted. "Shut up and let me think. Last night at the lean-to, while we were having our man-to-man talk, JoJo was giving me some kind of song and dance about the elves stealing Santa Claus and taking him for a ride."

"Get him up."

"Peter, no," Sheila wailed. "He's overstimulated already."

"So am I. Where does he sleep?"

Shandy headed for the staircase. Young Jackman leaped off the sofa.

"For God's sake, have mercy! You'll wake the whole damned pack of them. All right, if you insist, I'll get him. I'm sorry I opened my mouth."

He took a last pull at his grown-up vitamins and slogged upstairs. He was back in less time than Shandy could have hoped, preceded by a nine-year-old a good deal wider awake than his father.

"Pop says you want to see me, Professor Shandy."

"Yes, JoJo. I want you to tell me about the night you watched the elves kidnap my Santa Claus. Can you describe exactly what happened?"

The youngster wiggled and scratched. "Well, see, it

wasn't elves. I mean it was only this one elf and I didn't really see him steal it. He just had it."

"You mean the Santa Claus dummy was on the sled when you first caught sight of it?"

"That's right. See, what happened was, we had the Sunday School party that afternoon. It was a real drag, so me and Tommy Hoggins got to kidding around about who could drnk the most punch. They had this goofy punch, right, one bowl red and one bowl green. It was prob'ly just Kool-Aid or something, but anyway me and Tommy started mixing the two kinds together—"

"Like father, like son," Sheila murmured. "Never mind all that, JoJo. Professor Shandy doesn't want to hear about your tummyache."

"But if I hadn't drunk all that punch, I wouldn't have had to keep getting up and going to the bathroom," the boy pointed out reasonably. "That's how I saw the sled."

"Have you any idea what time it was?" Shandy asked.

"All I know is it must have been real late, because the Christmas lights were out and there was nobody around except this one elf, see, giving Santa Claus a ride on the sled. It was dumb. I mean, what's the sense of doing some oddball thing like that when there's nobody around to watch? I was going to yell down at him but then I thought I better not because I didn't want to wake up Mum and Pop and the brats," JoJo said virtuously.

"Did you put on the light in the bathroom?"

"I didn't have to. There's a little night light that's always on."

"That's right," Sheila put in. "We've had it ever since JoJo was a baby. Roger was always stubbing his toe on something when he had to get up in the night."

"That's because you always made me do the feedings when it was your turn."

Apparently Dickie and Wendy came naturally by their bickering. Shandy nipped the squabble in the bud.

"Then the elf never knew you were watching, JoJo?"

"How could he? I was upstairs and he was down on the ground. Anyway, he didn't look up."

"How could you tell where he was looking, if all the lights were out?"

"It's never pitch-dark when there's snow on the ground.

You ought to know that," the child replied loftily. "Anyway, I'm good at seeing in the dark. Ask Pop."

"That's right," said Jackman. "JoJo has exceptionally keen night vision. It comes in handy, considering the times and places Sheila chooses to drop the car keys."

Before the wife could get in her retort, Shandy asked, "How long did you watch the elf?"

JoJo shrugged. "I don't know. A couple of minutes, I guess. There wasn't much to see. He just came across—"

"Across from where?"

"Across the walkway. Like as if he was coming from the Enderbles', only he wasn't."

"How do you know?"

"Because the sleds aren't allowed to go in the shrubbery. Professor Enderble won't let 'em."

"But what if this elf disobeyed?"

"Then I guess Professor Enderble would get sore."

"So in fact all you can say for sure is that the sled was in the road when you first saw it, and it came to my house. Did it come to the front or the back door?"

JoJo hesitated. "I don't know. I thought it must be going to the front because I figured the elf was going to put Santa Claus back on the porch like you had it, but I couldn't tell because the spruce trees were in the way. Anyway, I guess maybe he never went to either door because I looked the next morning to see if the Santa Claus was back and it wasn't and I never saw it again."

"You didn't notice where the elf went after that?"

"No, I went back to bed."

JoJo squirmed a bit inside his new Christmas-present bathrobe, then blurted out, "I was sort of scared, if you want to know."

"Why? You didn't tell me that last night. Hey, come on. Get it out and you'll feel better." Jackman was, after all, a concerned father.

"Well, like I said, there was something funny about the whole scene. Like—I mean, I knew it had to be Professor Shandy's dummy on the sled but it—it didn't feel like a dummy. It was as if it was real but not alive. I don't know what I mean!"

He looked from one to the other, then said abruptly, "Can I go back to bed now?"

"Of course," Shandy answered. "Thank you, JoJo.

You've been very helpful. You may be interested to know that the elves brought back my Santa Claus yesterday, while you were camping. I put it in the cellar. And—er—it's still a dummy. Come and see it tomorrow, if you like."

"We're going to a hockey game," said Roger Jackman. "You run on upstairs, JoJo. Mum and I will be up soon. Very soon," he added with a meaningful look at their uninvited guest.

Shandy took the hint. "I'll be off. Sorry to butt in on you like this, but I had to know."

"Aren't you going to tell us why?" Sheila pouted.

"Later, perhaps. Right now, I wouldn't know what to say."

Shandy let himself out and stood for a moment on the doorstep, wondering what to do next. His own house stood next door, serene and inviting in spite of its gaudy bedizenments, and he was extremely tired. The snow was falling yet faster, caking on his overcoat sleeves and shoulders. There must be one hell of a traffic jam on Main Street by now. Perhaps visitors would be stranded and the college would have to put them up in the dorms. The gawkers would get their fill of Balaclava before this night was over. He'd about had it, too.

Nevertheless, Shandy turned his coat collar as high as it would go, jammed his gray felt hat down over his eyes, and trudged past his snug front door, up toward the glow of searchlights that still showed through the gathering whiteness to the northeast. Even as he walked, the lights dimmed and the noise of departing fire apparatus filtered down over the campus. The show was over.

But the trouble might hardly have begun. First it was a bludgeoning faked to look like an accident, now open murder and arson in one day. What was next on the agenda?

Arresting Hannah Cadwall wasn't going to solve anything. Only a nitwit like Mirelle Feldster could believe that. True, the police seemed to believe it, too, but he supposed they had to, once a jug of taxine turned up in her medicine cabinet and a whopping motive in Ben's bankbooks.

There was no such blatant evidence in Jemima's case. He was going to have one hell of a time convincing anybody that her body had been brought to his house on a sled, disguised by a Santa Claus mask.

Still, that had to be how it happened. The murderer having somehow managed to pinch one of those all-concealing elf costumes, waited in the shrubbery knowing she'd make a production of leaving the party early to go on her self-appointed rounds, because she always did. If anybody else happened along the path in the meantime, it didn't matter. The elf was just another trespassing student. The worst he could get was a scolding.

Perhaps she'd been offered a ride on the sled. That would explain why there was no sign of a struggle in the snow. Jemima would fall for a silly caper like that. She loved being involved with the students' pranks and, like Helen, she'd been wearing her party shoes instead of sensible boots.

Excited now, Shandy walked faster, manufacturing dialogue. "Come on, Mrs. Ames, I'll ride you to your door so you can change."

Then a whack on the head in the dark—Jemima never bothered with a hat, so it would be easy enough to land a killing blow—and that was that. The plastic cover designed to protect the riders' clothing would hide her telltale purple cloak, the Santa Claus mask would cover her face and head. The dummy, no doubt, had already been kidnaped and taken sleigh riding around the Crescent. Nobody would notice it wasn't a dummy any more.

Still, the murderer wouldn't dare hang around in public for long. The sled must have been dragged off somewhere, probably up on campus where it ought to be anyway, and hidden somewhere until the coast was clear. If the body did happen to be discovered any time during the evening, the plan to pass off the death as accident would have been spoiled, but how critical was that? Suspicion would no doubt fall on the student sled-pullers, but there was no great likelihood the bogus elf would ever be caught.

According to JoJo, the killer was still in costume when he brought the body back. Then how did Alice's fried marble get into the Cadwalls' bedroom? It couldn't have got caught up in a trouser cuff or pocket as Shandy had supposed—unless Ben himself had been the one to carry it back.

Was it possible the comptroller had tracked the murderer into the brick house and actually been standing close by when the dish was overturned? Would he have had

nerve enough to confront a killer in the act of dumping a
corpse?

No, but he might very well have tried to nail a student
who was carrying a joke too far, and that was what the
whole scene had been staged to look like. He could have
got into the situation without knowing he was risking anything other than his dignity. He could have hidden behind
the whatnot and spilled the marbles himself trying to get
at the elf, or more likely trying to get away. It would be
like him to keep quiet afterward and play a lone hand,
especially if he didn't know who was under the disguise
but thought he had a good chance of finding out. It was
also typical of Cadwall to believe he could pin down the
culprit before the killer got to him.

Did that mean Ben had got hold of a tangible clue to the
elf's identity? Shandy began to walk faster. If he had, the
evidence must have been kept in his desk at the office, that
sanctum sanctorum where not even his secretary would
dream of meddling. Since the office had been locked up
right after the body was found, there was a chance it
might still be there.

Normally, Grimble would be off duty by now and his
minions would never dare pass out a key in his absence.
Because of the fire, however, there was a good chance he
might still be around. Shandy only hoped he could get the
man to open the comptroller's office without insisting on
tagging along and wanting to know what the professor
was hunting for when Shandy hadn't the least idea and
probably wouldn't find it in any case. This was a stupid
wild-goose chase and he'd probably catch nothing but flu
out of it, if he hadn't picked up the bug already. Nevertheless, Shandy wallowed on.

He wished to heaven he knew where that dummy Santa
Claus had been kept after it was taken, and whether the
elves who brought it back were the same ones who'd staged
the original kidnaping. There was another point he hadn't
considered. Mirelle had seen two on Monday, but JoJo had
seen only one the night Jemima was killed. Was there a
second hiding somewhere then? Jemima was a big woman.
Getting her off the sled and up into the living room must
have taken plenty of muscle. Why had he been so ready to
assume one person could manage the job alone?

Shandy gave up trying to think straight and concentrated on fighting his way uphill. It was a sticky, wet snow that clung to his galoshes like fresh cement. By the time he caught sight of the security office, he was thinking only of getting in out of the snow and sitting down. His heart sank when he saw the small building was in darkness, but he tried the door anyway and for a wonder it opened.

For a moment, he was too preoccupied with catching his breath and beating the snow off his coat to realize that he was not alone. From behind the closed door of Grimble's inner sanctum, voices were audible. Though he could catch no words, he deduced from the low-pitched grunts and the high-pitched squeals that one was a man and one was a woman. The man was certainly Grimble, but who was the woman and what were they up to?

It didn't sound like conversation. It sounded like— Shandy suddenly realized what it sounded like and, being a man of delicacy, decided this was no time to come looking for keys. The decent thing would be to go straight away. But he was very tired and cold, and the office was warm. He felt for one of the wooden chairs that ought to be ranged along the wall, and found it. There was something hanging over the back, something soft and thick but wet, as though it had been out in the snow, a cap or muffler or some such thing. He fingered the knitted wool curiously. It was a cap, he decided, a long stockinet cap with three biggish openings knitted into one end. In fact, it was an elf mask.

Grimble.

Grimble, the one person who stuck out so far he couldn't be seen. Grimble, who'd managed to get Jemima's death passed off as an accident, who'd played the buffoon while Ben Cadwall was sitting dead at his desk, who had access to every house, every building, every room on Balaclava's campus, Grimble who could go where he chose and apparently take whom he pleased, judging from the sounds beyond the door. Grimble, who'd probably flummoxed his own keyboard in case some wiseacre like Shandy came nosing about wondering how somebody could get hold of a key without authorization. Grimble with the soul of a ferret and the morals of a buck rabbit. Who was more likely to get caught *flagrante delicto* by a pair of snoops like Jemima and Ben, and who was better equipped to get rid of them both before they could make out a provable case against him?

A provable case. That was the rub. What proof had Shandy now but a soggy head covering identical to twenty or thirty others? Grimble could always say he'd found the mask outside somewhere, and who was to convince the police that he hadn't?

As to having a woman in his office, that was a misdemeanor, not a crime. Shandy might carry the tale to President Svenson and Grimble might get fired, but that would solve nothing. Shandy wasn't a vengeful man, he was merely a good farmer. Once a dog started killing sheep, you had to get him away from the lambs. But you didn't shoot the dog unless you knew for sure he was guilty.

Not liking the job at all, Shandy tiptoed over to the inner office door and pressed his ear against the crack. It was no good. There was weather stripping around the edges to keep out drafts from the constantly opening outside door, and also perhaps to muffle sounds from within, since the place seemed warm enough where Shandy was. He started to loosen his overcoat, then buttoned it up again. If the outer office was this temperate, the inner chamber must be a pretty hot spot, all things considered. Maybe they'd opened a window at the back. Wearily, he went out again to face the elements. Something landed hard on his head, and he knew no more.

Chapter 22

"You're under arrest."

Shandy opened one eye, got a snowflake smack in the cornea, and shut it again. "What the hell are you talking about?" He had difficulty speaking, and this seemed due to the fact that somebody was sitting on his chest.

"I'm performing a citizen's arrest. Lie still or I'll clobber you." The voice was identifiable now. It was Shirley Wrenne's.

"Shirley," he began testily, "have you—"

"Why, Peter Shandy! I must say you're almost the last person I'd expect to find skulking around the security office."

"I wasn't skulking, damn it!"

He had been, but that was beside the point. "Get off me, you wanton hussy."

"I will not. I'm going to sit here till Grimble comes."

"Grimble's not coming. He's busy."

"Then you're in trouble, Shandy."

"What have you been drinking, for God's sake?"

Shandy struggled to get out from under the not inconsiderable weight, narrowly escaped being clobbered as promised, and at last managed to dump his irate colleague into a snowbank. Miss Wrenne fastened on his left ankle and had all but managed to divest him of his trousers when the lights in the security office went on and Grimble did in fact appear.

"What's going on here?"

"She's trying to arrest me."

"I am arresting him."

"What the hell for?"

"He was skulking."

"She's drunk."

"Wait a second. One at a time, damn it. Okay, Miz Wrenne, what's the scoop?"

"I caught him trying to break into the security office and bopped him one. He's a saboteur."

"I am not a saboteur," said the professor with what little dignity he had left, "nor was I trying to break into the security office."

"Tell that to the fuzz, buster."

"Now, just a minute," said Grimble. "Let's not get hasty. Professor, what was you doing?"

"I was looking for you," Shandy replied truthfully.

Miss Wrenne snorted. "The door's around the other side, in case you hadn't noticed."

Shandy realized his best defense was attack. "For that matter, what were you yourself doing here, Shirley?"

"Looking for saboteurs."

"Well, while you're horsing around out here bopping and clobbering innocent fellow faculty members, the saboteurs are probably up setting fire to President Svenson's pajamas," he snapped. "If you must play cops and robbers in the snow, why don't you go where the action is?"

"Yeah, that's right," said Grimble. "No hard feelings, Miss Wrenne, but we got security officers all over the place tonight. Why don't you go on home and get some sleep? Nice of you to take an interest," he added politely.

She was in no mood for courtesies. "Aren't you at least going to grill him?"

"Yeah, I'll do that. Professor, you go on into the office. I'll be back soon as I walk Miss Wrenne up the hill."

"Don't bother," snarled the woman. "I can take care of myself, thank you."

She vanished into the storm, and Shandy passed gratefully back into the security office. He looked for the elf mask, but it was not to be seen. He sat down on the chair where it had been, and began digging snow out of his pant legs. The security chief took the chair beside him.

"Okay, Professor, what did you want to see me about?"

"For one thing, I'd like to know what happened to that elf mask that was hanging on this chair a few minutes ago."

"Huh?"

"I was in here, Grimble, listening to you conduct your nocturnal revels. You forgot to lock the outer door."

"Jeez! How could I—" The security chief caught himself. "Look, Professor, you don't understand."

"Yes, I do. Who was she?"

For a long moment, Grimble said nothing. Then a sly grin stole over his beefy countenance.

"Hell, Professor, do I have to answer that? What do you think she was so steamed up about?"

"You are referring to Miss Wrenne?"

"Well, like they taught us back at the police academy, you got to consider the evidence. It's tough on them single dames in a place like this," he went on in a voice of compassion. "Hot to trot and no place to go. I was just bein' neighborly, as you might say."

"Damned decent of you," grunted Shandy. "Miss Wrenne must be a remarkably fast dresser. I trust President Svenson will be able to view the incident in its humanitarian aspect."

"Hey, look, you wouldn't rat on a guy?"

"Why hide your light under a bushel? Your motives were pure, weren't they?"

"Oh, cripes, you know what he's like."

"Yes, I do. That's why I believe you're in no position to be un-co-operative."

Grimble made a remark. Shandy chose to ignore it.

"Are you going to tell me what happened to that elf mask?"

"What elf mask?"

"The one that was hanging on this chair, soaking wet, about five minutes ago."

"I never seen no elf mask," the man muttered. "She must o' brought it in with her an' took it out again."

"Why?"

"How the hell do I know? I tell you I never seen no elf mask."

"I don't believe you," said Shandy, "nor do I believe it was Miss Wrenne you were canoodling with just now. However, I'm to tired to argue. What I want from you are the keys to the Administration Building and the comptroller's office."

"You can't go in there. They got it sealed up."

"We'll unseal it. Get the keys and let's go."

"Do I have to come, too?"

"Yes. If we run into any more self-appointed vigilantes, I'd rather they clobbered you than me."

Dragging the man who might be Ben Cadwall's murderer along on a search of the place where he'd died probably wasn't a brilliant thing to do, but Shandy wasn't operating by reason just now. Anyway, killer dogs weren't killers so long as the shepherd kept his eye on them. It didn't make much sense to leave him running loose in the dark either. Shandy repeated his order. Grimble made another remark and fetched the keys. Together but not talking, the two men ploughed through the storm to that square of old red brick from which Dr. Cadwall's rigid body had been taken just about twelve hours before. It wasn't until he was actually unlocking the office that Grimble asked the inevitable question.

"What do you want in here, anyway?"

"Evidence," said Shandy.

"What kind of evidence? They've already caught Miz Cadwall with the poison. She's goin' to be arraigned tomorrow."

"I know. That's why I have to get in here tonight."

"Oh, Christ on a crutch!"

"Look, Grimble, why don't you stay out here? Then you won't be able to see what I'm up to and your conscience won't bother you."

The security chief grunted and flung himself into the secretary's chair. Shandy flipped the light switch, shut the comptroller's door behind him, and stood wondering. Now that he'd gained entrance, his brain felt as numb as his overtaxed body. The point Grimble had raised was valid. What did he want in here?

Mostly, he wanted to flop down in Ben's comfortably padded swivel chair and take a nap. On second thought, he didn't. That yellow waxwork face, those half-open staring eyes, were still too clear in his mind's eye. He shoved the chair out of the way and knelt in front of the desk.

The police had locked the drawers and presumably taken the key, but Shandy had locked himself out of his own desk often enough to have learned a few useful tricks. In a matter of moments, he was peering into the comptroller's most secret place.

It was a terrible disappointment. If Ben had found any clues, he certainly hadn't kept them here. He hadn't kept much of anything except the tools of his trade and one drawer amply stocked with patent medicines.

Shandy poked through the assortment. This could be a convenient way to poison a dedicated hypochondriac, but how had the deed been managed? Antacids, each in its sealed packet. Aspirins smooth and unmarred, Band-Aids, a clinical thermometer, foot powder, antibiotic salve, cough drops wrapped in silver paper, sunburn lotion, heaven knew why, a box of tissues, and a half-empty bottle of nose drops. Now he knew what he'd come for.

"Grimble! Grimble, come in here a minute."

"What? What for?"

The security chief, who'd evidently been taking a nap in the secretary's chair, stumbled into Cadwall's office. "What's the matter now?"

"You're going to be a witness," the professor told him, watching his face carefully. "I'm going to take this bottle of nose drops out of the drawer, holding it very carefully inside this tissue in case there might be any fingerprints on it other than Dr. Cadwall's, which I don't expect there are, and drop it into this envelope."

"What the hell for?" Grimble didn't look anything but sleepy and truculent.

"Because you and I are going to take it over to the organic chemistry lab. You're going to unlock the place for me, and I'm going to analyze what's in the bottle."

"Oh yeah?"

"Yeah. Get moving, Grimble."

Chapter 23

Grimble snored. He had been snoring for hours, while Professor Shandy kept himself awake by counting every bottle, flask, pipette, test tube, and assorted whatnot in the laboratory. On the plastic laminated counter before him, Hannah Cadwall's fate hung in the balance.

No, by gad, it didn't! He shoved a cork into the vial that had just told him what he needed to know, packed it and the bottle of nose drops with scrupulous care into a small box he found, and pounded the security chief back to consciousness.

"Oh, Christ," moaned the man, "what now?"

"We're going to wake up the president."

"He'll kill us."

"That's a risk we have to take. Get your coat on."

The snowstorm wasn't going to amount to much. Already the flakes were falling few and far between, forming huge lumps as they collided in the air. But the cold was awful. Slopping along in his wet overcoat, Shandy wondered why he couldn't have waited till morning to show Svenson what he'd found. Then he caught sight of the chapel clock through a gray haze and realized it was morning. Almost half past five and he still hadn't managed to grab a wink of sleep. He'd begun to feel a personal hatred for the clever fiend who'd thought of putting taxine in Ben Cadwall's nose drops. He thought of punching Grimble in the mouth on the chance that he might be the right man, but hadn't the strength to do an adequate job.

The Svensons always claimed they kept farmers' hours, and apparently they did. By the time Shandy and his un-willing companion hove in sight of the immense white house on the highest part of the hill behind the campus, a light was burning in the kitchen. Sieglinde herself came to the door, more Valkyrie-like than usual in a long pale blue robe, with thick flaxen braids down over her shoulders.

"Peter Shandy! What do you here? Thorkjeld is still in bed."

"You'll have to get him up."

That was almost certainly the first direct order Mrs. Svenson had ever received from a faculty member. She gave Shandy a long, thoughtful look, then said, "Come in. Stand please on the mat while you drip."

Incredibly, the president came down. Thorkjeld Svenson was awesome enough in ordinary garb; swathed in acres of brown wool bathrobe, unshaven and red-eyed, hair twisted up into iron-gray horns at either side of his thun-derous forehead, he was terrifying.

"What do you want?" he roared.

Grimble cowered behind Shandy and tried to pretend he wasn't there. The professor quailed, but stood his ground.

"I want you to get Mrs. Cadwall out of jail. She didn't kill her husband."

"Ungh."

The president hurled himself into a vast wooden chair and held out one hand. Sieglinde put a cup of coffee the size of a washbasin into it. Shandy winced in envy and longing. At his back, Grimble whimpered.

"Grimble and I," he began, because in spite of every-thing he felt a twinge of compassion for the security chief, "have been working all night."

"Ungh."

"Realizing that the police case rests only on the thin evidence of taxine somebody planted in Mrs. Cadwall's effects—"

"Ungh?"

"Thorkjeld, listen to him," said Mrs. Svenson. "No

woman would be fool enough to keep such stuff after she had poisoned her husband with it. I certainly would not."

"Ungh!"

"Anyway," Shandy went on hastily, "we went looking for clues in the comptroller's office and found a bottle of nose drops."

"Yeah, that's right."

Seeing that the sky was not going to fall, Grimble decided to claim his share of the limelight. Shandy trod firmly on his toe and kept talking.

"This seemed a reasonable vehicle for a soluble poison with a nasty taste. The medication would disguise the flavor of the taxine, and by the time it trickled down the nasal passages into the throat, the victim would be almost certain to ingest a fatal dose."

"Ungh."

"So we took the bottle over to the organic chemistry lab and tested it and it's bung-full of taxine. You'd better take it down to the jail right away and tell them to let Mrs. Cadwall out."

At last the great man uttered what for him was a long sentence. "Why me?"

"Because you're more impressive than I am."

Sieglinde nodded. "That is true. Thorkjeld is impressive. You, Peter Shandy, are not. I will give you coffee."

"No, thank you. I'm going home to bed. Come on, Grimble."

"We might o' waited for the coffee," the security chief grumbled when they got outside.

"Don't be a jackass, man. Could you honestly sit down at that table and drink coffee with the president glowering at you from behind his whiskers?"

"No, I guess not," the man conceded. "Say, I guess I ought to thank you for—" he conquered his better feelings and turned off toward the security office.

Shandy wended his lone way downhill to the brick house, took a hot shower and three fingers of brandy, and climbed into bed. He did not wake until noon. His first conscious act was to telephone the library.

"Helen, can you meet me at the dining room?"

"I'd love to, Peter. Half past twelve?"

"Fine."

That barely gave him time to shave and dress, but he

managed. His overcoat was still sodden, so he grabbed the old plaid mackinaw in which he'd knocked about the turnip fields for more years than he cared to count. This was no time to fret over trivia.

He'd just snaffled the table least vulnerable to intrusion when Helen entered the dining room, wearing high boots and a brand-new bright red storm coat.

"I nipped down to the village first thing this morning and got myself some heavy-weather gear," she said. "Now I can give that nice man back his socks. How are you, Peter?"

"Ask me later. I haven't had time to think about it yet. Beef pot pie seems to be the *pièce de résistance*."

"Fine, if the beef isn't too resistant. My jaws are tired from arguing with Mr. Porble about the Buggins Collection. Peter, would you believe I actually got him to let me spend a little time there this morning, and he says I can go back after lunch?"

"Splendid. Would you mind sitting here beside me so I won't have to shout?"

As soon as they'd got their orders in, he began telling her in a low voice all that had happened after he'd left her the night before.

"My personal conviction, appearances to the contrary notwithstanding, is that it could not have been Shirley Wrenne who was—er—closeted with Grimble."

"Of course it wasn't," said Helen. "If it were, she wouldn't have come bashing away at the first man she met. She'd have made herself scarce, which I'm sure is what the other woman did while you were having your rumpus outside, not because women are ashamed of having sex these days, or say they aren't, but because she'd hate to have you know she was doing it with Grimble. He's not exactly love's young dream."

"I've been trying to think who around college would—er —succumb to a man like him. She'd have to be hard up for company."

"Or else the original I-don't-care girl," said Helen. "I'll get cosy with some of the secretaries, if you want. They're always the ones who really know what's going on."

"I'd be grateful," said Shandy. "Every fresh discovery I make seems to put me one step farther back."

"Nonsense, Peter. You're the only one who's doing anything constructive. Here, let me pour you some more coffee."

For a blissful second, Shandy was Thorkjeld Svenson, reaching out for the cup he knew Sieglinde would have ready. It wasn't the coffee that mattered, it was the caring. Helen was only showing common courtesy but a man could dream, even a man fifty-six years old who was almost certainly coming down with a rotten cold. He drank the coffee.

"After all your adventures," said Helen, "I feel silly telling you about my own little mystery. I thought it might possibly mean something, but—"

"Tell me anyway," Shandy urged.

"Well, it's just that—Peter, I have to confess to you that I have this ridiculous habit of counting things. I simply can't be left alone with more than three related objects for two minutes before I find myself totting them up. It's awful."

"I've always found it a source of innocent pleasure and sometimes of illumination," said Shandy.

"Peter, you don't!"

"I do. On that necklace you wore last night, there are seventy-four pearls."

"Seventy-five. There's a little one set in the clasp. It's always flipping over so you probably couldn't see it. Oh, Peter!"

Surely not even Thorkjeld and Sieglinde had experienced such a moment. When the stars quit reeling in the firmament, Shandy spoke again.

"You were saying—"

"Oh yes. As I believe I mentioned last evening, Dr. Porble let me go into the Buggins Room for just a short while late yesterday afternoon. There wasn't much I could do in those few minutes anyway, so I stood there like a ninny—sorry, comrade—and counted them. And it was such fun that this morning when I got in there again, I—"

"Counted them over, as any reasonable person would do. How many?"

"That's my mystery. Yesterday, there were two thousand, six hundred and thirty-eight. Today there are two thousand, six hundred and thirty-three. And the room was locked and nobody's been in there except me."

"That is odd."

The professor consumed a forkful of beef pie thoughtfully. "There's no chance you—er—"

"Got mixed up in my count? Would you?"

"Perish the thought!"

"There, see, you're outraged at the mere suggestion. We compulsive counters do not lose count. Even if I did happen to skip one, I couldn't be out by five whole, great, fat books, could I?"

"Not possibly."

"Then where did they go?"

"You're suggesting that somebody obtained entrance by some method as yet undetermined, and snitched them? Considering that nobody in all these years has ever willingly set foot in the place, much less taken away any books—"

"How do we know that?"

Shandy put down his fork. "We don't, do we?"

"Would Jemima have known?"

"She ought to, if anybody did. Do you think there's the remotest possibility any of those books is worth anything?"

"I'm wondering. The collection is old, Peter, much older than I'd been led to believe. I thought it would be all Warwick Deeping and Gene Stratton Porter, but Ulysses S. Grant's memoirs seem to be among the more recent publications. I happened to pick up a copy of *Vanity Fair* that I thought might be a first edition, and—and I think I'm going to get in touch with an old friend in Boston who knows a great deal more than is legal about the rare book market. Do you mind if I leave you?"

"Yes," said Shandy.

He bolted the last of his lunch and flung money on the table. "Come on, you'd better use the phone at my house. No sense in running up toll calls on Tim."

"Oh, I completely forgot to tell you, he called last night shortly after I'd got in the house. Jemmy has a baby boy. I'm shaky on the details because neither of us could make much sense of what the other was saying, but he sounded positively ecstatic."

"I'm glad."

Shandy was in truth happy for his old friend, but more immediately concerned with the question of whether Helen's call was going to turn up anything. It didn't take long to find out. After an exchange of pleasantries, she stated her problem and got her answer. He thought she was going to faint.

"Oh no! That's just not possible. Yes, I know you—but I simply cannot believe—and have you any idea how much —oh, my God!"

Shandy thought he'd better fetch the brandy.

Chapter 24

When he got back, she'd hung up the phone and was staring into space, her face as white as the snow outside the window.

"Good Lord, Helen, what did you find out?"

She drank some of the brandy. "Thank you, Peter."

She set down the glass with great care. "During the past several months, there's been a strange little trickle of rare books coming into the market through a dealer whom my friend refuses to name, which means he's a fence. They all have had the same odd-shaped bookplate steamed out of them. Two weeks ago, the dealer got hold of the poems of Currer, Ellis, and Acton B-B—"

"Here, take more brandy. Helen, that can't be true?"

"It is if my informant says it is. He claims the book is in mint condition and the dealer got it for five thousand dollars because who ever heard of Currer, Ellis, and Acton Bell?" Her voice was shaking.

"Currer, Ellis, and Acton Bell," Shandy repeated in a stunned tone. "Charlotte, Emily, and Anne. Their one joint publishing venture, paid for out of their own thin pockets and a complete financial bust. Ten copies sold, or something like that?"

"Six, I believe," said Helen. "The rest were used to line

trunks. Peter, I think I'm going to be sick. It's—it's like finding out Sir Parsifal had gone and hocked the Holy Grail."

The librarian wrung her hands in anguish. Shandy felt it only common courtesy to cover them with his own. The gesture led to further courtesies.

At last Helen murmured into his collarbone, "Peter, you're such a blessed comfort. I wish I didn't have to go."

"You don't."

"But Dr. Porble will be furious."

"To hell with Porble. How do we know he isn't a crook?"

"He'd never sell the Brontë sisters for a lousy five thousand dollars."

"He wouldn't know the Brontë sisters if they walked up and hit him over the head with their reticules."

"Then he wouldn't know enough to steal the book, would he? Peter, I really must go. Professor Stott will be coming in for his hog statistics and they're still not finished. I can't afford to get fired."

"Yes, you can. I should point out that what with having tenure in the rank of full professor, in addition to my royalties from the Balaclava Buster, et al., I am a man of not inconsiderable fortune."

"Whatever do you mean?"

"Lawful wedlock was what I had in mind."

"But you've only known me since Monday afternoon. Peter, you've been a bachelor—"

"Quite long enough. Nothing is more powerful than an idea whose time is come. You, as a woman of literary attainments, should know that. I'm not trying to rush you, Helen. I'm just—er—doing the preliminary spadework. A natural first step for a farmer to take."

"Then I may have time to think it over?"

"Of course. You—er—won't mind if I count the days?"

"I'd be disappointed if you didn't. I think I'd better go now. Thank you, Peter."

At least it wasn't a flat turndown. Shandy refrained from offering to walk her back up the hill, and sat down at his desk. He needed to collect his thoughts. Taking paper and pen, he started making a list.

Perhaps because his mind was running in that general direction, the first query he wrote down was, "Why would any woman in her right mind afflict herself with Grimble?" He could see but two possible explanations: either she was indeed damned hard up, or else she wanted something from him that she couldn't get any other way.

The one thing Grimble had that nobody else did was that keyboard in his private office. Was it actually possible one of the ladies Shandy knew—for she must somehow be connected with the Crescent as well as the college—could bring herself to commit such an act?

For five thousand dollars? Plenty of women had done it for less, and God alone knew how many books had been peddled out of the Buggins Collection by now. Even at cutthroat prices, the take must be impressive. Had the looting gone on over a long period of time, or was it the threatened fruition of his own long campaign to get the books into circulation that had inspired somebody to weed out the treasures first?

He wished he didn't keep coming back to the likelihood that he himself was responsible for the whole rotten chain of events. Doggedly, Shandy turned to another question. He was writing, "Who stole my Santa Claus?" when the doorbell rang.

It was a woman, and for one delirious moment he thought Helen might have returned to say yes. She proved, however, to be Hannah Cadwall.

"Peter, I came to thank you for getting me out of jail. The president says you stayed up all night hunting for taxine in Ben's nose drops."

"It had to be somewhere."

"But to think you'd do that for me! Peter, I didn't realize."

Oh, God, there was that look again, and this one's husband not even buried yet. Shandy backed away a step.

"Not at all," he replied stiffly. "Ben was a colleague, and I felt I owed you something in return for the capable way in which you managed Jemima's funeral."

"Oh, that."

Hannah strove not to appear deflated. "I'd forgotten poor Jemima. Well, I daresay the experience will come in handy now that I've got to do it over again for Ben. Harry the Ghoul ought to give me a cut rate."

She started to laugh, somewhat hysterically. Shandy remembered the brandy and she quieted down.

"Yes, I believe I would. Maybe it will take away the taste of that jail food. Peter, I simply can't tell you what it was like."

She proceeded to do so, however. It took Shandy some while to switch her off on a different track.

"Hannah, do you have any faintest glimmering of a notion who may have killed your husband?"

"Now, don't you start. Seventeen different policemen asked me that this morning, as soon as Dr. Svenson came roaring in like the Bull of Bashan and made them unlock the cell. Of course I don't. If I did, don't you think I'd have managed to talk my way out of being arrested in the first place?"

"But dash it, Hannah, you must know something? You lived with the man. Where did Ben get his nose drops?"

"Drugstore, I suppose, or at the Cut-Rate when we went shopping in the city. It's just a common brand you can buy anywhere. He always keeps—kept—I still can't get used to it—anyway, he'd always buy two, one for the house and one for the office. Ben had terrible trouble with his sinuses, you know. He claimed those nose drops were the only thing that ever helped him. Dr. Melchett tried to tell him it was the nose drops that caused the congestion, but of course he'd never get Ben to believe that."

"Would he have used them as soon as he got to the office?"

"I should think so, coming in out of the cold like that. He generally did."

Shandy had a thought. "Would he have done it that day after the funeral, when we all more or less arrived at your house in a bunch?"

"I suppose so. I had so many things on my mind just then, I wouldn't remember."

"Assuming he did, was he likely to go into the bathroom or somewhere and shut the door, or would he just bale the stuff into him wherever he happened to be?"

"Oh, you know Ben. He'd never miss a chance to perform in front of an audience. No misery ever loved company the way his did. That's the brandy talking, not me."

The professor nodded. "So undoubtedly at least some of the people there were treated to a discourse on nose drops. I daresay I'd have heard it, too, but I was preoccupied with Tim. That means anybody there could have got the

idea of buying a bottle of that same brand, doctoring it
with taxine, and planting it in Ben's desk with the virtual
certainty that he'd pump poison down his throat the next
morning."

"Why, yes, I suppose they could, if they could get in,
but how could they do that? Ben was always so careful
about locking up, even if he just stepped out to go to the
men's room."

"What about his secretary?"

"Not Myrnette Woodruff," said Hannah flatly. "Anyway, she's been down with flu ever since Christmas night,
because I called to let her know about Jemima's funeral
and she was too sick to come. She felt terrible to miss it.
And you needn't get any funny ideas about her and Ben
either. Her husband's Master of the Grange and they cele-
brated their silver wedding anniversary this past October.
Her daughter gave them a lovely party and Ben and I were
invited. That's wonderful brandy, I must say."

She drained her glass and looked hopeful. Against his
inclination, Shandy gave her a refill. This conversation
was probably going to wind up as an exercise in futility.
If she had anything of value to tell, that sharp state policeman would surely have got it out of her. All he himself
would be likely to get was a hard time. Still, one never
knew. He poured himself another modest tot and settled
back in his chair.

"Hannah," he said abruptly, "did Jemima ever mention
anything about books being taken from the Buggins Collection?"

"That's a crazy question, though, come to think of it,
she did. She was stewing one day about making him bring
it back."

"Making whom bring it back?"

"Oh, Peter, how can you expect me to remember a silly
thing like that, with everything else that's happened? Jemima was always in a swivet about something."

"For God's sake, woman, try!"

"Don't yell at me like that! Ben never yelled. He could
get pretty nasty sometimes, but he always kept his voice
down."

"I'm sorry, Hannah, but you've got to remember! Damn
it, the person who took that book is probably your husband's murderer."

"That's the stupidest thing I ever heard."

Mrs. Cadwall set down her twice-emptied glass and started gathering herself together. "I don't mean to be rude, Peter, I really do appreciate what you did for me, but I must say you're getting some awfully peculiar notions lately. Those plastic reindeer, for instance. Now, please don't take this the wrong way, but if I were you, I'd go and have a nice, quiet talk with Dr. Sidman."

She was out the door before Shandy could think of a way to convince her that he did not need a psychiatrist. Perhaps in fact he did, for a notion wilder than all the rest came surging through his brain. Quite forgetting what Mrs. Lomax was going to say when she found sticky glasses sitting on the walnut tables, he grabbed his ancient mackinaw and made a beeline for the Administration Building.

Miss Tibbett was only too happy to make Professor Shandy free of her files, and intimated ever so gently that she'd be happier still to grant other freedoms. Shandy pretended not to know she wasn't talking about the files.

"No, no, Miss Tibbett, I mustn't take up any more of your valuable time. Just leave me here and go on with what you were doing. Er—there is just one more thing."

"Yes?" she responded eagerly.

"I expect it's been chucked out years ago, but is there the faintest chance you still have the *curriculum vitae* Dr. Cadwall submitted when he applied for the comptrollership?"

"We don't chuck things out, Professor."

Gracious even in disappointment, Miss Tibbett produced the document that had been lying dormant for over a quarter of a century. Shandy read it avidly and made careful notes. He asked for another more recent dossier and made further memoranda. He fought down an impulse to kiss Miss Tibbett, after all, and rushed from the building. Now that the preliminary research indicated a hopeful prognosis, his next step was obvious. He must find out where in Sam Hill Patsville, Ohio, might be, he must get there as fast as possible, and he must hunt up some long-time inhabitant with a good memory and a penchant for gossip.

When he stopped at the brick house for pajamas and toothbrush and the spare hundred-dollar bill he always kept hidden inside the stiff front of his only boiled shirt, he found Mrs. Lomax itching to state her views with regard to sticky tumblers on walnut tables. Shandy wasn't interested.

"Never mind that. When you've finished here, I want you to take this note across to Miss Marsh. If she isn't there, leave it where she'll be sure to see it."

"Why? Where are you going?"

"Away."

He put on his respectable overcoat, now only somewhat damp, grabbed his hat and muffler, and dashed for Harry's Garage, where a car was already being gassed up to take him to the airport. Mrs. Lomax gaped after the professor, then went to the kitchen and steamed open his note. It read:

Dearest Watson,
    The game's afoot. Stay in the roundhouse till I get back. They can't corner you there.

Devotedly,
Arsène Lupin

"Well," Mrs. Lomax remarked to the teakettle, "they've all been saying he's gone soft in the head. Now I'd believe anything."

Chapter 25

Not until Shandy was halfway back to Balaclava Junction
did he remember that he'd been ordered by Mrs. Svenson
to bring Helen to tea on Thursday afternoon. He checked
with one of the airplane's stewardesses, who confirmed his
suspicion that this was indeed Thursday. There was no
way of finding out from here whether the engagement was
still on in view of Cadwall's demise, but he'd damn well
better show up, just in case. It was nip, tuck, and a costly
speeding ticket, but he managed to reach the library in
time to find Helen zipping up her new boots and casting
worried glances at the clock.

"Young Lochinvar is come out of the west!" she exclaimed.

"Very funny. Is it still on?" he gasped.

"Yes, but don't you want to sit down a minute and catch
your breath?"

"I'll breathe when we get there. Come on."

As it was already ten after four, Helen didn't ask the
questions that were obviously burning on her lips. Together they toiled up to the crest where the president's
house, white-painted and Palladian-columned in the tradition beloved of academe, rose in majesty out of the

snowdrifts. One of the several Misses Svenson, tall and fair as a young birch tree, let them in.

"Good afternoon, Professor Shandy, and this must be Miss Marsh. We're so glad you could come. I'm Ingeborg. Please come in. Mother is in the living room."

From the array of coats and boots in the front hall, they could see this was a party of no mean proportions instead of the intimate family tea they'd anticipated. In a way, Shandy was glad. It meant a stupendous smorgasbord after the chilly artifacts of plastic and cardboard that airlines and fast-food restaurants are pleased to call food. It meant tiny glasses of akvavit and large cups of hot tea to warm the cockles and cheer the spirit. It meant lots of people to cushion him from the full impact of President Svenson, but it also meant noise, confusion, a necessity to make small talk that would prevent his being able to mull over what he'd found out in Patsville, Ohio, and how it fitted in with the things he already knew. He decided to concentrate on the herring and postpone the mulling.

Helen Marsh, although no more prepared than he for the gala assemblage that met their eyes, was by no means out of countenance. Her well-made light blue dress and modest pearls were entirely appropriate, her smile unstrained, and her conversation ready. He was proud of her. He'd tell her so if he ever got a chance to speak to her again. They'd barely made their manners to Sieglinde when Professor Stott claimed her and led her to where the good things were piled highest, talking hog statistics with unwonted animation the while.

Shandy possessed himself of a plateful of sandwiches, a nip of akvavit, and a cup of tea, thinking to retire into some corner and refresh himself in peace. It was not to be so.

"Shandy, I want you."

"Certainly, President," he managed to articulate around a mouthful of rollmop, "if Mrs. Svenson doesn't mind."

Intimating that he didn't give a damn whether Mrs. Svenson minded or not, the great man led his victim into the library, and shut the door.

"Talk."

"What do you want me to say?"

"Don't be flip, Shandy. Damn it, I told you on Sunday

to get this mess cleared up, and you've let it go from bad to worse. Now they've attacked my power plant."

"How bad was the damage?"

"Not bad," Svenson admitted. Then he roared, "Any is bad! Why, Shandy? Why?"

"I think I know why," the professor replied, "and also who and how. The trouble is, I have no stickable evidence yet."

"Horsefeathers! Get 'em in here. I'll make 'em talk."

"That would be one approach," said Shandy cautiously. "However, I—er—think I can manage something that would be more convincing in court than—er—confession under duress."

"I don't trust you."

Shandy slammed down his cup and sprang out of the chair. "I don't give two hoots in hell whether you trust me or not. I'm the one who's been victimized, I'm the one who got this mess shoved down his throat, and I'm the only one who's lifted a hand to straighten it out. I'm tired and I've got a rotten cold and I'm goddamned fed up with being badgered. If you want me to resign here and now, consider it done. If you want me to finish this job right, get the hell off my back and let me do it."

"By yumping yiminy!"

For a full thirty seconds, President Svenson stood snorting through his hairy nostrils like a bull about to charge. Then his lips curled skyward. He began to chuckle. It turned to a guffaw that brought Sieglinde hurrying into the room.

"Thorkjeld, what are you laughing at?"

"Shandy just told me to go to hell."

"Can you not go quietly? You frighten our guests."

"She's mad at me for leaving the party," said the president morosely. "It's Shandy's fault, Sieglinde. All right, Peter, I'll give you till tomorrow noon. Come and eat herring."

"Er—thank you, no. I seem to have lost my appetite."

"Eat herring!"

The professor ate and found it, after all, good. Nevertheless, the hollow feeling at the pit of his stomach remained even after he and Helen were settled back at the brick house and he was telling her what he'd found out and what he'd deduced and she was reacting altogether to his satisfaction.

"Peter, that's brilliant! I'm sure you're right."

"But how can I prove it? If I don't show up with the goods at twelve o'clock tomorrow, Svenson will be nailing my flayed pelt to the chapel door by a quarter to one."

"And Sieglinde will be right beside him, holding the hammer. I do like her so much."

"De gustibus non est disputandum."

"Oh, don't pull that professorial stuff on me. If you were nailing up President Svenson's hide, wouldn't you like having me caddy for you?"

"Yes, and it's a splendid suggestion. Helen, would you really?"

"That's a big commitment. I'll have to ponder the aspects."

"Don't pussyfoot, woman. Yes or no?"

"Peter, do you realize you could have any woman on this campus?"

"Dash it, I don't want any woman on this campus. I want you, to keep those she-wolves at bay."

"Is that all you want me for?"

"No. Helen, what in God's name am I am going to do?"

Miss Marsh leaned back on the sofa, happening to encounter Shandy's arm. She did not draw away and he did not encourage her to do so. It was quite a while before they again addressed the problem under discussion. When Helen did speak again she sounded somewhat breathless, as well she might.

"Back in Victorian days, the gentry used to have beaters who'd flush the birds for them to shoot. What you need is a beater."

"Often as not, the hunter missed the bird and hit the beater."

"That's the chance we beaters have to take. Do you or do you not want me to hold the hammer for you?"

"Helen, if anything should happen to you—"

"Peter, nothing is going to happen to me. Let me do this for you and"—she planted one more light kiss on his glowing cheek—"maybe you can do something for me sometime."

"What are you going to do?"

"Just this."

She walked over to the telephone, studied the college directory, and dialed a number. She got her bird.

"Hello, this is Helen Marsh from the library. I'm the new assistant for the Buggins Collection, you know, and I've just happened on a note Mrs. Ames wrote to herself about a book you borrowed from the collection. She was apparently rather worried about getting it back. Oh, you did? Are you quite sure? You see, I've started the cataloguing, and I've run into some very disturbing problems. Some of the most valuable books in the collection are missing, and the one you took happens to be on the special list."

There was a noise on the other end of the line. Helen listened, then laughed merrily. "But of course we have! You don't think Dr. Porble would let such valuable acquisitions go unlisted, do you? The staff are making a careful check now and if we don't turn up the missing books, we're going to get special investigators—yes, of course. I understand perfectly. Perhaps if you took another careful look around—thank you so much. Then I'll expect to hear from you. Good-by."

She replaced the receiver. "Over to you, Arsène."

Chapter 26

"Helen, you're stuck with the toughest job. You'll have to get on that phone and somehow convince Lieutenant Olivetti that we haven't both gone crazy. Explain who you are and make it sound impressive. Give him the facts and tell him to deploy his people on all roads leading out of Balaclava Junction, but not to interfere till I say so."

"Peter, you're not intending to face a two-time murderer alone?"

"No, not alone. Oh, Christ! Call the police. Hurry!"

He grabbed his jacket and rushed out of the house, downhill after an elf who was dragging an empty sled at a fast clip. The student was in complete costume with the elf mask pulled down over the face, but he'd suffered enough from this particular nuisance to recognize the form and gait beyond any doubt. Shandy put on a frantic burst of speed, took a flying leap, and landed on the sled.

"Turn around," he ordered.

"Huh?"

Taken aback, the sled-puller stopped short. "Hey, I can't take a passenger just now. I'm—doing an errand."

"For Grimble?"

Whatever else she might be, Heidi Hayhoe wasn't

213

stupid. She picked up the sled rope again. "Where to, Professor?"

"President Svenson's house."

"All the way up there?"

"Yes, damn it, all the way up there. Get cracking!"

"There," said Mirelle Feldster from behind her parlor curtain. "He's gone loopy for sure. Just as well I didn't—"

"Didn't what?" asked her husband.

Mirelle's answer, if there was one, was drowned by yells from outside. Strolling gawkers, intrigued by the sight of Shandy, grim-faced as Scrooge, riding behind a straining, swearing, furiously sprinting elf. "Hi-yo, Santa Claus!" they shouted. A few tried to push or jump on the sled, but Shandy turned on them a face so savage that they fell back, staring and muttering.

The girl must be incredibly strong to keep up such a pace. The professor felt no remorse for what he was doing to her. Heidi couldn't be in such a desperate hurry unless she'd already got the tip-off, and Helen needed every minute he could gain to reach Olivetti and start the police moving. He stuck with the sled until they reached the end of Svenson's driveway.

"This far enough?" the student panted.

"It will do."

Shandy handed her a five-dollar bill. "Here. I know you always expect ample payment for your—er—services."

"Forget it."

Furious, she slammed her body down on the sled and began coasting downhill, trying to make up for lost time. Shandy hoped she'd come a cropper, but didn't wait to find out. He hurried up to the presiden't front door and thumped until another of the Svenson daughters let him in.

"Professor Shandy! But the party's over."

"That's what you think, young lady."

"Mother's gone to lie down," she stammered. "Daddy—"

He brushed past her and strode into the library, where Thorkjeld Svenson lay sprawled in a gigantic easy chair before a television set, watching John Wayne get his sombrero pierced by flying bullets. Shandy flicked the "off" switch.

"You want action, President. Get your coat and your car keys."

"Why?"

"Because I say so. Move!"

Incredibly, Svenson did.

"Daddy, where are you going?" called the daughter.

"Ask Shandy."

But Shandy had not waited to be asked. He was already behind the wheel of Svenson's beat-up Chevy.

"Is there any gas in this heap?"

"Who knows? Where are we going?"

"To head 'em off at the pass."

He crunched into first gear for the sharp pitch down to the road where he and Helen had got stopped the night before, then into high, casting worried glances at the gas gauge. It said "half," but there was no telling what that meant. Svenson's car, like its owner, was a law unto itself.

Shandy had counted on Helen's surprise attack to force their prey into doing something stupid, and it had. They picked up the trail with no difficulty at all. He didn't even have to work hard at keeping the other car in sight, since it was obvious where they were heading.

Once only, Svenson spoke. "There's a state trooper chasing us."

"Good," said Shandy. He blinked the lights a few times, and trod harder on the gas pedal. The engine coughed ominously. Cursing with great feeling and expression, he turned into a filling station. The police car started to follow him in, but he waved it on.

They lost minutes, but not too many. When they ran inside the airport terminal, two state policemen in uniform were standing near the door, trying to look nonchalant. Shandy rushed up to them and one murmured, "Boarding. Gate number six."

"Good. Come on."

Sure enough, there they were, clutching their boarding passes and the take-on luggage they must have kept packed and ready ever since they murdered Jemima. The man was tall and burly, clad in a rough dark overcoat and a black lambskin hat much like the garments President Svenson had on. The woman was almost as big as he. She wore a plain blue tweed coat, a blue Angora beret, woolly gray gloves, and enormous black leather boots. Under the beret showed a great knot of flaxen hair.

"Sieglinde!"

"President, no!"

Shandy flung himself upon the howling berserker and held back with all his might until the police could close in. "That's not your wife."

It was not Sieglinde. It was Heidi Hayhoe, mistress of disguise and, on the evidence, of Bob Dysart. Snarling, Svenson fought to get at her.

"Trollop!"

"Oh, hey, listen," cried the girl with a nervous giggle. "Anybody can happen to dress like somebody else. I've worn this outfit lots of times."

"She probably has, President," said Shandy. "I expect this pair of fun-loving pranksters has impersonated you and your wife on numerous occasions. At—er—motels and so forth."

"Arrgh!"

"Sure, what the hell?" Dysart, as always, was quick to see a chance. "You fellows know how it is. I'm a yang, she's a yin. Look, President, I know the rules about faculty-student relationships as well as you do, so let's just say I resign for reasons of moral turpitude as of here and now. I'll drop you a line and make it official, but right now my friend and I have a plane to catch, which we're going to miss if we don't run like crazy."

He was so plausible as a philanderer caught in the act that he might even have got himself and Heidi out of the boarding gate, if Shandy hadn't reached over and wrenched open the tote bag he was carrying. In it were Cotton Mather's *Wonders of the Invisible World* and the original two-volume edition of Hamilton's *Federalist*, uncut. Dysart hadn't had time to steam out the Buggins Collection bookplates.

The pair were brought back to Balaclava Junction under heavy guard. Grimble was taken into custody and brought down to confront them. He lost his nerve and ratted. Then Heidi Hayhoe ratted, leaving Bob Dysart with nobody to rat on. In due time, the judge, showing a fine sense of what was appropriate, threw the book at him.

For Shandy the adventure ended where it began, in the brick house on the Crescent. He'd called Helen from the airport, and again from Ottermole's office to say he was bringing company back. She had a fire going, sandwiches cut, coffee brewed, and sherry at the ready. Sieglinde

Svenson, whom they'd collected when they dropped the president's car off, nodded her beautiful head.

"Now you have a home, Peter. Sherry, please. Also for Thorkjeld."

"And you, Porble?"

"Might as well."

The librarian was looking stunned and apprehensive. He still didn't know why they'd dragged him from his own fireside at this hour of the night, but it could be for no good reason.

"Take some yourself, Peter," Helen urged, "then for goodness' sake tell these people everything, from the beginning."

"Well," said Shandy, "I suppose you could say it started with the marbles."

He described once more how he'd found Jemima while hunting for his missing marble, how the errant sphere had turned up in Cadwall's bedroom and thus led him to discover the comptroller's body.

"I expect we'll find out somewhere along the line that either Dysart or Heidi tipped over the dish while they were staging the accident. They'd think it a clever touch, no doubt. Cleverness as opposed to intelligence was, you might say, the keynote of the whole operation. That ought to have made me think of Dysart right off the bat, though I'm ashamed to say it didn't."

"He took an awful risk," said Helen, "killing Mrs. Ames in his own house. At least, I suppose he must have."

"Oh yes. But he had a very pretty scheme worked out. He got her alone in the bedroom, whacked her on the head with a piece of two-by-four or some such thing, held edge-on so that it would leave the right kind of dent, and shoved her body under the bed. He then tossed that extremely noticeable and unmistakable purple cape out the window to Heidi, who was waiting below in her elf costume, having brought her sled to the house and stashed it out of sight. She covered her head and body with the cape and walked down the path in plain sight of the window, with Dysart making sure everybody noticed her going."

Porble winced. "I was one of them. My wife said, 'I'm afraid Jemima isn't quite herself tonight,' and Dysart laughed as though it was the funniest thing he'd ever heard."

"No doubt he was delighted to see his plan working so well," Shandy remarked. "Once she was well inside the shrubbery, the girl got rid of Jemima's cape. I expect she folded it as small as she could, then stuck it overhead among the branches, knowing the people going home from the party wouldn't be apt to look up. They'd tuck their chins into their collars and watch where they stepped on that slippery path. Then all Heidi had to do was step out and mingle with the crowd. Mary Enderble and Roger Jackman probably did see her, but paid no attention because the Crescent's always swarming with students in elf costume and Heidi's been taking particular pains to make herself noticed by barging about with her sled where she's not supposed to be."

"And getting away with it because she's a natural-born performer," said Helen. "People don't mind having the star take the stage."

"Especially not when they're related to wealthy alumni," Porble added nastily.

Shandy ignored the interruption. "I expect Dysart devoted the rest of the evening to getting his wife as drunk as possible while himself pretending to drink a great deal more than he did. He might even have given her a sedative, although," remembering Adele and her cough medicine, "that may not have been necessary. Anyway, once Adele was safely out of the picture and the Illumination over for the night, Heidi Hayhoe came back. Jemima was a big woman, but Heidi is an amazingly strong girl, as I found out earlier this evening. She and Dysart between them would have no trouble carrying the body downstairs and getting it on the sled, disguised in the Santa Claus mask off the dummy Heidi and no doubt some of her cohorts had pinched from my porch and—er—made sport with.

"Probably he then lay low for a few minutes while she dragged the sled over here. The Jackman child happened to catch her doing it, but of course all he actually saw was one of the elves riding Santa Claus around on a sled, as they'd been doing all evening. Interestingly enough, though, he seems to have got some kind of subliminal impression about the situation because he suddenly became frightened and scooted back to bed. If he'd stayed up, I daresay he'd have seen Professor Dysart taking a late-night stroll around the Crescent to sober up from his own party.

When Dysart disappeared among my spruce trees, the child would think he'd sought shelter for—er—personal reasons."

"Not bad," said the president.

"No, actually, it was pretty good. If they hadn't overdone the cleverness by bringing in that unnecessary step stool and overturning the marbles that should have been safely out of the way, I might never have noticed anything fishy about the so-called accident. Except, of course, for the missing door key."

"That's where Grimble comes in, I suppose," said Porble.

"Exactly. Heidi got it from him using the same—er—methods Delilah used on Samson. I would not have believed an attractive young woman could be so—er—"

"I would," said Helen. "I told you what she was the minute I laid eyes on her, but you didn't listen."

"Good men never believe there are any bad women," said Sieglinde. "That is why good women have a duty to keep them from running loose and getting into trouble. These are excellent sandwiches, Miss Marsh."

"Thank you," said Helen, somewhat flustered. "Peter, what about the keys? She had one to the library, too, didn't she?"

"Dysart did. I expect she took them from the security office either with or without Grimble's knowledge, had them duplicated, then replaced the originals—er—next time around."

"My God," said Porble faintly.

"Why the Buggins Collection?" demanded the president. "Nobody else," he shot a javelin glance at the librarian, "thought it worth bothering about."

"And Peter," said Helen.

"And I," said Sieglinde. "Though I did not mean for Thorkjeld to appoint Mrs. Ames."

"I did it because you nagged me. It's all your fault."

"In any event, it was the Buggins Collection that killed her," said Shandy. "I suspect Dysart, having got hold of the keys, used to make his raids whenever he saw the chance. He could duck out into the corridor on the pretext of using the men's room and even if someone did happen to find him exploring the Buggins Room, there's nothing so very remarkable about an academic's showing a desultory interest in old books. However, Jemima, once she became assistant, also developed the habit of making whirlwind visits to the library. She happened to catch him in the act of taking one of the books. I suppose he told her Porble had said it was all right and, knowing what a slapdash sort of person she was, simply hoped she'd forget the incident. But Jemima didn't forget and kept nagging at him to return the book, which of course he couldn't do because he'd sold it. Furthermore, the fact that she knew he'd been in the room at all made him Suspect Number One if the thefts ever were discovered, and a stumbling block to a highly lucrative enterprise even if they weren't. He'd probably decided to get rid of her even before her—er—taking umbrage at my Ilumination decorations suggested a method. I hope so, anyway."

"But what about Dr. Cadwall?" Sieglinde wanted to know. "Did he, too, know that Professor Dysart had taken the book?"

"Dysart probably thought he did because Ben was so inquisitive and his wife a close friend of Jemima, who was a great talker. However, he had another reason to be afraid of the comptroller. He knew that Ben had grown up in a small Ohio town with Adele, who's a good bit older than she would have us believe, and that in fact the two were once engaged."

"So?"

"So when Ben started taking public issue with the way Adele's money was being thrown around, Bob must have got worried. You see, Ben also knew that while Adele had, as advertised, come into her parents' fortune, being rich in Patsville, Ohio, doesn't necessarily mean quite the same thing as being rich in Dallas or Palm Beach. Since he'd almost married into the family, Ben had a pretty shrewd idea of how much she actually inherited, and of course he signed Bob's pay checks. It was obvious to him that the Dysarts' total income simply was not big enough to sustain their flamboyant life style for any extended time. The logical inferences were either that Bob was getting additional funds from some undisclosed source or that he intended to blow every cent he could milk from Adele's estate and then ditch her for somebody else. Since both surmises happened to be true, and since Ben was in a position of real power at the college, I expect Dysart considered him far the greater threat."

"Still, if Professor Dysart was planning to elope with Heidi Hayhoe, why did he not just go and not kill these good people?"

"Oh, I don't think he intended to clear out so soon. He'd spun that yarn about Ben's getting poisoned coffee intended for him, and then got his girl friend to torch the power plant in order to support the idea that he was being persecuted by saboteurs. I expect he thought he could keep it going until he'd finished plundering the Buggins Collection. He's an imaginative chap, you know. He must have enjoyed himself a great deal, ripping off a fortune from under Porble's nose and having an affair with a student in defiance of the college's strictest rule."

"You know," Helen mused, "it's conceivable that by forcing Professor Dysart's hand, we may have saved that girl's life. Do you think he ever really meant to take her with him?"

"That's a good question," said Shandy. "He wouldn't dare leave her behind alive, of course, and I'm not at all sure what he meant to do with her once they got away. The police found a ransom note in his pocket, that he'd evidently written in the car while she drove and meant to post from wherever they were going. I don't know if he actually thought he could get the college and Heidi's wealthy relatives to pay a large ransom to imaginary kidnapers, or if he was just setting the stage to kill the girl and do a vanishing act himself so he'd be presumed dead and left free to enjoy his loot. The man was absolutely dumbfounded when they arrested him, you know. I don't believe it had ever once entered his head that he couldn't outsmart the whole world."

"He outsmarted me, at any rate," Porble muttered. "I'm not going to offer any excuses, President. I was derelict in my duty, and I'm resigning here and now."

"You'll resign when I say so," roared Svenson.

"That is wise, Thorkjeld," his wife approved. "Dr. Porble was right to concentrate on the work that means most to the college. Miss Marsh will help us get back some of the stolen books, and as for the rest, why should we regret losing what we never knew we had? The money at least will not be lost."

"How?" demanded the president.

"There will be much publicity when the wicked Dysart

and his young strumpet come to trial. This will be unpleasant for us, but we shall take a vigorous stand on the side of good and right and you will be dignified and majestic for the photographers and next year many more thousands of people will come to our Illumination and thus we gain back the money."

"Hoist with my own petard!" Shandy groaned.

"And you, Peter Shandy," Sieglinde went on unheeding, "will let the ladies of the committee select your decorations. You are not to be trusted. Thorkjeld, we must go."

Professor Shandy shook his head. "I can't believe this nightmare is over. I suppose as the last—er—item on the docket, one of us ought to go over and explain to Adele Dysart that her husband's spent all her money, killed two of her neighbors, and tried to elope with an oversexed undergraduate. President, you—"

"Not me! I delegated you to clean up this mess, Shandy, and by Yesus, you're still delegated. Go."

"Just one minute, Dr. Svenson," cried Helen Marsh. "If you think you're going to send this innocent man into that—that vampire's nest—"

"I do."

"Then," she sighed, "I suppose I'll have to go with him."

"To hold the hammer?" Shandy asked in the tone of a man who will brook no further shilly-shallying.

"Yes, Peter," she replied. "To hold the hammer."

"What the hell are they talking about?" demanded the president.

"Never mind," Sieglinde told him. "He knows and she knows. You do not need to know. Come, Thorkjeld, it is past your bedtime."

CHARLOTTE MACLEOD

"Suspense reigns supreme" <u>Booklist</u>

THE BILBAO LOOKING GLASS 67454-8/$2.95

Sleuth Sarah Kelling and her friend, art detective Max Bittersohn are on vacation at her family estate on the Massachusetts coast, when a nasty string of robberies, arson and murders send Sarah off on the trail of a mystery with danger a little too close for comfort.

WRACK AND RUNE 61911-3/$2.75

When a hired hand "accidentally" dies by quicklime, the local townsfolk blame an allegedly cursed Viking runestone. But when Professor Peter Shandy is called to the scene, he's sure it's murder. His list of suspects—all with possible motives—includes a sharp-eyed antique dealer, a disreputable realtor, and a gaggle of kin thirsty for the farm's sale!

THE PALACE GUARD 59857-4/$2.50

While attending a recital at a fashionable Boston art museum, recently widowed Sarah Kelling and her ardent lodger Max Bittersohn witness the disposal of a corpse from an upper-story balcony to the garden below. A life-threatening hunt for the murderer exposes and international art scandal and unveils yet another museum murder!

"Mystery with wit and style" <u>Washington Post</u>

Also by Charlotte MacLeod:
THE WITHDRAWING ROOM   56743-4/$2.25
LUCK RUNS OUT   54171-8/$2.25
THE FAMILY VAULT   62679-9/$2.50
REST YOU MERRY   61903-2/$2.50

AVON PAPERBACKS